About the Author

Sharon Booth writes about love, magic, and mystery. Her characters may be flawed, but whether they're casting a spell, solving a mystery, or dealing with the ups and downs of family life or romance, they do it with kindness and humour. Sharon is a member of the Society of Authors and the Romantic Novelists' Association, and an Authorpreneur member of the Alliance of Independent Authors. She has been a KDP All-Star Author on several occasions.

She likes reading, researching her family tree, and watching Doctor Who, and Cary Grant movies. She loves horses and hares and enjoys nothing more than strolling around harbours and old buildings. Take her to a castle, an abbey, or a stately home and she'll be happy for hours. She admits to being shamefully prone to crushes on fictional heroes.

Her stories of love, community, family, and friendship are set in pretty villages and quirky market towns, by the sea or in the countryside, and a happy ending is guaranteed.

If you love heroes and heroines who do the best they can no matter what sort of challenges they face, beautiful locations, and warm, feelgood stories, you'll love Sharon's books.

Books by Sharon Booth

There Must Be an Angel
A Kiss from a Rose
Once Upon a Long Ago
The Whole of the Moon

Summer Secrets at Wildflower Farm
Summer Wedding at Wildflower Farm

Resisting Mr Rochester
Saving Mr Scrooge

Baxter's Christmas Wish
The Other Side of Christmas
Christmas with Cary

New Doctor at Chestnut House
Christmas at the Country Practice
Fresh Starts at Folly Farm
A Merry Bramblewick Christmas
Summer at the Country Practice
Christmas at Cuckoo Nest Cottage

Belle, Book and Candle
My Favourite Witch
To Catch a Witch
Will of the Witch

How the Other Half Lives: Part One: At Home
How the Other Half Lives: Part Two: On Holiday
How the Other Half Lives: Part Three: At Christmas

Winter Wishes at The White Hart Inn

Christmas at Cuckoo Nest Cottage

Bramblewick 6

SHARON BOOTH

Copyright © 2019 Sharon Booth.

Paperback published 2022
Cover design by Green Ginger Publishing

The moral rights of the author have been asserted.
All rights reserved. No part of this publication may be reproduced, stored in any retrieval system, or transmitted in any form, or by any means electronic, mechanical, photocopying, recording or otherwise, without the prior written permission of the publishers.

This book is a work of fiction. Names, characters, businesses, organisations, places and events other than those clearly in the public domain, are either the product of the author's imagination or are used fictitiously. Any resemblances to actual persons, living or dead, is entirely coincidental.

ISBN: 9798367058376

"No person is your friend who demands your silence or denies your right to grow."

~ Alice Walker

Holly Carter
Receptionist at Bramblewick surgery, lives alone in a rented house at the edge of the village, next door to Lulu Drake at Cuckoo Nest Cottage.
Lewis Palmer
Gardener at Kearton Hall, Kearton Bay. New resident of Bramblewick. Friend of Jackson and Abbie, tenant of Nell and Riley MacDonald.

Anna Blake
Head receptionist at Bramblewick Surgery. Mother of Eloise, stepmother of Gracie, wife of Connor Blake.
Connor Blake
GP at Bramblewick surgery. The Blakes live at **Chestnut House**, former home of Dr Gray, Anna's late father.
See *New Doctor at Chestnut House*

Nell MacDonald
Proprietor of the village café and bakery, Spill the Beans. New mum to baby Aiden.
Riley MacDonald
GP at Bramblewick surgery. Husband of Nell and dad of Aiden. The MacDonalds live at **The Ducklings**.
See *Christmas at the Country Practice*

Rachel Johnson
Practice nurse at Bramblewick Surgery. Mother of Sam. Daughter of Janie.
Xander North
Real name Alexander South. Famous actor now

concentrating on local theatre and running **Folly Farm** as an animal sanctuary with his fiancée Rachel and her family.
See *Fresh Starts at Folly Farm*

Isobel Clark
Known to everyone as Izzy. Teacher at Bramblewick Primary School. Best friend of Anna Blake.
Ash Uttridge
Teacher at Bramblewick Primary School. Partner of Izzy. The couple live in **Rose Cottage**.
See *A Merry Bramblewick Christmas*

Abbie Sawdon
GP at Bramblewick Surgery. Mother of three. Lives at **The Gables**.
Jackson Wade
Teacher at Bramblewick Primary School. Best friend of Ash. Lives in **Helmston**.
See *Summer at the Country Practice*

Chapter 1

Lewis stepped out of the hallway onto the path and breathed in the damp, November air. The wooden door behind him clicked shut and a key turned in the lock.

'So, what do you think?'

Lewis eyed the pretty blonde woman who was smiling up at him and nodded. 'It's great. Perfect.'

She laughed and they headed round the side of the building towards the street. 'Well, I wouldn't go that far. I know it's basic but it's a reasonable price and the location is perfect, don't you think?'

They were standing in front of the shop now, on what passed for Bramblewick's main street, and his glance took in the row of stone-built, red-roofed shops, the pretty village green, and the gurgling beck that threaded its way through the village just a few feet in front of him.

He grinned. 'Well, there's a pub at the end of the street so that's a pretty big tick in its favour for a start. I may pile on the pounds living above a bakery though. The smell coming from downstairs was to die for.'

She tutted, patting him playfully on the arm. 'Get away with you! You could do to put on a bit of weight anyway.' Her big blue eyes widened in horror, and she clasped a hand to her mouth. 'God, that sounds awful. I don't mean you're too skinny honestly. I was just —'

'Chill, no offence taken,' he reassured her. 'Truth is, I *am* a bit on the skinny side. Can't seem to put weight on no matter how much I eat.'

'Lucky you.' She sighed. 'I only have to take a tray of sausage rolls out of the oven and I gain half a stone. It's a curse. So,' she brightened again and tilted her head to one side, her expression hopeful, 'are you interested? Do we have a deal?'

Lewis rummaged in his pocket and pulled out a crumpled bag of pear drops. 'Want one?' he asked, offering her the bag.

She shook her head. 'No thanks.'

'Don't blame you. Taste like nail varnish and they rot your teeth.' He grinned, displaying a set of perfect, pearly white teeth which he took far too much care of to let such a fate befall them.

'Why eat them then?'

'Better to eat pear drops than smoke cigarettes. I quit three months ago, and pear drops are the only things that stop me succumbing. No idea why. One of those psychological quirks that someone smarter than me would no doubt have a weird and wonderful explanation for. A month's rent and a month in advance did you say?'

'That's fair enough isn't it? I mean, I know it sounds a lot, but it seems to be standard practice and—oh, Holly! Holly, over here!'

Lewis raised an eyebrow as his prospective landlady

seemed to forget all about him for a second. She raised her arm and waved frantically, and he followed her gaze, seeing a young brunette, wrapped up in a red duffle coat and a long grey scarf, crossing the low stone bridge over the beck.

'Did you get it?' His companion—Nell—clearly had more important things on her mind now than whether he was interested in renting her flat. As the brunette neared, he realised she was struggling under the weight of several shopping bags and rushed to help her.

'Well, aren't you a gentleman?' Nell beamed at him as he returned and placed three bags on the pavement beside her. 'Holly, this is Lewis. Lewis, this is my friend Holly.'

The brunette plonked two more bags down beside the others and smiled up at him. 'Pleased to meet you, Lewis. Thanks ever so much for the help.' She turned to Nell, clearly excited. 'I got it!'

'Fabulous!' Nell sounded delighted. 'I was really worried you'd back out at the last minute; you were so adamant it was a waste of money.'

'Yes, well, I nearly did,' Holly admitted. 'But when I saw it on the rail and realised it was the last one in stock too, I just couldn't resist. It will be worth it won't it?' She sounded doubtful and Nell squeezed her arm, as if reassuring her.

'It will. Promise. Gosh, Lewis, I'm so sorry. Listen to us jabbering away when we're supposed to be discussing rent.'

'My fault,' Holly said. 'I've been trying to decide whether to buy this really expensive dress or not and

Nell kept telling me I should go for it but... sorry, I'm doing it again, aren't I?' She glanced at the bunch of keys in Nell's hand and frowned. 'Did you say rent? Are you going to look at the flat?'

Nell nodded. 'He's already seen it. Just waiting for his verdict aren't I?' She gave him a meaningful look.

Lewis shifted the pear drop from one cheek to the other while he reached into the inside pocket of his overcoat and pulled out his wallet.

Nell squealed. 'Does that mean you want it?'

'I definitely want it,' he agreed. 'Cash okay?'

'More than okay.'

Holly tucked a strand of her hair behind her ear and said slowly, 'I thought you weren't going to rent the flat out again after Riley moved out?'

'I wasn't going to,' Nell admitted. 'But it seemed a shame to just leave it sitting there, especially since it had new carpets and had been decorated when he lived there, and besides,' she gave Lewis an apologetic glance, 'the money will go a long way towards childcare fees, now I'm back at work full time. You've no idea how expensive it is to put a baby into nursery. Riley nearly passed out with the shock of it all.'

Lewis counted the money and handed a bundle of notes to Nell. 'It's all there,' he assured her.

'You'll need a receipt,' she said.

He shrugged and tucked his wallet back in his inside pocket. 'I trust you.'

Holly's eyes widened and Nell tutted. 'You shouldn't trust me, not with that much money. You don't even know me. Look, come and warm up in Spill the Beans, and I'll write you out a proper receipt while you have a coffee.'

He considered for a moment then nodded. 'Okay. Might as well check out your café anyway. I have a feeling I'll be spending as much time in there as I will upstairs.'

Nell beamed at him. 'Coming, Holly?'

Holly shook her head and reached for the bags of shopping. 'No thanks. I've got to drop some of these groceries off at Lulu's and then I'm going home to get ready for tonight.'

Nell glanced at her watch. 'Already? You've got hours yet.'

'I *need* hours to make myself look passable, new dress or no new dress,' Holly said.

'Do you live far? Do you need a hand with those bags?' Lewis asked.

Holly stared at him, and he shuffled uncomfortably, feeling he'd said something wrong.

'Thank you,' she said carefully. 'I'm fine, honestly. But it was very kind of you to offer.'

'No worries.' He shrugged and stuck his hands in his pocket, suddenly awkward.

As Holly hurried away, Nell called, 'See you tonight, Holls!'

She turned back to him, a frown creasing her forehead. 'Bless her,' she murmured.

Lewis wondered what she meant by that, but decided it was none of his business.

'Coffee then?' he said cheerfully.

She looked blank for a moment, as if she'd forgotten

all about it. 'Oh yes, coffee.' She smiled at him. 'And a receipt. And I'll get you a proper tenancy agreement drawn up by the end of the week too. Trust me indeed! You're far too nice for your own good.'

***

Holly had soaked in the bath for ages and was finally more relaxed. It had taken ages for the tension to ebb out of her and she was almost reluctant to leave the bathroom behind. Usually, she jumped in the shower and was in and out within a few minutes, but she was so nervous and stressed that, for once, only the bathtub would do.

Not that her bathroom was one she usually liked to linger in. It was ancient and ugly, with chipped tiles and old-fashioned taps and a toilet cistern held together with bits of string and sticky tape. She'd done her best with it, keeping it immaculately clean, laying a cheerful citrus-coloured bathmat over the ugly, black vinyl tiles and hanging a bright orange blind at the metal-framed window, but it was far from being her favourite room in the house, and that was saying something.

Still, with a few scented candles, some perfumed bubble bath, and soft music playing from the radio on the landing, Holly could almost forget about her dingy surroundings. If she didn't look up she could pretend that the black mould on the ceiling wasn't there, and the lavender fragrance from the bubble bath masked the musky smell of damp that lingered in the room no matter what she did to prevent it.

She needed this time to calm down. She was churned up, and not just about the party although, Lord knows, that was making her nervous enough. It was Nell's flat that had done it. Why hadn't she asked? Why had she left it so long? Now it was too late, and it was her own fault.

She'd mentioned to her boyfriend, Jonathan, that she didn't think she could stand living at the cottage any longer. Her landlord did nothing as far as repairs went, and the place was depressing and squalid. It had occurred to her that the flat above Spill the Beans was empty. The last occupant, Riley MacDonald, had moved out to be with Nell, and they were now happily married with a young son, living in Nell's cottage, The Ducklings. Since then Nell hadn't bothered to look for another tenant and had mentioned once or twice that she couldn't be doing with the hassle of vetting tenants and collecting rent.

'But the thing is,' Holly had said excitedly to Jonathan one evening as they sat together on the sofa, watching some action film he'd been keen to see, 'I'm sure she wouldn't mind if it was someone she knew well. And after all I *am* her friend.'

'Huh?' Jonathan tutted and paused the film, clearly annoyed at the interruption. 'What are you on about now?'

'Nell's flat,' Holly said patiently. 'The one above Spill the Beans. I'm going to ask Nell if she'll rent it to me.'

'Why the hell would you do that?'

Holly had felt the familiar lurching in her stomach at the scorn in his voice.

'I really can't stand it here much longer. It's getting me down. Nell's flat's only small, but it's clean and dry and warm, and I know she'd do any repairs if they were needed and —'

'Don't be stupid.' Jonathan's tone was dismissive. 'You're too old to be living in some grubby flat above a shop, for crying out loud. Besides, you told me yourself that she doesn't want a new tenant. Why put yourself through that?'

'Through what?'

'Rejection! She's going to have to turn you down and then what will happen? You'll feel awkward for asking, and she'll feel awkward for saying no. Your friendship will be damaged and for what? Just because you have a sudden fancy to live in some flat, as if you're Bridget Jones or something. You have a perfectly good grown-up house here. You're not a student you know.'

'I know that! I wasn't...' Holly's voice trailed off as Jonathan pressed the play button on the remote control and settled back to continue watching his film. She'd stared at the screen blindly for a few moments, her thoughts jumbled and her throat full as she battled not to cry.

Jonathan had patted her knee, not even glancing at her. 'Cup of tea would go down a treat, babe.'

So she'd pushed all thoughts of approaching Nell to one side, and now she'd lost out to this Lewis man. How could she have been so stupid, so cowardly? She should have had the nerve to ask. She was useless, that was the truth of it.

As she rubbed herself dry with a large, fluffy, purple

towel, Holly realised that, when Lewis handed over the deposit money to Nell, he'd taken away her last bit of hope—the hope she hadn't even realised she was still harbouring. She honestly thought she'd resigned herself to staying in this dump, and to not approaching Nell about the flat. When she saw Lewis accept the tenancy of the place, she'd understood, far too late, that she'd still nursed the thought that, one day, she would pluck up the courage to ask Nell if she could move in. What had she been waiting for? How much worse could things get here really?

She padded into the bedroom and sank gloomily onto the bed. A glance at the clock revealed that she had less than an hour before Jonathan would arrive. They'd agreed he would pick her up at seven and they'd head to Abbie's house, The Gables, together.

Her eyes fell on her new dress, hanging on the back of the door, and she felt a stirring of pleasure. She really had looked good in it when she tried it on in the changing rooms of the shop in Helmston, and even though it was quite expensive she just hadn't been able to resist.

Jonathan didn't really approve of her wasting money on clothes, but she hadn't bought anything new for ages, and this was special. A one off. She was so looking forward to the party and it wasn't as if they got to socialise much was it? She deserved this one night, didn't she?

Her forehead creased as she tried to remember the last night out they'd had together. She remembered they'd gone out on her birthday—but that didn't really count as they'd gone to the pictures to see some Marvel movie she wasn't particularly interested in.

They'd missed the last get-together her friends had, she thought sadly. Izzy's and Ash's engagement party. She'd have loved to be there, and had planned to go right up until the last minute, but then she and Jonathan had argued, and he'd told her to go without him and she really hadn't been in the mood for it...

Before that it was the christening of Nell's and Riley's baby, Aidan, but they'd argued that day too, and it had all got spoilt. It was her own fault. She'd neglected him. She'd known perfectly well that he hardly knew anyone there, but she'd been so pleased to see everyone that she hadn't spent enough time with Jonathan after the service. No wonder he'd felt pushed out. She shouldn't have been so thoughtless.

Jonathan had paid for that week away in Majorca of course, and that had been fun in a way. At least they'd had plenty of sunshine and she'd hardly annoyed Jonathan at all the whole seven days.

She sighed and gathered her makeup bag, hair straighteners, perfume... rummaging in drawers and cupboards for the bits and pieces she needed to make herself halfway presentable for the party. She must remember to wrap Abbie's gift and write on her birthday card. She shouldn't have spent so long in the bath. If she wasn't ready when Jonathan arrived he wouldn't be best pleased with her.

In the event she was ready by ten to seven and a few glances in the mirror left her feeling optimistic for once. The dress was in vintage nineteen-twenties style, with a deep red mid-thigh length knit lining, overlaid with pretty black mesh with black sequins and beading, that finished in a scalloped hemline with a long black fringe that fell to just below the knee. She felt incredibly sexy in it—something she hadn't felt in ages she realised. With her dark chestnut hair straightened to perfection and carefully applied makeup, she thought that, for once, she could hold her head up and make Jonathan proud.

She gathered the gift bag containing Abbie's birthday present and card, picked up her beaded clutch bag and hurried downstairs to await Jonathan's arrival. There was a peculiar sensation in her tummy, like flapper girls were dancing the Charleston in there, as she imagined his pleasure when she opened the door, and he beheld her in her twenties-style glory.

It was gone ten past seven before the knock on the door came, by which time she'd worked herself up into a state of nerves. Determined not to mess things up as she usually did, she opened the door and smiled lovingly at her boyfriend, telling herself that it didn't matter if he was late, and it certainly wasn't worth putting him in a bad mood by mentioning it.

Her smile dropped as he glanced at her and wrinkled his nose in distaste. 'What in God's name have you got on? You look a right state.'

Holly's stomach plunged as the despondent flapper girls sank to their knees. She felt stupid and tugged at the dress, wondering why she'd ever thought it suited her.

'Have you, er, brought a change of clothes with

you?'

It wasn't like him to dress down for a party. Jonathan liked to be admired and took great pride in his appearance. It seemed unlikely that he'd choose to go to the party in old jeans and a rust-coloured jumper that had seen better days.

'Going where?' He pushed past her and headed into the living room, plonking himself down on the sofa and linking his hands behind his head as he stared up at her, a challenge in his eyes. 'We're not going anywhere tonight are we?'

Holly felt the blood drain from her face. 'It's the party, remember? Abbie's party? The GP at work. It's her birthday and we—'

'I know who Abbie is, for crying out loud. Another one of your cronies, so how could I forget? We had this conversation, remember?' Jonathan's eyes softened and he reached out to take her trembling hand. 'Holls, we agreed didn't we? You know I had to work today, so we decided we'd not bother. We were going to stay in and order a takeaway, watch telly, relax. Remember?'

Holly bit her lip, struggling to recall the conversation. 'I know you said you had to work today …'

'Yeah, and I said I'd be exhausted. Far too tired for a party. You were great about it. I said you should go on your own, but you insisted you'd rather stay with me.' He shook his head, looking sad. 'I wouldn't have come if I'd known you were still going. You should have told me if you'd changed your mind, Holls. I've come all this way from Whitby, and I'm already knackered, and now I have to go home again while you go to some bloody party. Cheers for that.'

'I thought—' Holly rubbed her forehead, bewildered. 'I don't remember saying that. I thought we'd agreed to go to the party—both of us. You never said anything about being too tired.'

'Are you calling me a liar?' Jonathan's chin jutted out in a challenge.

'No, no, of course not. It's—I just—my memory...' Her voice trailed off and she sank onto the sofa beside him, feeling defeated.

He sighed and pulled her to him. 'Bless you, you never know what day it is most of the time do you?'

Holly blinked away tears, not sure what to think any more, but grateful for the kindness in his tone.

'I'll go and get changed,' she murmured. 'Then we can order that takeaway.'

She began to stand but Jonathan tugged her down beside him. He cupped her chin in his hand and turned her face towards him.

'Look, I can see you really want to go, so even though you've messed me about a bit and I'm pretty tired and hardly dressed for the occasion, I'll go with you. No, no arguments,' he said, holding up his hand as she began to protest. 'I can see how much it means to you and I know your memory's been a bit dodgy lately. Not your fault. You can't help yourself. If you don't mind me going dressed like this I'm game if you are.'

Holly considered him doubtfully. He would look out of place, and surely that would make him *feel* out of place? He'd be bound to get edgy and cross again. She wasn't sure she had the energy to deal with another scene.

'It's okay,' she said. 'I don't mind missing the party, honestly.'

'But I do,' he said, as he pulled her to her feet and handed her the clutch bag she'd dumped on a chair. 'Let me do this for you, Holls. I may be tired but I'm not so tired I can't make an effort for my girlfriend. Just try to be a bit less forgetful in future, eh? It can be really stressful, trying to keep up with your mood swings and your frequent changes of mind. That's all I ask, okay?'

Holly nodded and he grinned. 'Great. Come on then. Let's get to this party.'

But as Holly closed the door behind them she realised she'd never felt less in the mood for a party. It was all spoilt, now that she'd messed things up again, and Jonathan didn't even like her dress. If her own boyfriend thought she looked stupid what would everyone else think? What a waste of money it had been. People would be laughing at her. She really wished she had the energy to persuade Jonathan to stay in for that takeaway after all.

Chapter 2

'Holly, you came! Come in, join the madhouse.' Abbie sounded genuinely delighted when she opened the front door of The Gables and beamed down at her. For a moment, Holly forgot all about her nerves and felt almost like her old self, excitement bubbling inside her at the sound of music and the buzz of chatter from within the house.

'Happy birthday!' She handed her hostess the gift bag, which contained some rather delicious-smelling toiletries from an expensive shop in Helmston and stepped into the hallway.

'Oh, you shouldn't have. I told you not to waste your money,' Abbie chided her. She opened the bag and the waft of perfume reached Holly's nose, making her close her eyes in bliss. It was heavenly. She'd been almost tempted to keep the gorgeous slices of soap, which looked good enough to eat, for herself.

'On the other hand,' Abbie said, sniffing appreciatively, 'I'm rather glad you did. How wonderful does this smell?'

Holly smiled, pleased that Abbie approved, then her stomach swished nervously as Jonathan, who was still standing on the path outside, cleared his throat rather loudly.

'Sorry! I've kept you waiting haven't I?' Holly practically shoved Abbie out of the way to make plenty of room for him to join them in the hallway.

Abbie looked a bit startled but turned a pleasant smile on Jonathan. 'So sorry. I didn't realise you needed a separate invitation to come in,' she said sweetly.

She glanced briefly at him, and Holly's nerves increased as she realised how inappropriately he was dressed for a party. Abbie looked gorgeous and had clearly gone to a lot of effort tonight, and there was Jonathan in his old jeans and jumper.

'Do close the door please, Jonathan. Let's get you both a drink. I love your dress,' Abbie said, as she put an arm around her and steered her towards the living room.

Holly glanced worriedly over her shoulder to make sure Jonathan was following. He scowled at her, and she gave him a pleading look. *Please don't get cross tonight.* Why on earth hadn't she made sure he was safely inside before she'd given Abbie the birthday present? She'd forgotten herself again, charging straight in, letting excitement get the better of her. Jonathan was quite right; she was totally thoughtless at times.

Abbie's living room was cheerfully decorated with bunting and banners proclaiming, "Happy Birthday". A table at one end of the room groaned with food and there was a trolley in one corner loaded with various bottles of spirits. Around thirty people had already arrived, milling around, spilling into the hallway, hugging each other, shrieking greetings, calling over to

Abbie that they absolutely loved what she'd done to The Gables.

Already feeling overwhelmed, Holly awkwardly smoothed down her dress and looked for a friendly face.

'Holls! You made it!' Izzy's greeting had the same mixture of surprise and delight as Abbie's had done, and despite her relief at seeing someone she knew well Holly frowned, wondering why both friends were going so over the top. She noticed Izzy eyeing her dress and flushed; she felt awkward and ugly, and wished with all her heart she'd worn one of her old dresses that they'd all seen before and wouldn't pay any attention to.

'Hi, Jonathan. Nice to see you. Wow!' Izzy's eyes widened. 'Holly, that dress is amazing.'

Holly felt a wave of nausea. Amazing? Code word for bloody ridiculous no doubt. What had she been thinking? It was a real one-off, this dress. An attention magnet. The last thing she needed. Jonathan was right, she must look stupid.

'Expensive mistake,' she said lightly. 'Where's that drink, Abbie?'

Abbie tutted. 'Expensive mistake nothing. It looks fantastic. You look gorgeous, Holly.'

Holly felt Jonathan's arm go around her and her tension increased. It was good to be in the safety of his embrace, but on the other hand she was all too aware that the two of them must look ridiculous together. She'd gone way over the top in her choice of outfit, whereas he hadn't bothered to dress up at all. No wonder people were staring at them. She heard murmuring coming from some of the other guests and her face started to heat up. She wanted to go home.

'What would you like to drink?' Abbie asked, her gaze passing from Holly to Jonathan and back again. Holly could see the amusement in her eyes. She must find their attire very funny.

'Anything. I don't care,' she said, wishing she could add, 'just bring me a jugful of the stuff.'

Jonathan squeezed her. 'She'll have a soft drink,' he said firmly. 'And a beer for me please. Sorry I'm not dressed up for a party,' he added. 'I kind of had it sprung on me, and this is the result.'

'Really?' Izzy raised an eyebrow. 'You were invited weeks ago.'

'Yes I know, but Holly and I had agreed to stay home.' He rolled his eyes playfully, the picture of tolerance and patience. 'I've been working all day and we thought we'd have a quiet night in, but then she changed her mind at the last minute so...' He smiled at them and shrugged. 'I expect it was because of the dress. She was so excited about it I suppose she thought it was too good an opportunity to miss to show it off. I don't mind really. Just that if I'd known we weren't staying in I'd have dressed more appropriately, obviously.'

He ruffled Holly's hair affectionately and she tried to avoid Abbie's gaze. Now her friend would think she didn't really want to attend her birthday party, and she didn't remember even considering declining the invitation.

'Right, well...' Abbie cleared her throat and glanced at Izzy, as Holly's face burned and she shifted miserably, Jonathan's arm still clamped firmly around her shoulders. 'Are you sure you only want a soft drink, Holly?'

'Soft drink?'

Holly's spirits lifted slightly as Riley MacDonald, also a GP at the surgery where Holly was a receptionist, wandered over and pulled her out of Jonathan's embrace and into a gentle hug of his own.

'You want to try that pink gin that Nell's on,' he told her, in his soft, Scottish burr, nodding over to the far end of the living room where his wife was chatting to their friends, Anna and Connor, a glass of something distinctly alcoholic in her hand. 'It's all the rage you know, gin. Get the party going, eh? You can have a soft drink later.'

'She needs to pace herself,' Jonathan said. 'She does tend to go overboard a bit. You know Holly.'

'Aye, I do. Life and soul of any party,' Riley said. His tone was even and his expression pleasant, and Holly wondered why she sensed an edge suddenly.

'Pink gin sounds lovely,' she said. 'I'll just have the one, just to taste it,' she added hurriedly, giving Jonathan an appeasing smile.

He smiled back. 'Fine. If that's what you want.'

'Pink gin it is then,' Abbie said. She hurried off and Riley stepped back, eyeing Holly admiringly.

'Now, I'm not much use with clothes and fashion and all that business,' he admitted, folding his arms, 'but I have to say, you look really good tonight, Holly.'

'Scrubs up well, doesn't she?' Izzy agreed.

'Aye, she does. That dress is like something out of an old film—like an Agatha Christie movie or something.'

'I'd take that as a compliment,' Izzy said, laughing. 'It's the best he can manage, knowing Riley.'

'Holly!'

Holly's heart sank as suddenly a whole crowd of people swooped upon her: Connor, the third GP at the surgery; his wife, Anna, who was head receptionist; Izzy's fiancé, Ash; Abbie's eldest daughter, Isla; and Nell herself, all converged on her, exchanging remarks about the dratted dress as they hugged her.

'That's so cool!' Isla, who was only thirteen but already looked like Abbie in miniature, with her long, tawny hair and blue eyes, gazed at the dress in awe. She reached out a hand and stroked the black beading on the mesh overlay. 'Bet it cost a fortune. Did it?'

'Isla! You don't ask questions like that.' Abbie had returned, carrying a beer for Jonathan and Holly's pink gin. 'Sorry about that,' she said. 'My daughter's still learning how to socialise. She's been feral for far too many years.'

'Charming,' Isla said.

'Where are Bertie and Poppy?' Holly asked, glad of a change of subject. Abbie's two youngest children must be in bed she supposed, but anything to take people's minds off her clothes.

'At Folly Farm,' Abbie said. 'And they've taken Willow and Alby with them,' she added, referring to her dogs. 'Rachel's mum very kindly said she'd look after them all for the night, but we thought Isla was old enough to stay here and enjoy the party. She's a young lady now, as she's constantly reminding me.'

'Does that mean I can stay up 'til the end?' Isla asked hopefully.

'Ten o'clock we said,' Abbie grinned, ruffling her hair. 'Don't push your luck.'

'Where's Jackson?' Anna, having given Holly a hug and whispering, 'You look gorgeous,' in her ear, turned her attention to their hostess and her partner, much to Holly's relief.

'On his way,' Abbie said.

'On his way?' Nell screwed up her nose. 'Is he still living in Helmston then? Thought you two would have moved in together by now.'

'He's here all the time anyway,' Isla said. 'Don't know why he doesn't just make it official.'

'There's plenty of time for all that,' Abbie said firmly. 'It suits us to have a bit of space. He's here about half the week, but it's good for him to have his own place too. It's still early days.'

'But things are going well?' Izzy asked.

Ash grinned. 'Judging by the big smile that seems permanently plastered to Jackson's face, I'd say they're going very well.'

Jackson, Abbie's partner, was a teacher at the local primary school, where Izzy and Ash also taught. They were good friends with Jackson—Jackson was going to be best man at their forthcoming wedding—so they were delighted that he'd finally met the woman of his dreams, and even more delighted that she was another of their friends. They were both romantics at heart.

'He should be here any minute,' Abbie said, glancing at her watch. 'And Xander and Rachel are on their way too.'

'Ooh, and guess who's here, Holls,' Nell said, her voice eager. 'You'll never believe it, but—'

The door opened behind them, and they all turned to see a tall, fair-haired young man enter the room. He stopped dead and held up his hands as all those pairs of eyes fixed on him.

'Whoa, what did I do?'

He had a deep, sexy voice, Holly thought fleetingly, then pushed the thought from her mind, ashamed.

'Lewis, you remember Holly?' Nell asked, as Holly's heart sank when Jonathan straightened beside her.

'Of course. How could I forget?' He smiled politely at her, and she smiled stiffly back.

'Your knight in shining armour,' Nell added, seeming determined to ruin Holly's evening. 'He helped her with her shopping, like a proper gentleman,' she told no one in particular.

'How kind of you,' Jonathan said, slipping one arm around Holly's waist as he shook Lewis's hand.

Lewis shrugged. 'No big deal,' he said comfortably. 'Anyone would have done the same.'

'I couldn't believe it when I saw him arrive,' Nell said. She turned to Anna and Connor. 'This is the young man who's renting the flat above the shop. Took the tenancy today didn't you, Lewis?'

'Welcome to Bramblewick, Lewis,' Anna said, smiling at him.

'How do you know Abbie?' Connor queried.

'Lewis is a gardener,' Abbie said, before Lewis had the chance to explain. 'Jackson hired him for me and he did a sterling job I must say. We've been friends ever since.'

'So you're the one responsible for turning that wilderness outside into a vision of loveliness?' Nell beamed at him.

'Good job,' Riley agreed. 'Might have to hire you to do something with our garden. It's okay for now, but when wee Aidan starts toddling we're going to need more space for him to wander around without hurting himself. Needs to be child friendly.'

'Oh, Lewis isn't working for himself any longer,' Abbie said. 'He's got a full-time gardening job now and—'

'I'm sure I can fit it in,' Lewis said. 'Maybe in the spring?'

'That would be grand,' Riley agreed.

There was silence for a moment then Lewis said cheerily, 'Is that it then?' He nodded at Holly, smiling.

She blushed to her hair roots. 'Sorry?'

'The famous dress. The one you had your doubts about buying.'

Holly gulped. Beside her, Jonathan took a long, slow sip of beer. 'Er, yes, this is the one.'

He nodded. 'Right decision.'

He was just being polite, friendly, she thought desperately, but she could have cursed him. Now he'd put all the attention back on her again. She saw her friends exchange glances and her heart sank.

'That's what we said,' Izzy said firmly. 'She looks fantastic doesn't she?'

Holly drained her glass. 'This pink gin's lovely,' she gabbled. 'Any chance of another?'

'Steady on, for heaven's sake.' Jonathan gave a short laugh and shook his head. 'Got to watch her. She's a demon with a few drinks inside her.'

'Really?' Anna frowned. 'I've always found her to be nothing but good fun.'

There was a distinct chill in the air and a long, awkward silence. Holly longed to go home. This was all far too stressful. Why hadn't she listened to Jonathan and stayed home instead? They could have been curled up on the sofa now, watching one of his favourite films, eating a takeaway.

She was grateful when they heard the front door open and close and the muttering of voices in the hallway. Then the living room door opened again and in walked Jackson, followed by Rachel, who was the practice nurse at the surgery, and her fiancé Xander. Holly was so relieved about the distraction that, for a moment, she didn't notice what everyone else had clearly seen straight away. There was a general murmuring and exclamations of surprise and delight and Holly focused once more as the crowd turned away from her and towards Jackson.

'You look so different!'

'Oh my word! I can't believe it!'

'When did you do that? I never thought I'd see the day.'

She realised that Jackson had shaved his beard off,

and that he looked suddenly younger and rather handsome and incredibly sheepish. He was gazing at Abbie, an undisguised appeal in his eyes.

'What do you think?'

Abbie threw her arms around him and hugged him, and Holly saw her whisper something in his ear. His expression changed and he lost that wary look, as a smile lit up his face.

'Wow, Jackson!' Isla gazed at him in astonishment. 'You look, like, *young*!'

Jackson ran a finger over his top lip and shrugged, clearly embarrassed. 'I thought it was time for a change. Is it really okay?'

'You look ever so handsome,' Rachel assured him.

'And Isla's right. You do look younger,' Nell added.

Ash beamed at him. 'Nice one, mate.'

Jackson smiled back at him. 'I thought it was time. New beginnings and all that.'

Abbie slipped her arm through his. 'Definitely.'

'What do we have to do to get a drink in this place?' Xander asked. He kissed Abbie on the cheek. 'Happy birthday!'

'Happy birthday,' Rachel and Jackson chorused.

'Drinks,' Abbie said, laughing. 'Ooh, and I'll get you another pink gin, Holly.'

Rachel and Xander turned to Holly and their eyes widened. Xander whistled.

'Wow-ee! That's quite a dress,' he said, sounding admiring.

'Gorgeous, Holly,' Rachel said. 'You look amazing.'

Holly couldn't believe it. What more did she have to

do to distract attention from herself? As everyone turned once more to look at her, she managed to unclamp Jonathan's arm from around her waist.

'Excuse me,' she murmured, head down as she turned towards the door, 'I need the bathroom.'

She shot out of the living room and headed towards the stairs. She couldn't remember whether The Gables had a downstairs loo or not, but it didn't matter if it did. She wanted to put as much distance as she could between herself and all those people down there who kept insisting on staring at her and making comments about this stupid dress. It was so obvious that they thought it ridiculous, and she couldn't help but agree. Why had she ever thought it would look good? She looked as if she were going to some fancy-dress party.

She bolted the bathroom door behind her and leaned against it, slapping her palm to her forehead in exasperation.

'Stupid, stupid, stupid!'

She caught sight of herself in the bathroom mirror and felt sick. She looked like a clown with all that makeup. What must they all think of her? No wonder Jonathan was so ashamed of her half the time. She slid down the door and landed in a heap on the floor. Hugging her knees she stared unseeingly at the bathroom window, wondering how long she could hide up here, and how long she would have to stay before she could reasonably make her excuses and head home. However long it was, it was too long.

***

Lewis hadn't intended to stay at the party for more than an hour or so. He hadn't been sure about accepting the invitation at all, but he liked Abbie and Jackson, and since he was moving to Bramblewick it made sense to get to know as many of the villagers as possible. Now that he was here, he found he was quite enjoying himself. People were exceptionally friendly and keen to talk to him.

It wasn't long before he was picking up snippets of information about them all and putting names to faces, and Abbie and her friends made quite certain that he wasn't left out of any conversations, including him at every opportunity and giving him no chance to feel alone.

Right now they were discussing some wedding—or rather, two of them. It seemed that Rachel and Xander were getting married just before Christmas, and Izzy and Ash's big day was only five weeks away.

He was embarrassed to admit, even to himself, that his mouth had dropped open in shock when Xander North had walked in. Xander North! Lewis didn't watch much television but even he knew this famous actor, who starred in an historical detective series called *Lord Curtis Investigates*.

Lewis felt a sudden sadness, remembering how his mum had watched the first series and raved about it, swooning over the dashing and handsome aristocrat with a secret. How excited she'd have been to be here tonight, and to meet Xander for herself. But she'd never even got to see the second series. Life could be very unfair sometimes.

He squared his shoulders and took another sip of beer, determined not to wallow in grief. Not tonight. His mum would want him to enjoy himself, make friends, and that's what he intended to do.

'Sorry, what did you say?' he asked, realising that Abbie had said his name.

She smiled. 'You were miles away. I was just telling them all about your new job at Kearton Hall.'

'Ah, right. Well, not exactly new. I've been there a few months now,' he pointed out.

'What made you give up your own gardening business?' A dark-haired woman—Anna he thought her name was—looked at him questioningly. 'Only, I'd have thought working for yourself would be a dream come true.'

'When there's plenty of work on it is,' he said. 'Trouble is, throughout the winter months I struggled massively to make any money. Besides, I often found myself doing general labouring in the gardens round here—digging and weeding and tidying up. Which is fine,' he added hastily, 'but there wasn't a lot of opportunity to design and landscape, and that's what I really love.'

'And do you get the chance to do that at Kearton Hall?' Nell asked.

He smiled. 'It's something different every day,' he said. 'The family's keen to restore the gardens and make them a real feature for visitors to explore. Lady Boden-Kean takes a huge interest. She plans to set up a kitchen garden to supply the house with all its vegetables and herbs, and she also wants the main gardens to have different zones. We're looking at setting up a sensory garden, a children's area, and a cottage garden, for example.'

'Sounds like you're loving it there already,' Riley said. 'So you think you made the right decision, taking up paid employment instead of working for yourself?'

'Early days,' Lewis admitted, 'but right now I'd say yes, without a doubt. I look forward to going to work every day. Not everyone's so lucky.'

'Very true.' There was a general nodding of heads and murmurs of agreement.

'What brought you to Bramblewick?' Rachel asked.

'I'm living up past Staithes at the moment,' he explained. 'When the bad weather comes it's going to be a nightmare getting to Kearton Bay. I need to be this side of the Hall, where it's more sheltered. And to be honest, I'm sick of sharing with my two flatmates. I think I've grown out of all that. I'd like a bit of space, somewhere of my own. Property's way too expensive in Kearton Bay and Farthingdale—that's if you can manage to find somewhere to rent. Most of the houses and flats there are holiday lets. I had to look further afield, and Bramblewick's not that far away. Plus, if you want the absolute truth, Nell's flat was the cheapest place I found—of the ones that were liveable that is.'

Riley nodded. 'Told you we should have charged more,' he said, nudging Nell.

She laughed. 'Oh shut up. I'm glad you saw our advert, Lewis. I'm sure you'll be a model tenant and that you'll be very happy here.'

'Fancy you working at Kearton Hall though,' Izzy said. 'That's where Rachel and Xander are getting married.'

Lewis raised an eyebrow. 'Really? No doubt I'll be getting orders about the flowers very soon then.'

'From Tally?' Rachel asked.

Lewis nodded. 'Yeah. You've met her then?'

'Oh yes, she's lovely isn't she?'

'Who's Tally?' Nell asked.

'Wedding planner at Kearton Hall. She's quite young but seems to know what she's doing.' Rachel shivered. 'Can't believe it's next month. I'm so nervous.'

'No need to be nervous,' Anna said, a twinkle in her eyes. 'Just because thousands of Xander's adoring fans might find out where you're getting married and turn up at the Hall to gatecrash the wedding.'

'Don't!' Xander shuddered. 'I have nightmares about that. We've done everything we can to keep the venue secret, not to mention the date. I really hope that it works.'

'Well, I haven't even heard a whisper about it,' Lewis reassured him, 'and I work there. I think they've been very discreet about it, don't worry.'

'Good to know,' Xander said. 'I take it you'll keep this under your hat.'

Lewis raised a glass to him. 'No worries on that score, I assure you.'

'Excellent.' Xander turned to Ash. 'Not long until your big day is it? You must be scared stiff.'

Izzy shivered. 'Don't know about Ash but I'm petrified.'

'It'll all be fine,' Ash promised her, putting his arm around her.

'I don't know how he stays so calm,' she admitted. 'I'm a nervous wreck. Still, the main thing is we'll be married, and we'll have all our friends there with us to celebrate.' She spun round to look at Lewis, almost spilling her glass of wine in the process. 'You must come too! Honestly, you'll be very welcome.'

He shook his head, certain that she'd only asked out of politeness. 'I wouldn't dream of it. As you say it's a day for you and your friends. You barely know me.'

'Oh, but you're a friend of Abbie's and Jackson's,' she insisted. 'That makes you a friend of ours.'

'And you're my friend too,' Nell added. 'You should come!'

'Seriously, mate,' Ash told him, 'you'd be very welcome there. We're having a buffet, so it's not as if there won't be a place for you. We'd like you to be there.'

'That's very kind of you,' Lewis said, genuinely touched.

'That's settled then!' Nell said, squeezing his arm.

'Well, I—'

'I'd give it up, Lewis,' Riley advised him. 'You may as well go along with it. You're one of us now,' he added in a spooky voice.

Lewis grinned. 'Well, in that case, thanks very much. I'm always up for a buffet.'

'Good man!' Xander clapped him on the back approvingly.

'Holly's been gone a long time,' Abbie said,

frowning. 'Do you think she's all right?'

'I don't know, but Jonathan certainly seems to be doing fine without her.' Riley narrowed his eyes as he peered over Connor's shoulder to where Jonathan was standing, glass in hand, chatting in a rather intimate way with a couple of young women who seemed to be hanging on his every word.

'Looks like he hasn't even noticed Holly's not here,' Nell muttered.

Lewis took a sip of his beer as his companions gave each other knowing looks and mumbled in disparaging tones about Holly's boyfriend.

'I take it this Jonathan's not that popular,' he ventured at last.

They all looked at each other and he shrugged. 'Sorry, none of my business.'

'We can hardly blame you for asking when we've not exactly hidden our feelings from you,' Nell admitted. 'I don't want you to think we're usually like this, Lewis, 'cos honestly, we're not. We're a friendly bunch, really we are. Just that, well, Jonathan is—'

'Vile.'

There was a moment's silence then Anna burst out laughing. 'Say it like it is, Rachel, why don't you?' She shook her head slightly. 'Goodness knows what you must think of us, Lewis.'

Rachel looked sheepish for a moment, but there was defiance in her eyes. 'Sorry, but he is. I don't trust him. The thing is, Lewis, if you knew Holly—I mean, if you'd known her before she met *him*—well you'd understand.'

'Right enough,' Riley admitted. 'I don't think of any of us feel comfortable with what he's done to her.'

Lewis pictured the smiling, rosy-cheeked brunette who'd carried the shopping home from Helmston and chatted to him outside Spill the Beans. He thought about the clearly awkward and uncomfortable young woman at the party, who'd shot upstairs at the first opportunity, seeming desperate to get away from everyone's scrutiny and apparently incapable of taking a compliment. Just what *had* Jonathan done to her?

At that moment, Isla wandered over to join them and the subject was dropped.

Lewis drained his glass. 'Any chance of another beer, Abbie?' he asked. 'Then I'd better think about calling a taxi.'

'So soon?' Abbie looked disappointed. 'But the party's hardly started, and I haven't blown out the candles on my birthday cake yet.'

'I know but it's a long way home. I only came to wish you a happy birthday, and to show my face to my new neighbours. Tick, tick. Job done, I can head home and get an early night. I'll be up at dawn tomorrow to start packing.'

'Ooh, exciting.' Abbie hugged him. 'All right, fair enough. But another beer first, okay?'

'Definitely,' he said, smiling.

Ten minutes later, glass in hand, he made his way into the garden. It was bitterly cold. The autumn chill was giving way to the bite of winter already, despite it still only being November. He leaned against the kitchen wall and stared out over the landscape he'd created for Abbie over the previous few months. He couldn't see much detail in the darkness, but he didn't need to. He knew every inch of this garden and remembered clearly how he'd tackled each section of it, transforming it from a mess of tangled weeds into a beautiful space, with a wildflower patch, water feature and a lush, green lawn for the children and dogs to run around on.

His thoughts turned to all the packing he had to do. His flatmates wouldn't be much use. He could well imagine them pulling things out of their various boxes and bags and insisting they belonged to them.

They hadn't had a particularly well-equipped kitchen when he'd moved in and had come to rely on him to provide even the necessities. He closed his eyes, wishing he could afford to let them have it all and buy new stuff for the flat, but he didn't have the money to replace it.

It was a good job the flat was furnished, and the carpets were in good condition. It had been decorated by Riley too, so that saved him a job and the expense. It was just all the faff of moving his stuff over to Bramblewick. Still, it would be worth it. This seemed like a nice village, and he couldn't deny that living above a café and bakery was going to be a huge bonus. Cooking was definitely not his strong point.

His eyes flew open as he sensed someone beside him.

'Oh, hi. We wondered where you'd got to. Thought you were still upstairs.'

Holly hesitated. 'I—I was just about to go back

inside. I've been out here for ages.'

'You must be freezing.' Lewis frowned. He'd only been out here a few minutes and he was cold already. She only had that thin, sleeveless dress on. He could see her breath coming out in wisps of mist in the dark night air. She was shivering. He took his jacket off and draped it around her shoulders.

'No honestly, I'm fine.' She wriggled away from him but he insisted.

'You'll catch your death,' he told her, realising with a jolt that he sounded like his mother. She'd always told him to wrap up and keep warm. He'd lost count of how many scarves and pairs of gloves she'd bought him over the years.

Holly seemed to give in pretty quickly. Evidently, she was secretly relieved to snuggle into his jacket, and she pulled it tighter to her, leaning beside him against the wall. They stood in silence for a few moments, listening to the buzz of chatter and the music coming from within the house.

'Aren't you going to ask me what I've been doing out here?' Holly said suddenly.

Lewis didn't look at her. 'I suppose if you wanted me to know you'd tell me.'

He sensed her turn towards him, felt her gaze upon him.

'You're a strange man,' she said at last. 'I've never known anyone like you.'

Now he did look at her. 'Thanks very much,' he said.
'Sorry, I didn't mean—sorry.'
He frowned. 'It's okay. I'm not offended. I was

joking.'

'Oh.' She rubbed her forehead, sounding confused. 'I don't always know.'

'Well,' he said, wanting to reassure her, 'I'm not the easiest person to read apparently. It's been said many times.'

'I suppose,' she said, sounding reluctant, 'I ought to go back in.'

He thought about what her friends had said. *I don't think any of us feel comfortable about what he's done to her.*

'You don't like parties then?' he said cautiously.

She didn't reply, but he could make out that she was chewing her lip and seemed deeply unhappy about something.

'Jonathan will be getting really annoyed with me,' she said eventually. 'He hates being left alone and he doesn't really know anyone. I shouldn't have stayed out here so long.'

Lewis thought about Jonathan, deep in conversation and in full flirt mode with those two women in the living room. He hardly looked lonely, and it was doubtful he'd even missed Holly.

'He's a grown man,' he said. 'I'm sure he's fine.' *And he hasn't exactly come looking for you to make sure you're okay, has he?*

'But it's not fair. He's not even dressed for a party and it's all my fault. We'd agreed not to come tonight you see. But I forgot.'

'Did you?'

She stared at him, then her shoulders slumped. 'I'm not sure,' she admitted, sounding thoroughly confused.

'I don't remember saying it, but I must have done. Why else would he turn up wearing his old jeans and jumper?'

Oh, I can think of a reason.

'He only came because of me. He didn't want to disappoint me.'

What a superstar. He could feel the tension in his shoulders and tried to relax. No point discussing it with Holly. She would jump to Jonathan's defence. He'd seen it all before.

The kitchen door was pushed open, and a giggle reached their ears. Two people lurched onto the patio then stopped dead as they noticed the two figures leaning against the wall.

'Holly!' Jonathan's joviality was clearly forced. He was shocked to see her, no question. Lewis had to hand it to him though, he masked it well. 'I was hoping you were out here. I've looked everywhere for you.'

Lewis watched, feeling sympathy for her as Holly's gaze took in the woman standing beside Jonathan. 'Have you?'

'Yes. I was beginning to think you'd abandoned me.'

The woman tutted and headed back indoors. Holly seemed unable to speak.

Jonathan reached out and touched the sleeve of the jacket she was huddled into. 'What's this?'

'My jacket,' Lewis said evenly. 'She was cold, so I lent it to her.'

Jonathan folded his arms. 'Well, you really are a knight in shining armour aren't you? First the shopping and now this. What do you say, Holly? Found a real hero here, haven't you?'

Holly clutched the front of the jacket. 'Who was that girl, and what was she doing out here with you?'

'Are you serious?' Jonathan glared at her. 'I've spent the last forty minutes hunting high and low for you and you dare to accuse me of—'

'I'm not accusing you of anything,' Holly said. She jutted out her chin and glared back at him. For a moment, Lewis could imagine the old Holly that her friends had talked about. The one with spirit and confidence. He rather liked this version of her. 'All I said was, who was she? And why did you both come out here?'

'We were looking for you of course, what do you think? I'd honestly begun to believe you'd left, and Gina offered to help me look for you. The garden was our last resort. Bloody hell, talk about suspicious.'

'I'm not suspicious,' Holly said, though Lewis suspected she was lying through her teeth.

'I should bloody well think you're not, considering you're the one who dragged me to this damn party in the first place and you've hidden away all night.' He looked from her to Lewis and back again. 'And while we're on the subject of suspicion, what the hell are you doing out here with *him* anyway?'

'I wasn't out here with him,' she protested. 'I've been out here ages on my own.'

'Yeah right.'

'It's true,' Lewis said, though he felt no obligation to placate Jonathan. 'I'd just come outside as Holly was making her way back indoors. She was shivering so I lent her my jacket.'

'If she was going back in, why is she still standing outside with you then?'

Lewis didn't have an answer to that one. He wasn't really sure himself.

'I was trying to pluck up courage to go back in,' Holly confessed.

'Courage? For what?' His tone was all scorn.

To face you again, no doubt, Lewis thought. She'd been worried about leaving him for so long and was probably dreading a scene.

'I don't know,' she said miserably.

Jonathan tutted. 'I can guess. That bloody stupid dress! I knew you'd feel overdressed. What the hell possessed you anyway? Anyone would think we were at a costume ball. Trust you to go overboard.'

Lewis clenched his fists as Holly hung her head.

'Actually, I think she looks absolutely stunning,' he heard himself say. 'And that dress is beautiful. It's nice to see someone make a real effort. So many people just don't bother, do they?'

His tone was pleasant, but he knew, as his gaze took in Jonathan's own shabby attire, that the meaning was clear.

Jonathan stared at him for a moment but when Lewis didn't look away Jonathan did.

The kitchen door opened, and Jackson peered out. 'There you all are! I'm just about to light the candles on Abbie's cake. You wouldn't want to miss out on singing Happy Birthday to her, would you?'

Jonathan nudged Holly. 'Give the man his jacket

back,' he commanded. 'We're going home.'

Lewis really hoped she would argue, but he had a feeling she'd be all too glad to leave. Sure enough, she looked relieved, and couldn't hand Lewis the jacket fast enough.

'Thanks ever so much for lending it to me,' she said. 'It was so kind of you.'

'Not a problem,' he assured her. 'Any time.' He smiled at her, and she smiled back.

Jonathan grabbed her arm and pushed her into the kitchen, following close behind.

'Everything okay, Holly?' Jackson asked, his voice sharp.

Lewis heard her reply, 'Fine thank you. Sorry.'

There was some muttering and then Jackson leaned out to look at Lewis. 'What was all that about?'

Lewis sighed. 'Just Jonathan, determined to show us all who's in charge.'

'Huh!' Jackson rolled his eyes. 'Are you coming inside?'

'Sure. Give me a minute. I'll just put my jacket back on.'

Jackson hesitated then nodded. The door closed and Lewis was left alone in the darkness once again. He shook his head slightly and tried to calm his disturbed thoughts. *Not my business*, he told himself as he shrugged his jacket back on.

As he dug his hands into his pockets, he touched the bag of pear drops and pulled one out. If ever he needed a cigarette it was now. Sadly for him, a pear drop would just have to do.

Chapter 3

Holly winced as the kettle slammed onto the worktop and, after flicking the switch, Jonathan began to hunt around in the cupboards for mugs, clattering cups and plates and banging cupboard doors in the process. There was absolutely no need for him to do so. He knew perfectly well where the mugs were kept. Holly knew he was making a point and wondered what she could say to placate him.

Then again, she knew from experience that nothing she said would help. If anything her attempts to coax him out of his bad mood usually made him worse. Resigned to her fate, she kept silent and continued to scroll down her Facebook timeline, even though she wasn't taking in a single word of any of the posts.

A few minutes later a mug of tea was slammed down on the table in front of her.

'Thank you,' she murmured.

Jonathan didn't reply, rummaging in the bread bin for two slices of wholemeal bread to stick in the toaster. His back was to her, but Holly could feel waves of resentment radiating from him. She sighed inwardly and tapped the Twitter icon. Maybe there was something to distract her on there.

It was hard to concentrate though, when she could hear Jonathan's sulk travelling across the kitchen and hitting her smack in the face. It was funny really how he could be so noisy when he didn't say a word. He had a real gift for sulking; like a toddler who'd been refused sweets at the checkout, or a teenager who'd been banned from using the computer for a day or two. Except, of course, that he was a grown man and surely he should have grown out of sulking by now?

She put down her phone and took a sip of her tea.

Jonathan leaned against the worktop, aggressively biting chunks out of his toast. His brows knitted together as he ate, and he even chewed angrily.

Holly racked her brains for something to say to break this horrible atmosphere. She hated days like these. They were so awkward and made her feel worthless, as if she'd failed him but wasn't quite sure how. He hadn't come to bed last night but had slept on the sofa. She suspected that, if it wasn't so expensive to get a taxi to Whitby at that time of night, he'd have gone home.

They'd walked back to her house in silence, and he hadn't said a word to her last night, not even when she told him she was going up to bed and wished him goodnight. She hadn't even been sure he'd still be there when she got up that morning. She hated to admit it, but there was a part of her that wished he hadn't been.

'Do you want me to nip to Maudie's and get you a paper?' she ventured at last, knowing how much he enjoyed his Sunday morning ritual of sprawling on the sofa, flicking through the tabloids and reading out bits of so-called news to her.

'I'll get one on the way out,' he said briefly. He popped the last bit of toast in his mouth and dropped the plate into the washing up bowl in the sink. 'Right, that's me done.' He glanced at his watch. 'Bus will be here in ten minutes so I'll get off.'

'You're going home?'

'Nothing much to stay here for is there?'

Holly bit her lip. 'I'm sorry,' she mumbled.

'Forget it.'

'No really, I am. I shouldn't have left you alone for so long, especially as we were with my friends, not yours. I was being selfish.'

Jonathan opened the door of the under-stairs cupboard and reached for his jacket, which was hanging from a hook on the door. He shrugged it on and bent down to pick up his trainers.

'Jonathan, you don't have to go do you?' Holly pushed her tea away, feeling sick. 'It's Sunday. We can have a nice day together. I'll go and get you a newspaper and then I'll cook us both a roast dinner. I bought a chicken especially.'

He tied the laces on his trainers, yanking at them quite aggressively. 'I think it's better if I go home.'

'But I've said I'm sorry.'

'Yeah, for hiding away all evening.'

'Well, that's what you're mad at me for isn't it?'

He didn't reply.

'Is it something else? Have I done something else to annoy you?'

He zipped up his jacket and headed down the hall

towards the front door.

Holly half stood. 'Jonathan! What did I do?'

'You should know,' he replied, throwing open the door and stepping outside without even glancing back.

The front door slammed shut and Holly stared at it, her stomach churning. It would be days before he contacted her again. She knew the routine by now. There was nothing she could do but take her punishment. She wished she knew what, exactly, she was being punished for.

***

'Well, this is a nice surprise, I must say.' Lulu beamed at Holly as she ushered her into the kitchen of Cuckoo Nest Cottage. She hurriedly cleared the clutter from the worktops so that Holly could set down the loaded tray she was carrying. 'Nice bit of Sunday dinner. Been a while since I had that I must admit.'

Holly felt a prickling of shame. Her neighbour, Lulu, or Louisa Drake to give her her full name, was in her eighties, and suffered badly from arthritis, swollen legs, and various other ailments. Holly visited her most days to check up on her, do a bit of housework and maybe make her a sandwich or heat up some soup, but she'd been so busy lately with Jonathan that she hadn't cooked her a decent meal for ages. She also knew, deep down, that if Jonathan hadn't stomped off home earlier it wouldn't have occurred to her to make any dinner for Lulu even today. Why hadn't she thought of it before? Maybe, she thought, peeling back the foil on the plates,

Jonathan was right. She was selfish and thoughtless and stupid and all the other adjectives he frequently used to describe her.

'Ooh, a nice bit of chicken, and two Yorkshire puds.' Lulu's face creased as she smiled in delight. 'Thanks ever so much, Holly. I was just wondering what to have for me dinner, but it wouldn't have been anything like this. I do love a Yorkshire pud.'

Holly laughed. 'Well, let's tuck in then. And it's proper mashed potato too, none of that frozen stuff you hate so much.'

'Even better,' Lulu agreed.

Holly put the tin foil in the bin and carefully carried the plates over to Lulu's ancient pine table. The two of them took their places and for the next fifteen minutes or so the only remarks they exchanged concerned the food, which Lulu pronounced delicious and a credit to Holly's cooking skills. Holly shrugged off the compliments, but it did feel nice to be in the company of someone who wasn't judging her and finding her wanting.

'Go and put your feet up in the living room,' she told Lulu, 'while I wash these pots up and make us a cup of tea.'

'I can make the tea,' Lulu said but Holly was having none of it. 'Go and sit down,' she insisted. 'Get those legs up. You know what the doctor said.'

Lulu's legs were permanently swollen, and one was almost double the size of the other. The doctors had advised her that she should lie with her legs higher than her heart for at least thirty minutes, four times a day, but Lulu struggled to obey them as she found lying flat boring.

'The kettle can be boiling while I wash up. It's no trouble honestly.'

Lulu patted her on the shoulder and did as she was told. Holly got on with the jobs in hand, but her mind kept wandering to Jonathan and what he was doing now. He should be home, even though the buses were rather unreliable on Sundays. Always supposing he'd gone home of course. She remembered the girl who'd been with him last night at the party. Gina, did he call her? He'd assured Holly they were only searching for her, but had they been? Or had they gone out into the garden for some other purpose? Panic knotted her stomach as her imagination went into overdrive. What if he'd arranged to meet her today? Is that why he'd left so early?

After drying her hands she picked up her mobile and called his number. It rang a couple of times then a voicemail message from Jonathan played. Holly frowned. It usually rang a lot longer than that. Had he rejected her call?

Trembling, she waited for the tone then left him a message. 'Jonathan, it's me, Holly. I, er, I was just ringing to check that you got home okay. You know, what with the, er, buses and everything. I—' she gulped, 'I really am sorry about last night. I—I love you. Bye.'

'In his bad books again are you?'

Holly spun round, shocked to see Lulu standing in the doorway, her arms folded, and her lips pursed.

'Just a misunderstanding,' she said lightly. 'Now, cup of tea.'

'Misunderstanding my eye,' Lulu said. 'Always got something to complain about hasn't he? Never known such a moaner in all me life. Like a big, daft kid.'

'It was my fault,' Holly insisted, spooning sugar in the mugs.

'Course it was. I'd expect nothing less,' Lulu told her.

'Go and sit down.' Holly swallowed down the lump that had suddenly appeared in her throat. 'You're supposed to be resting your legs.'

'Oh, I know. That's all I ever hear.'

'Well it's true. Look at the size of your left leg especially. You need to get it propped up on cushions.'

Lulu tutted. 'All very well telling me to rest that leg, but what's me other leg supposed to be doing in the meantime?'

Despite her misery Holly couldn't help but laugh.

Lulu grinned at her. 'That's better. That's more like my Hollybobs. Wondered what had happened to her to be honest. Nice to see you smile once in a while.'

'You make me sound like a right misery,' Holly protested.

'If the cap fits.' Lulu tutted and made her way back into the living room.

A moment or two later Holly followed her, carrying two mugs of tea.

Lulu nodded her thanks as she shuffled around on the sofa, making herself comfortable.

'What a palaver this is,' she muttered, lifting her leg with both hands, and plonking her foot down on a cushion. 'This settee isn't built for comfort, that's for sure. Not when you're my age, any road.'

'Do you need any help?'

'Nowt you can do about it, love. It is what it is.' Lulu sighed and reached for another cushion to support her back a little. 'If it's not me leg throbbing it's me neck, or me hands. Look at these claws. I ask you!' She held up gnarled, twisted fingers for Holly's inspection. 'Ready for the knacker's yard, I reckon.'

'Don't say things like that,' Holly said. 'It upsets me.'

'Happens to us all,' Lulu pointed out, not sounding particularly worried about it. 'And truth to tell, when you can't even go for a nice walk in the countryside, even though you live in a pretty village like Bramblewick, there doesn't seem much point to it all.'

'Do you really think that?' Holly was aghast. 'I had no idea.'

Lulu smiled. 'Only in me darkest moments, don't worry. Most of the time I'm quite happy. Long as I've got David Dickinson to watch on an afternoon I'm right as rain. By, it makes me laugh that programme. All them greedy so-and-sos trying to get a fortune for that old tat.'

Holly had no idea what Lulu was talking about, since she'd never really had the opportunity to watch daytime television and probably wouldn't, even if she had, but she nodded and smiled back, grateful that Lulu had something to entertain her. It must be a boring life she mused, feeling guilty.

Lulu had really gone downhill during the last five years or so. Before that she'd been lively and healthy, out and about in all weathers and active in village life. It was sad to see how much she'd declined. It had happened so slowly and gradually that Holly hadn't realised how much she'd changed.

She'd known Lulu all her life, having lived next door to her since she was born. Even when her parents' marriage had broken up and they'd both moved on to other homes and new lives, she'd managed to take over the tenancy and stay put.

She knew no other home and Lulu had been the one constant in her life. When her father moved out, and then her mother remarried and left to be with her new husband, Lulu had still been there, just yards from Holly's front door. Holly's house was at the end of a small row of tiny cottages on the edge of Bramblewick, but Cuckoo Nest Cottage stood separate to those and was twice the size of each of them, with a garden that was larger than all of theirs put together. It was the bane of Lulu's life, since she could no longer take care of it. It wasn't so bad now, as everything was beginning to die off and growth had declined drastically, but in the summer the grass seemed to double in height every week. Holly did her best with the lawnmower and strimmer, but she wasn't much of a gardener.

She thought about Lewis, reckoning that he would love to be let loose on Lulu's garden. Remembering Lewis though probably wasn't a good idea. He must think she was an absolute fool, standing out there in Abbie's garden, freezing to death because she was too embarrassed to go back inside, even to fetch her coat. He was a kind man though, and hadn't pushed her for explanations, which was a good job, since she wouldn't have been able to offer one. Was that why Jonathan was cross with her she wondered. Was he jealous?

She felt a tiny seed of hope within her, and almost hugged herself in delight. It made sense, surely? And if Jonathan was jealous of Lewis, that meant he still loved her. He would never have reacted so badly if he didn't.

'What are you smirking about?' Lulu's suspicious tones cut through her thoughts, and she blinked and straightened, reaching for her mug of tea.

'Sorry, miles away. Just thinking about those people you were talking about on the antiques programme.'

Lulu narrowed her eyes. 'Sure you were. You were thinking about that manchild again no doubt. All you ever think about these days.'

'Don't be silly,' Holly said, but she couldn't deny it to herself. When she got home, she would try ringing him again, reassure him that he had no reason to be jealous. Lewis was just a bloke she'd happened to bump into. Jonathan was the love of her life. He need never doubt that.

Chapter 4

Holly flicked listlessly through the television channels, her nose wrinkling as she dismissed each one in turn. There was nothing that she fancied watching, though to be fair that was probably more her fault than the programme makers. Her heart wasn't in it. She couldn't settle to anything. She glanced over at her phone where it lay redundant on the coffee table. She had checked and double checked that the volume was on full, but there had definitely been no call or text. Nothing.

Three days! She threw the remote control beside her on the sofa and grabbed a cushion instead, burying her face in it as she hurled herself down and pleaded with herself not to cry. As she lay there, cushion held tightly to her face, she closed her eyes to blink away the tears and told herself that it would pass. It always did. He would forgive her eventually and then all would be well again.

But what if this time it wasn't? The fear gnawed away at her, making her feel sick. Supposing, this time, he'd moved on. Decided that she really wasn't worth the trouble. That she'd let him down one time too many.

If only he'd answer her calls, then she could talk to him, tell him again how sorry she was for leaving him alone at the party and reassure him that nothing was going on between her and Lewis. He had to believe that. She would make him believe it.

The knock on the door almost stopped her heart from beating. She threw down the cushion and lay there, eyes wide as her heart recovered itself and went into overdrive, hammering hard in her chest. Could it be...?

Hardly daring to breathe, she got to her feet and headed into the hallway, her legs feeling weak with fear. *Don't get too excited*, she warned herself. *It could be anyone—canvassers, religious missionaries, even early Christmas carollers for goodness' sake.*

'You took your time. Were you asleep?' Jonathan stood on the doorstep, hands behind his back, a wide smile on his face.

Holly's stomach somersaulted. 'Jonathan! I'm sorry, I didn't know it was you.'

He narrowed his eyes. 'Who else would it be? Were you expecting someone?'

'Of course not! It's just, I haven't heard from you in three days and—'

'I know, I've really missed you. Have you missed me?' He thrust a bunch of flowers and a box of Maltesers into her hands. 'For you.'

Holly looked down at them, astonished. 'For me? Why?'

'Like I said, I missed you.' He gave a short laugh. 'Well, come on then, Holls, are you going to invite me in or what? It's freezing out here.'

'Oh of course. Sorry.' She stepped aside and he pushed past her, kicking off his trainers and throwing his jacket casually on the stairs.

'I'll just put these in water,' she called as he strolled into the living room.

'Coffee would be great too,' he replied. 'Warm me up a bit. God knows I need it, and it's always like a fridge in this place.'

Holly had to admit that the central heating in her home wasn't as efficient as it should be but try telling that to her landlord. He didn't give a monkey's. She could freeze to death for all he cared. Right now though, a warm feeling was spreading through her that even the chill in the house couldn't prevent. Jonathan was back and it seemed he'd forgiven her.

She put the kettle on and while it was boiling she filled a vase with water and began to trim and arrange the flowers. They were lovely. He was so thoughtful. She was a bit surprised by the Maltesers though, considering Jonathan was always ribbing her about her weight and made quite pointed remarks whenever he saw her eating anything too fattening. It just showed how much he loved her, she supposed. She would be able to enjoy those later since she could eat them with a clear conscience and Jonathan's approval.

A few minutes later she carried the vase into the living room and placed it carefully on the windowsill, then went back into the kitchen for Jonathan's coffee. He was lying on the sofa, remote control in hand, and he'd already found a film he wanted to watch. Holly put his mug on the coffee table then sat down in the armchair.

'Cheers, Holls. I'm ready for this.' Jonathan swung his feet onto the floor and reached for the drink. 'It's freezing out there you know. I've had a nightmare journey from Whitby, I can tell you.' He winked at her. 'Early night for us, eh? We can get all warm and cosy under that duvet. I've brought my toothbrush.'

Holly knew she should be delighted, and she was, of course she was. Just that...

'Where have you been for the last three days?' She tried not to sound too cross about it, but his casual behaviour, as if nothing had happened, was rattling her. How could he just waltz back in like things were fine? Did he have any idea how miserable she'd been?

He blinked. 'What are you on about? You know where I've been. At work. Where do you think?'

'I haven't heard from you for three days,' she persisted. 'I've rung you loads of times, and you didn't answer. You could have at least texted me to tell me you were all right—that we were okay.'

A coldness came into his eyes, and Holly's stomach plummeted. She knew that look. She'd pushed him too far and he would retreat from her again. Why did she always have to open her big mouth?

'I know it was my fault,' she added hastily. 'And I really am sorry that I left you alone for so long. You were right,' she told him, knowing how much he enjoyed being told that. 'About the dress I mean. I did feel stupid in it. It was too much. That's why I disappeared. I felt like a fool, so I hid away, but that had nothing whatsoever to do with you.'

Jonathan sipped his drink slowly then nodded. 'I knew that, Holls. No need to explain. I felt really sorry for you, that's all. I didn't know what to say and that's why I stayed away. How could I face you after what happened?'

For a moment, the girl in the garden flashed through Holly's mind and she swallowed. 'What—what happened?'

'What they said,' he explained, shaking his head sadly. 'I don't know if they realised I was listening or not, and I don't even think they cared if I was. But you tell me, Holly, what was I supposed to do? How did you expect me to react when all I heard was insults about my own girlfriend?'

Holly stared at him. 'What are you talking about?'

He sighed. 'Your so-called friends, that's what. They were all huddled together, and I could hear them, laughing about your dress and making fun of you. They were saying how you always go over-the-top, how you can never just be, well, *normal*.' He hesitated then ploughed on. 'They were talking to that bloke. You know, the tall, gangly blond one. They were telling him how you had a reputation for being loud and a bit silly at parties. One of them—it might have been Anna, I'm not sure—said you showed them up sometimes, but then Izzy—I think it was Izzy anyway—she said not to be mean because it wasn't really your fault. It was just the way you were, and you couldn't help yourself. Someone said, "Yes, but honestly, that dress!" and they all laughed. I couldn't listen any longer, really I couldn't.

I walked away because I might have said something I'd regret, and no matter how I felt about it I know they're your friends and you care about them.'

Holly felt sick. "They really said all that?'

'Oh, sweetheart, I'm so sorry. I didn't want to tell you, but the thing is I couldn't face you. Afterwards, I mean. I didn't know what to tell you, or if I should even mention it at all. I had to stay away while I calmed down and thought things through. I decided this morning that you had a right to know. If it was me being discussed and mocked by my mates I'd want to know, and who am I to keep it from you? Are you okay?'

'But—' Holly shook her head, confused. 'They wouldn't. I mean, are you sure you heard it all right?'

'Believe me, I heard. And I wasn't the only one. Half the room heard. Your new friend seemed to find it all most amusing.'

'Lewis?' Holly's face burned. What on earth must he think of her? 'But, if you were angry with my friends for what they said, why did you take it out on me?'

Jonathan looked bewildered. 'Take it out on you? What the heck are you talking about? As if I would do that.'

'But you didn't speak to me! And you practically accused me of flirting with Lewis.'

Jonathan reached over and took hold of her hand. 'Aw, Holls, you've got me all wrong. You should know me better than that by now. Come on, love, as if I would do that. I didn't speak to you because I was too busy trying to figure out in my head what to say to you, and whether I should say anything at all. And the only reason I was put out to see you with Lewis is because I knew that, just minutes beforehand, he'd been laughing at you. I couldn't stand seeing him with you, pretending to be nice.' His lip curled in disgust. 'Offering you his jacket, for crying out loud. What a hypocrite. You'd have thrown it back at him if you'd heard them all, I promise you that. Now you tell me, how did you expect me to behave, eh? How would you have felt if you'd heard my pals mocking me? You wouldn't have liked it would you?'

Holly shook her head, feeling dazed. 'No, no of course not.'

Jonathan watched her for a minute, then he gave her a sad smile and patted the sofa beside him. 'Come and sit here. My Holly needs a cuddle, right? Come on.'

As he held out his arms to her, Holly found herself compelled to walk into them. She practically fell on the sofa, and he wrapped her in a tight embrace.

'It's okay, love, it's okay. I know it must be hurtful to you and I'm sorry. I hate that it's me, of all people, who had to tell you about this. Please don't be too upset. For one thing they'd been drinking, and you know how that affects people. Anyway, you've always got me, you know that don't you?'

Holly closed her eyes, imagining her friends standing around gossiping about her, laughing at her new dress, and pitying her for never getting things quite right. They always called her their party girl, she remembered. Funny, she'd always thought it was a term of affection. How had she not realised that it was their way of mocking her?

She put her arms around Jonathan's waist, glad of the safety and protection he offered.

'I've really missed you,' she whispered tearfully.

'I've missed you, too,' he told her, stroking her hair. 'It's all right, Holly. Don't get upset. I love you so much. Nothing will ever change that—especially not your so-called friends.'

Thank God for Jonathan, she thought, blinking away the tears. It seemed he was the only one in the world she could really rely on to be honest with her.

Chapter 5

Holly nodded over at the elderly gentleman sitting two rows from the front in the reception. 'Mr Woodhouse? Dr Blake buzzed you in a moment ago.'

He cupped his ear and leaned forward slightly. 'Sorry, love, what did you say?'

'Dr Blake will see you now,' she said, a bit louder and clearer.

He gave her the thumbs up and shuffled across reception towards the corridor and Connor Blake's consulting room. Holly glanced ruefully at the electronic server that hung on the wall above various National Health Service leaflets and pamphlets. It had only been installed a few months ago and was supposed to make life easier for patients, but many of them still seemed to ignore it and waited to be called through by the receptionist. It was the same with the touchscreen check-in. Hardly anyone used it. They would rather queue at the desk and wait for her or Anna or Joan to book them in. Technology wasn't particularly popular in Bramblewick.

Seeing that Mr Woodhouse was the last patient for the morning, Holly began to do the bits and bobs that were needed before surgery closed for lunch. Her least favourite job was making sure that all the samples in the sample bin were correctly labelled and secure, ready for the "lab man" to call.

After pulling on latex gloves she quickly checked them all, relieved that all seemed well. Just in time too. She'd no sooner removed and disposed of the gloves and applied antibacterial gel to her hands than he arrived, giving her a cheery wave as he walked through the main reception doors. He was closely followed by one of the chemists' delivery drivers, who had called to collect prescriptions.

Holly was kept busy for the next few minutes as she flicked through the prescription drawer, collecting all the scripts that were ready to go to that particular chemist. Most prescriptions these days were sent electronically, but there were plenty of patients at Bramblewick who didn't trust computers and refused to accept anything other than paper.

By the time the prescriptions had been signed for, the lab man had left, and Mr Woodhouse was making his way back to the reception desk.

'Dr Blake says I've got to see the practice nurse for blood tests. He's written down what I need,' he informed her, handing her a piece of paper.

Holly nodded and checked Rachel's appointments on screen. 'We're a bit short on appointments,' she admitted. 'The earliest I can manage would be next Friday at nine-thirty. Is that okay for you, Mr Woodhouse?'

'That'd be smashing, Holly. Thanks very much.'

She quickly wrote his appointment details on a card

and handed it to him.

'How's Louisa doing?' he queried. 'That leg of hers still bad is it?'

Holly nodded. 'I saw her this morning before work. It wasn't too good, but it's her arthritis that's really playing her up this week. I think it's the cold weather. She's in ever so much pain, though she always denies it to me. One of the doctors is going to visit her this lunchtime, so we'll see.'

'Aye. Thought I hadn't seen her out and about much lately.' He sighed. 'Comes to us all though, doesn't it? Not that you'd know about that and won't for many a year. But one day you'll find out. It's not nice you know, when most of your friends drop off the perch and the ones you've got left are practically housebound. We all used to have such a laugh together. Such a shame.' He straightened. 'Mind you, I can't complain. Ninety-two and I still play bowls you know. Life in the old dog yet. Best get off, you'll be wanting to put the shutter down. Give my love to Louisa won't you?'

'I will, Mr Woodhouse. Thank you.'

Holly watched him walk away, deep in thought. The way things were going she'd have no one to miss when she got old. Her so-called friends weren't friends at all as it turned out, and she'd barely spoken a word to them for the last couple of days. How could she trust them now, knowing what they thought of her?

She logged off the computer and pushed the button to close the electronic shutter. As it rattled its way down she tried to summon her courage. She would just have to hope that everyone was busy for lunch, then she wouldn't have to talk to any of them.

Abbie, Riley, and Connor would be heading out on visits and Anna might be popping home to check on Chester, Gracie's rescue dog.

Chester was a six-year-old, wiry grey chap with one eye and a misshapen ear. He'd been badly treated and Gracie—Connor's eleven-year-old daughter—had fallen in love with him at first sight. Odd really, because she'd spent months studying all the different breeds of dog that she would be happy to own, and had made a shortlist of her favourites, and Anna had been convinced that, if there were none of those at the rescue centre Gracie would walk away without a backward glance.

Yet there had been not one, but *two* of Gracie's favourite breeds of dog available for adoption, and she hadn't looked twice at them. Her heart had been completely won over by a battered survivor, and there was no turning back. She was absolutely devoted to him, and he repaid her love and kindness tenfold. Anna and Connor loved Chester as much as Gracie did, even though it did mean that one of them always had to rush home at lunchtime to let him out and top up his water bowl.

Joan, who had come to the practice to cover Anna on maternity leave but had ended up staying part-time, only worked mornings or afternoons, so was never around at lunchtimes.

That only left Rachel, and she sometimes went home to Folly Farm to see Xander and her mum. Holly might just be lucky and be able to eat her lunch in peace.

Anna and Abbie were still in the office though when she went through from reception.

'Not going home to let Chester out?' she asked Anna, trying not to sound disappointed.

'Connor's popping by since he's got a visit that way. I'm working through so I can leave a bit early. I've got a final fitting with Izzy later, so we've got to be in Moreton Cross by half past four at the latest.'

Anna was going to be matron of honour to Izzy, who was marrying Ash at The Sea Star Hotel in Starfish Sands, near Filey. Izzy hadn't wanted any other bridesmaids, and Holly had been relieved to hear it. She only wished Rachel had been of the same mind.

She thought gloomily of the emerald green gown that Rachel had selected for her bridesmaids. It was beautiful, particularly when teamed with the faux fur stole that would stave off the winter chill, but Holly couldn't help feeling it would show off every lump and bump and reveal just how much fatter than her fellow bridesmaids she really was.

She wished she hadn't eaten that box of Maltesers, but it had seemed almost as if Jonathan was giving her permission. Usually he complained about her weight, but when he'd bought her the chocolates as a gift, it seemed as if he were saying that she was all right as she was. She had a horrible feeling that had been wishful thinking on her part, as she'd simply been looking for an excuse to scoff the lot.

'I don't know. It's all wedding talk round here lately,' Abbie said, smiling. 'Anyway, I can't stand here talking dresses, much as I'd love to. I've got visits to go on and I'd better get on with it or I'll be late for afternoon surgery. Ooh, before I forget, Anna did you ask Holly about the training?'

Anna groaned. 'Totally forgot. Holly, how would you feel about training to be a phlebotomist?'

Holly frowned. 'You mean, take blood from patients? Why?'

'Well, you know we're short of nurse appointments. Rachel's snowed under, and since a lot of her time's taken up with routine blood tests, it makes sense to train one of us for the job so we could help when she's particularly busy.'

'But why me? Why not you or Joan?'

'I can't see Joan being keen and besides you've been here longer than she has. As for me—to be honest, I've got enough to do, being head receptionist. And I thought you'd enjoy it. There'd be a small pay rise and, well, it might give you a bit of confidence, having that extra responsibility. What do you think?'

Holly's anxiety levels surged. Anna was right, it *was* extra responsibility. What if she wasn't up to the job? If she messed up she could do some real harm.

'I—I don't think so,' she muttered.

Anna looked surprised. 'Really? Look, why not take some time to think about it? There's no rush. Let me know when you decide.'

Abbie put her hand on her shoulder. 'I think you'd be great at it,' she assured her. 'The patients love you, and you're so good at putting them at their ease.' She stepped back, considering her. 'Are you okay? You've been ever so quiet today.'

'She's been quiet all week,' Anna said, giving Holly an anxious look. 'Not herself at all. What's up, Holls?'

'Nothing. Why should there be anything wrong?'

Anna and Abbie exchanged glances and Holly was instantly on her guard. What secret message were they passing between themselves? Clearly they had an opinion about her.

'Things okay with you and Jonathan?' Abbie's tone was casual, but Holly wasn't fooled.

'Perfect,' she said, forcing a smile. 'He brought me flowers and chocolates the other night. Just to say he loved me.'

'Well...' Abbie gave her a weak smile in return. 'That's lovely.'

'Yes, it is,' Holly said defiantly. 'We're very happy. He loves me just as I am. I may not be perfect, but it doesn't matter to him. He's wonderful.'

Abbie watched her steadily for a moment then cleared her throat. 'Right. Great. I'll be off then. See you both later.'

She headed out of the office and Holly avoided Anna by hurrying into the kitchenette to collect her sandwiches from the fridge, feeling that they would choke her if she so much as tried to eat them.

***

Lewis curled his hands around the mug of hot coffee and closed his eyes in bliss. Just what he needed. His face was numb with cold and a few minutes' rest plus a much-longed-for drink was like a gift from heaven.

'By heck, you look happy. What's made your day?'

His eyes flew open, and he grinned as Bernie, the estate manager at Kearton Hall, entered the staff room, carrying a mug of his own—no doubt filled to the brim with Bernie's favourite Yorkshire tea, "made so strong that a spoon could stand up in it", as he often said.

'A bit of warmth and this,' he said, nodding at the coffee and settling back in his chair, closing his eyes again for a moment as the heat from the radiator soothed his aching bones.

'You're easy pleased, I'll say that much for you.' Bernie grinned and sank down into the chair opposite him. 'Busy morning?'

'I've been clearing up fallen leaves,' he replied. 'Raking the lawns and the flower beds and dredging the ponds. Not my favourite job, but necessary.'

'Oh, aye.' Bernie nodded, sipping his tea thoughtfully. 'Don't forget the first wreath-making workshop's coming up. Hope you've bin gathering bits of greenery and berries and the like.'

'Of course. And I hope you've been collecting pheasant feathers and pine cones as instructed,' Lewis replied, a twinkle of amusement in his eyes as Bernie pulled a face.

'Not like I have owt else to do is it?' he said.

'Well, it was your wife's idea,' Lewis pointed out. 'You can hardly complain.'

Bernie settled back in his chair. 'I can't, but it's never stopped me.' His face wrinkled into a smile. 'I suppose it's a good idea of Darcey's, though. I mean, ten workshops they're running this year, and charging fifty quid a head. Fifty quid!' He shook his head, clearly bewildered. 'Some people have nowt better to spend their money on. And what do they get for that fifty quid, eh? A flipping Christmas wreath they could've bought ready-made for half the price at Helmston Market. They even have to bring their own secateurs and gardening gloves.'

'But don't forget they also get a mince pie and a glass of mulled wine,' Lewis pointed out with a smirk. 'Absolute bargain I'd say. Besides, there's nothing to beat that feeling of satisfaction at a job well done.'

'If you say so.' Bernie took a long gulp of tea and smacked his lips together in appreciation. 'Daft buggers can pay all they like. All I care about is that it's more money coming into the estate. That's what we're all working for, at the end of the day.'

'And a fine team we make,' Lewis said.

'Aye, happen we do.' Bernie nodded. 'Got plenty of orders for Christmas trees this year too.'

'Already? Still, nothing beats a real Christmas tree,' Lewis mused. 'I might get one myself for my new flat. Of course it would have to be a small one, but it would be nice to have a real one for a change. I've had artificial ones for the last few years.'

'Settling in all right in your new home?' Bernie enquired.

'It's great,' Lewis said, genuinely enthusiastic. 'It's great to have a place to myself again, after sharing with two other blokes for ages. And I can't deny living over a café and bakery is fantastic. You should taste the pies and pasties they make. I'm in serious danger of getting fat.'

Bernie spluttered with laughter. 'Get away with you. Seen more fat on a greasy chip. Like a whippet you are.' He patted his own stomach and shook his head. 'Look at this! This is the love of a good woman, that's what this is. Never had a weight problem until I married Darcey. I should be on a diet by rights, but like I said to her, I need padding for winter, being out in all weathers. Insulation right? She couldn't argue with that.'

They settled into a comfortable silence, sipping their drinks, each lost in their own thoughts. Lewis was musing on tomorrow's work already. He would be working in the greenhouses, potting some bulbs, covering the hellebores, and bringing them inside, so they'd flower a little earlier than usual. He had a couple of large greenhouses that needed checking over and plenty of maintenance jobs: getting rid of spent crops, cleaning, disinfecting, ensuring the heating and lighting were correct and there was adequate frost protection. Not his favourite month in the garden, he had to admit, but it would all pay dividends soon enough.

'Right, I suppose I'd better get off,' he said, taking his empty cup over to the sink and washing it out.

'Not having any dinner today?' Bernie drained his own mug and joined him at the sink. 'You need to keep your energy up. You'll have to come over to The Gatehouse one night, lad. Have a bit of tea with me an' Darcey. She said she'd like to get to know you better.'

Lewis nodded. 'I'd like that. Thank you.' Darcey

worked at Kearton Hall too, managing the house itself. She didn't have much to do with the grounds, so he rarely saw her, but she'd seemed friendly on the few occasions he'd bumped into her and after all, if she was married to Bernie, she must be nice enough he reasoned. 'I think I should reassure you, though, that I'll be eating later. I'm going to nip back to Bramblewick first, to register at the surgery. I more-or-less got my orders from the staff there the other night.'

'Better to be safe than sorry,' Bernie said. 'Off you go then. I'll talk to Darcey about dates for your tea and let you know. See you later.'

The drive from Kearton Bay to Bramblewick was uneventful and Lewis pulled into the car park behind the surgery, switched off the engine, and patted the dashboard of his battered old van.

'Well done,' he told it. He knew it was ridiculous, but it had become a superstition to always thank the old girl for getting him from A to B without incident. She was so old now that it was a miracle she even started, so any journey completed was a triumph.

He walked round to the front of the building, impressed by its smart, shiny exterior, which looked reassuringly professional, even if it didn't exactly fit with the style of the village. He could see there had been a recent extension, which made him think that someone had great faith in the practice. Anyway, he knew Abbie quite well and trusted her. Connor and Riley had seemed decent enough chaps. He hoped they were as good at their job as they were at making a stranger feel welcome.

The automatic doors slid open, and Lewis entered a fairly large, carpeted area, with an expansive seating area and a long reception desk.

There was an electronic server on one wall, and racks of the usual NHS leaflets fixed about the room. He eyed the one about stopping smoking, wondering if he should pick it up, but then decided the pear drops were doing the job. Although if the craving didn't vanish altogether within a month or two he might have to investigate the weight loss clinic more thoroughly.

There was a queue of four people ahead of him, and Lewis joined the line. Within a minute or two, several more people entered the surgery and stood behind him. He realised that he'd picked a busy time of day. It was just after lunch, and people were queueing to make appointments. He glanced at his watch, hoping he'd get back to Kearton Hall in time to eat before restarting work.

The receptionist smiled at him as he finally reached the front of the queue. She was auburn-haired and middle-aged and had kind eyes.

'How can I help you?'

He peered at her name badge. 'Good afternoon, Joan. I was wondering if I could register as a patient here? I've just moved into the area you see.'

Joan looked surprisingly disconcerted by the fact. She glanced at the queue behind him and tutted. 'Oh, right. Just a minute, love.'

She stuck her head round the door and yelled into what he presumed was an office, 'Holly! Can you give me a hand on reception please?'

Something fluttered in Lewis's stomach. Hunger, he supposed. He seemed to get even more hungry when Holly rushed into reception and took her place at the other end of the desk.

'If you'll just move over there, love,' Joan said, gesturing to Holly. 'I'm dealing with appointments you see.'

He nodded and left the queue behind, sauntering over to where Holly was tapping something into a computer. She looked up expectantly and he saw, with some dismay, that she'd been crying.

'Oh, hello.' She was clearly taken aback to see him. 'I wasn't expecting—How can I help?'

'Abbie said I needed to register here, now I've moved from Staithes. I suppose it is too far to go if I need to see a GP.'

'You're out of their catchment area anyway,' she said. 'Don't look so worried. It's pretty easy to register.'

'Glad to hear it,' he said, smiling. 'Form filling's not my thing.'

She handed him a couple of forms and told him how to fill them in and where to sign.

'You'll need two forms of ID,' she added. 'Have you brought anything?'

He nodded, handing her the birth certificate and the driving licence that he'd shoved in the glove compartment.

'When you've completed the registration form and the health questionnaire, I'll make you an appointment for a new patient check-up,' she told him.

Lewis took a seat and began to fill in the forms. It

didn't take him long and he was back at the desk before Holly, who had nipped into the office. When she returned, he handed them to her and after quickly reading through them she nodded. 'That's fine. Here's your ID back. I'll just find you an appointment.'

She stared at the computer screen, clicking and scrolling for what felt like forever.

'So what happens at this new patient check?' he asked eventually.

'Haven't you had one before?'

'Probably, but that was a while ago. Or I may have dodged it completely. Is it scary?'

For the first time she smiled. 'Terrifying.'

He grinned. 'That's better.'

She had dimples in her cheeks when she smiled he noticed. Cute. Shame she usually looked depressed.

'What's better?'

'You, smiling. It cheers me up.'

'I suppose every time you see me I look unhappy,' she mused. 'You must think I'm a real misery guts.'

'I just think it's nice to see you smile,' he said carefully. 'You have a lovely smile. You should show it off more often.'

She flushed slightly and turned her attention back to the screen. He watched her growing increasingly harassed.

'Problem?'

'We're a bit short of nurse appointments,' she admitted.

'No worries. I can make one another day.' Happy to, he thought.

'I suppose that's my fault, too,' she said, and he watched, feeling helpless as tears sprang into her eyes. 'Oh, heck!' She dabbed at them furiously. 'What the hell is wrong with me lately?'

She cast a nervous glance over at the other receptionist, but the queue had vanished, and Joan was busy typing.

'How,' Lewis whispered, 'could it possibly be your fault that there are no nurse's appointments?'

'You'd be surprised,' she whispered back.

'I'd be amazed,' he told her. 'Go on, dazzle me.'

She hesitated then shrugged. 'Okay then. We only have one practice nurse. You know, Rachel?'

He nodded.

'Well, she does all the blood tests you see, as well as everything else. It's too much for her really, so the practice is going to pay for one of us receptionists to train as a phlebotomist.'

'Brilliant,' he said. 'And are you the chosen one?'

'Yes,' she said gloomily. 'At least, I was. I turned it down earlier, and now everyone will think I'm an idiot and it will probably fall on Anna, and she's got enough to do already.'

He frowned. 'Okay, so why did you turn it down?'

'Because—' She shook her head. 'Oh, I'm sorry. Why would you be interested in any of this? You only came here to register.'

'But I am interested.' He smiled encouragingly at her. 'You wore my jacket. I feel that makes us friends.'

She laughed. 'Fool!'

'That's me. So indulge me. Why wouldn't you want

to be a phlebotomist?' He winked at her. 'Is it because you can't spell it and don't want to have to write it on your CV?'

'Certainly not,' she said, but he was relieved to see a gleam of amusement in her eyes. Better than tears, that was for sure.

'Just me then,' he said. 'I couldn't spell it to save my life.'

'I could spell it. I just couldn't do it,' she admitted.

'I find that very hard to believe,' he said. 'You're a bright, capable woman. Why wouldn't you be able to do it?'

'I'm not bright or capable,' she assured him. 'I'd mess up, no doubt about it. I—I seem to get very muddled lately.' Her eyes filled with tears again. 'It's all a bit of a mess actually.'

He could imagine it was, and he didn't need any help to figure out why. Poor Holly. She didn't deserve any of this.

He rummaged in his jacket pocket and brought out a crumpled paper bag. 'Have a pear drop?'

She peered into the bag. 'You and your pear drops! You're getting quite a reputation for them you know. Pear Drop Man.'

'There are worse things,' he pointed out.

'True enough. Hmm. I shouldn't really...' She glanced over at Joan who was paying them no attention whatsoever. 'Go on then. Thanks.'

She managed to separate one from the lumpy mass inside the bag and popped it in her mouth. Lewis did the same, thinking he really ought to get back to

Kearton Hall. He was going to be late at this rate, never mind not having any lunch.

'You ought to have more faith you know,' he said, uncomfortably aware that speaking with his mouth full of boiled sweet wasn't a great look. 'Your colleagues clearly do, or they wouldn't ask you.'

'Huh!'

He raised an eyebrow. 'You disagree?'

The reception doors slid open, and a couple of people entered, heading straight for Joan.

'I know what they think of me,' she burst out suddenly.

'I'm sorry?'

'What they were saying to you,' she said, staring at him, her expression defiant. 'I know what they told you about me at the party.'

He felt uncomfortable, remembering how her friends had expressed concern for her and how they'd worried that Jonathan was having a negative influence on her.

'Your friends care about you,' he murmured, not sure he should be getting involved in all this.

'Care about me? And that's why they made fun of me is it?'

'Made fun of you?' He blinked, confused. Where had she got that idea?

'I knew that dress was a mistake,' she admitted, tapping a pen nervously on a notepad. 'I should never have worn it, but even so. They didn't have to be so cruel about it.'

'Holly, I'm sorry, you've lost me,' Lewis said. 'Who

was making fun of you? Because, believe me, I didn't hear anyone mocking you and I certainly didn't hear anyone being cruel about you.'

She looked at him, clearly uncertain. 'You were laughing at me,' she said, her voice low. 'You don't have to deny it. I was told.'

'Told by whom?' He shifted the pear drop into his right cheek and stared at her, bewildered, then his mind cleared. 'Is this what Jonathan said, by any chance?'

She crunched the sweet for a few moments, clearly contemplating whether to answer. 'Does it matter?'

'Yes. It matters a lot, because whoever told you that any of us were laughing at you or being cruel got it all wrong. No one was laughing at you. The consensus among your friends was that you looked sensational in that dress, and I agreed. You did.'

Holly looked doubtful as she gulped down the remains of the pear drop. 'Sure I did.'

'Well,' he said lightly, 'I'm not going to spend the next hour arguing with you about it, but I will say that I'm not in the habit of telling lies, and I don't play games either. You looked lovely at the party, everyone thought so. Believe it or not, but don't doubt your friends. They care about you, trust me. They care about you more than you can possibly imagine.'

She bit her lip and he saw the confusion in her eyes. She wanted to take his word for it, he could tell, but something was stopping her. Jonathan, no doubt. What the hell had that louse told her?

Lewis's fists curled in anger. He could well imagine. In fact, he didn't have to imagine. He'd heard it all before, many times, and he'd seen the result that those tactics could have. Jonathan was harming Holly more than she could know. It was such a waste.

'You should tell them about your worries. I'm sure they'd reassure you.'

'I don't think so. Look, I'd better go and help Joan.' She pushed back her chair and stood. 'If you call the surgery in a day or two we'll try to find you an appointment, okay?'

He narrowed his eyes. 'You're changing the subject.'

'I'm at work, and I've taken long enough to register a new patient don't you think?'

He couldn't deny that, nor that he needed to get back to work himself. 'Okay, fair enough. Thank you for all your help. I'll inform your bosses that you're an exceptionally kind and competent receptionist.' He winked at her, and she grinned, making his heart leap. 'See you later, Holly.'

'See you, Lewis.'

He stuffed the ID in his inside jacket pocket and strolled out of the surgery. At least he'd made her smile again and hopefully put her mind at rest a little. She was really messed up, and he knew exactly who was to blame for that.

Not your business, he reminded himself again. *It's between Holly and Jonathan. Besides, she's got loads of friends. She doesn't need me sticking my oar in.*

Yet he knew, as he walked towards the car park, that it was no longer as simple as that. Holly had gradually become his business, and he didn't even know how it had happened.

Chapter 6

Holly rushed home from work after a busy day, intent on preparing a tasty meal for Jonathan, who would be arriving at her house at about seven o'clock. She'd bought steaks and his favourite beer-battered onion rings and was just trying to decide whether to do him his beloved chips or go with jacket potatoes when he called her to tell her that he wouldn't be round that night after all.

'I've got an early start tomorrow, love, and I'm tired out. All that travelling to and from Whitby, it gets too much. Gonna take a night off. Okay, babe?'

'But you can stay over,' she protested. 'You usually do anyway.'

'Yeah, but I'd still have to drive over to Bramblewick, and I can't be bothered. I need a night off.'

'I could come to yours if you like,' she offered. She was sitting in the living room of her little house, staring at the anaglypta on the walls. She was almost sure she could see a damp patch forming in one corner. 'I don't mind.'

It would be a long haul and she could really do without it, seeing as she'd have to get two buses, but it was better than sitting in this dump all alone.

'No, don't be daft. That's a heck of a journey and at this time of night it's just not worth it. Besides, how would you get to work for eight in morning? No, let's just take a rain check, okay? I fancy an early night anyway. We'll meet up soon enough. Maybe the weekend?'

The weekend? But it was only Monday! Holly forced herself to sound unconcerned. 'Sure, that's okay. I'll see you soon. Love—'

The call had ended. She stared at the mobile in her hand and tried to quell the uneasiness she was suddenly feeling. Now what? The clock on her phone said ten past seven. What to do to take her mind off it all?

Lulu! The steaks could wait.

Holly jumped up and rushed into the hallway. She pulled on her boots and duffle coat and let herself out of the house, slamming the door behind her, glad to see the back of the place even if only for an hour or two.

Lulu was delighted to see her, if surprised.

'Fancy coming out in this weather. You must be crackers.'

'Lulu, you only live next door,' Holly reminded her as she followed her lifelong friend into the living room.

Cuckoo Nest Cottage was probably twice the size of her own home yet felt much cosier. It was older than the terrace of houses Holly lived in by over a hundred years, and was the last house in Bramblewick, with a view over open countryside and the beck that meandered its way out of the village and onto the moors. A small bridge, not far from the cottage, crossed the beck, and she often saw children playing Pooh Sticks on there in milder weather, just as she'd done as a child.

Lulu had moved into Cuckoo Nest Cottage when she married. It had been in her husband's family since his grandparents' day, and he'd been born in the very bedroom that Lulu now slept in. It was sad to think that, since they'd had no children, she was the last Drake to live there.

'Not attached to yours though, am I?' Lulu reasoned. 'You've still had to walk a fair way and it's dark. I don't like you being out in the dark, you know that.'

'I come home from work in the dark during the winter months,' Holly reminded her. 'And I set off for work in the darkness each morning too, so popping next door seems pretty insignificant to me.'

'You'd argue black was white,' Lulu grumbled. 'Sit yourself down and I'll put kettle on.'

'You will *not*,' Holly informed her. 'You sit *your*self down and I'll make us both a nice hot chocolate.'

'So that's what you've come for,' Lulu said, a twinkle in her eye. 'Might have known. Why don't you just buy your own blooming hot chocolate, eh?'

'Why do I need to do that when I can come here and get it for free?' Holly said, laughing.

Lulu shook her head and sat down on the sofa, lifting her legs up to rest on a couple of cushions. 'You're a cheeky madam,' she said, as Holly turned towards the kitchen. 'While you're in there you can make us some toasted teacakes. They're in the bread bin. Just fancy a hot buttered teacake. What do you say?'

Holly grinned. 'Sounds perfect. Won't be long.'

The kitchen at Cuckoo Nest Cottage was quite large these days. It had originally been much smaller, but a storage room and a walk-in pantry had both been knocked out in the sixties so that the three spaces became one big one. The kitchen units were about twenty years old, but it was still a thousand times nicer than her own kitchen Holly thought, as she sliced teacakes and popped them in the toaster.

She loved Cuckoo Nest Cottage and always felt at ease there. Probably because she'd played there ever since she could remember and had spent many summer days running around the garden, while her mother and Lulu exchanged gossip from their deckchairs. She'd even stayed over on many occasions, sleeping in one of Lulu's spare bedrooms.

After Lulu's husband had died, Holly's mum had thought it would be nice for her to have some company at night, so Holly had been dispatched to keep their neighbour's mind occupied and stop her wallowing in grief. Holly didn't really think it had worked, but Lulu certainly seemed to appreciate having her around, and it had been good for Holly to escape her parents' endless arguments too. Cuckoo Nest Cottage had been a home to her like her own place never had.

She loaded a tray with two mugs of steaming hot chocolate and two small plates of hot buttered teacakes, and took them into the living room, where Lulu was glued to *Emmerdale*. It was her favourite programme, and Holly realised she'd only managed to get any conversation out of her previously because it had been the advert break.

She put Lulu's drink on the coffee table, handed her the teacakes and sat down, nibbling at her own teacakes, and waiting patiently for the soap to finish. Every so often Lulu would shake her head, tut, and tell one of the characters off for something they'd said or done.

Holly tried not to smile as Lulu gasped and directed an angry tirade at the screen. 'You're letting him get away with that? By heck, I know what I'd have done. You're lucky you're not locked up, you bugger.'

She watched fondly as Lulu chewed her teacakes, a frown on her face as she stared disapprovingly at the antics of the Emmerdale residents.

As the end credits rolled, Lulu tutted, shook her head, and reached for her hot chocolate, muttering, 'Who writes this rubbish?'

'I don't know why you watch it,' she told her. 'All you ever do is criticise it.'

Lulu stared at her, appalled. 'Are you mad? Best thing on the box, that is.' She took a sip of hot chocolate and watched Holly shrewdly. 'No Jonathan tonight then?'

Holly twisted the bracelet on her wrist as she tried to look unconcerned. 'No. It's been a long day for him at work and he needs a break. Can't blame him. You know how far it is from Whitby.'

'Never stopped him before,' Lulu said reasonably. 'Usually stays over anyway. What's different tonight?'

'Crikey, Lulu, we're not joined at the hip!' Holly gave

a laugh which she thought sounded impressively authentic. 'We can go a whole night or two without seeing each other you know.'

'I should hope you can.' Lulu placed her empty plate on the coffee table and settled herself as comfortably as she could manage, her back to the cushions which she'd stacked up behind her against the arm of the sofa. 'So, have you given this job any more thought?'

Holly wrinkled her nose, wishing she'd not confided in her friend about Anna's suggestion. 'I don't think it's for me,' she said carefully.

Lulu gave a big sigh. 'Thought you'd say that.'

'Well,' Holly said defensively, 'it's a lot of responsibility you know.'

'Is that your opinion, or Jonathan's?'

'Mine, of course.'

'Oh, yeah? Really?'

'Really! Jonathan doesn't know anything about it.'

Lulu's eyes widened. 'Thought you told him everything. Why haven't you mentioned this?'

Holly shrugged. 'Didn't seem worth it unless I decided to take on the training, and since I've decided not to do it there's no point really.'

'Is it 'cos you think he wouldn't approve?' Lulu demanded.

Far from it, Holly thought. As far as Jonathan was concerned she was sure he would only be able to see it as an improvement on what she already did. He was frequently scathing about her job as receptionist at Bramblewick Surgery, insisting that all she really did was pick up the phone and click a computer mouse a few times during the day.

'It's hardly rocket science,' he told her dismissively one night, as she'd told him wearily of the awful day she'd had at work, with cross patients who couldn't get appointments, terse conversations with a hospital secretary who'd insisted some test results had been sent over, even though they were nowhere to be found in the system, a broken photocopier that had caused loads of delays, and an impatient chemist who was demanding a prescription for a patient right there and then, even though none of the doctors were in the building to sign it.

Jonathan really had no idea what it could be like she thought. Every day brought new problems and fresh challenges. It was never as simple as booking appointments and handing out prescriptions, whatever people like him believed. She wished!

If she'd told him she was going to train as a phlebotomist, he might have found a little more respect for her. It sounded so clever and professional, and even Jonathan must see that it carried responsibility, even if he was blind to the weight of responsibility she already carried in her present role.

But the truth was, Holly couldn't bring herself to say yes. She was too afraid of making a mistake, of causing damage. She might get the samples mixed up, or label them incorrectly, or lose them, or even worse, harm the patient when she attempted to take blood. It was all too scary. Maybe a year or two ago she'd have accepted the job without a second thought, but she'd changed a lot since then. Maybe, she pondered, it was because she'd been at the surgery long enough now to understand all the things that could go wrong. Maybe she'd just grown up. Either way, she had enough to deal with. She didn't want to take on anything else.

'I'm sure Jonathan would be very proud of me,' she told Lulu. 'I just don't feel it's for me, that's all.'

Lulu sighed. 'Aye, well, it's your business I suppose. Seems a shame though if you ask me. You're in a rut, Holly, and you really need to break out of it.'

Holly thought that was a bit unfair. She was, after all, doing her best. It wasn't her fault that she didn't have a high-flying career. She didn't have the brains to go much further professionally, and yes she was trapped in that horrible cottage, but what was she supposed to do about that? She was a receptionist in a doctor's surgery, and made little more than minimum wage, despite the level of responsibility and pressure the job entailed. How was she supposed to afford somewhere decent that was close enough to get to work every day? North Yorkshire was a pricey region, and this area was popular. Look how far from Kearton Bay Lewis had settled, all because Nell's flat was the cheapest he could find.

She wrinkled her nose, thinking once again that she should have approached Nell first. It would have been perfect for her. Then again, it was further from Lulu and her friend needed her to be there every day.

'Did the doctor come today?' she asked.

'Oh, aye. It was Dr Sawdon this time. I like her. Very friendly and chatty. Not that Dr Blake and Dr MacDonald aren't friendly and chatty, but it's different with a woman isn't it? You can say a bit more; be a bit more honest about private things, like.'

Holly dreaded to think what Lulu had opened up to poor Abbie about. Holly had been on the receiving end of Lulu's "honesty" several times and, quite frankly, it had made her toes curl.

'She was telling me about the party,' Lulu said. 'That Lewis fella sounds nice. Did her garden didn't he? Might get him to do mine next spring. Lord knows, it could do with it.' She paused. 'Dr Sawdon said he lent you his jacket. Kind of him wasn't it? Not many gentlemen left in the world, but she seems to think he's one of them. What do you think?'

Holly thought about Lewis's visit to the surgery last week. He'd demonstrated, yet again, that he was kind and considerate. He'd done his best to cheer her up and seemed genuinely concerned about her.

There was something about him, she mused. He was laid back, casual, yet he had a way of coaxing information out of her, even though he never pushed her to answer any questions and seemed not to mind whether she spoke to him or not. She quite liked his company, she realised. He was easy to be around. What was it he'd said to her? *I don't lie and I don't play games.* That was reassuring, she thought. And, she had to admit, whatever he said sounded amazing. He could recite the telephone directory and it would be enthralling to listen to, as he spoke with that deep and rather sexy posh voice of his.

Her face heated up at the thought and she took a long gulp of hot chocolate, ashamed of herself.

'Well?' Lulu repeated. 'What do you think?'

Holly flicked back her hair and smiled guiltily at her friend. 'Yes, he's nice enough,' she said airily. She noticed the eager look on Lulu's face and pulled herself together. 'But if you ask me,' she added, 'he eats far too many pear drops.'

Chapter 7

Holly shook with a mixture of rage, fear and misery as she splashed her way along the rain-soaked pavement towards the surgery. She'd never felt less like going to work in her life she realised, as her hand closed around the folded envelope in her pocket, and the shock of its contents hit her all over again.

How could this be allowed to happen? And what the heck was she going to do about it? It was really all she needed she thought, on top of everything else. She reached the side door of the surgery just as Anna arrived.

'Nice weather for ducks isn't it?' Anna beamed at her. 'Cheer up, it might never happen.'

Holly pursed her lips, curbing the urge to snap back. Why did people always say stupid things like that? For all they knew, "it" already had. It certainly had in this case.

She wished she'd not popped home for dinner. She rarely did, as she mostly brought sandwiches to work with her, but she'd forgotten to prepare them the previous evening, having been at Lulu's until fairly late, and she'd slept through her alarm, only waking half an hour before she was due to start work. It had been a case of, quick shower, get dressed and get out of there. Not even time for a cup of tea, that's how pushed for time she'd been.

So for once, Holly had headed home for dinner and had discovered the envelope lying on the hallway carpet when she pushed open the front door. She hadn't suspected the worst. Why would she? She'd carried it through to the kitchen, dropped it carelessly on the worktop, and heated up some soup.

It was only when she was sitting down, tray on her lap, that she'd opened the envelope as she waited for the soup to cool a little. Funnily enough, upon reading the letter within she'd quite lost her appetite. The soup had been poured down the sink and she hadn't even bothered to make a drink, that's how shocked and worried she felt. So Anna's thoughtless comment was the last thing she'd needed to hear.

Rolling her eyes but saying nothing, Holly punched the passcode into the keypad on the wall and stepped forward as the door swung open. Without waiting for Anna she strode into the surgery, heading for the small cloakroom off the filing room where she could hang her duffle coat.

'What's the matter with you?' Anna queried, close behind her and already unbuttoning her own coat. 'Has something happened? Your face didn't look like that when you left earlier.'

'Nothing to worry about,' Holly said bitterly. 'Just life as usual.'

Anna frowned. 'What's up, Holls? If you want to talk—'

Holly almost crumbled. Her stomach was churning with nerves, and she felt a bit sick as she contemplated her choices. Not that she had many of those. Or any, come to that. Anna had always been such a good listener and so kind, but...

She recalled Jonathan's words to her one evening, as they'd discussed why she never got to see his friends any more.

'Not being funny, Holls, but they don't like being around you. Don't take this the wrong way, but you can be a bit depressing.'

'Depressing?' Holly had been horrified. 'What do you mean? I'm not depressing!'

'Look, I don't mind,' he'd reassured her. 'I'm used to you after all, and I understand that you've got issues. But my friends don't really know you, and all they see is your miserable face. They've got it into their heads that you're one of those people who always looks on the dark side. You know, glass half empty. And I mean, they've got a point haven't they? Be honest. You're not much fun. But it's okay, I get it. Everyone's different aren't they? We can't all be laughing and joking all the time, and I love you anyway, just as you are. But anyway, that's why no one comes round to mine when you're there. They don't feel comfortable around you.'

Holly had been shocked to the core. Is that how she came across? Was she really that person? She hardly recognised herself in the description Jonathan had just given her, and yet...

When she thought about it carefully, she realised she had been a bit gloomy lately. Rachel had jokingly patted her on the shoulder the other day and said brightly, 'Cheer up, Holls. It wouldn't kill you to put a smile on your face. They're free you know!'

It was just a casual, throwaway remark, but given what Jonathan had just told her it found its mark. Holly was wounded and nursed Rachel's comment to her. Now, as she remembered her conversation with Lewis, when even she had admitted that every time she met him she looked unhappy, she realised that her reputation as a misery guts was probably well-founded. No wonder people avoided her. Who wanted to spend time with someone so negative?

'I'm fine,' she said, forcing herself to smile at Anna. 'Just dying for a cup of tea, that's all. And really hoping there are some of those chocolate biscuits left in the cupboard, 'cos I'm starving.'

Anna smiled back but looked uncertain. 'I think there are, yes. I'll put the kettle on before the shutters go up.'

'I can do it,' Holly said. Really she thought, the cheeriness she'd managed to inject into her tone was Oscar-winning. She had no idea she was capable of such great acting.

Within a few minutes, the surgery whirred into life again. Joan arrived for her afternoon shift, carrying vanilla slices fresh from Spill the Beans for their break; the doctors came back, and after their usual huddle in the office where they exchanged murmured information about their visits, they headed into their respective consulting rooms. Patients began to arrive for afternoon appointments. The prescriptions were brought out of the locked cupboard and placed on the desk in reception. Computers were switched on, passwords entered, systems activated. The shutters went up and it was business as usual.

Holly was kept busy, booking in patients, making further appointments, scanning, photocopying, taking prescription requests, dealing with the delivery drivers, and doing a multitude of other jobs that ensured she barely got time to enjoy her afternoon break, never mind dwell on the letter in her coat pocket.

Even so, it was there at the back of her mind. The knowledge that her whole life was about to be turned upside down. An eviction notice from her landlord! All right, she hated her house, but it was the only home she'd ever known, and she had nowhere else to go. So what on earth was she supposed to do now?

***

'I know there's summat up with you, so why don't you just spit it out?' Lulu winced as she sat down and shifted round on the sofa so that she could lift her legs up once more.

'Never mind me. Are you okay? Is it your legs that hurt or the arthritis?'

Lulu shrugged. 'Take your pick. And stop changing the subject.'

She rarely complained about her aches and pains, which Holly thought extremely noble of her.

'Just one of them things,' she'd told Holly once, when Holly had expressed how unfair it all was. 'We've all got summat to bear haven't we? This is my burden. Let's face it, it could be worse. Especially at my age.'

Lulu made a determined effort at least to walk around the garden most days, doing her best to ignore the pain, and she tried not to sit down for too long. She also, despite her grumbles, mostly obeyed the doctors' orders and kept her legs elevated four times a day, even though she found it boring and frustrating. It seemed all wrong to Holly that she suffered so much. Honestly, if anyone had the right to be miserable it was Louisa Drake, but she stayed remarkably cheerful.

'Don't give me that look. I'm all right honestly,' Lulu told her now. 'Dr Sawdon popped in to see me earlier and she's given me some new medication, so things will be looking up soon won't they?'

Holly nodded, overcome with affection for her friend. It was fair to say that Lulu was more like family. Holly would do anything for her.

It didn't stop Lulu from telling Holly what she thought though, and she wasn't one to be fobbed off either.

'Now, like I said, you can stop changing the subject and tell me the truth. What's rattled your cage today, eh?'

There wasn't much point trying to fool her, Holly realised. Anna and Joan had seemed to believe that she was okay, but Lulu knew her inside out. Besides, she was nothing if not persistent. She'd never let it go until Holly gave in and told her the truth.

'I got a letter on Tuesday,' she admitted.

'Oh, aye? I'm guessing it wasn't to tell you you'd won

the lottery?'

Holly sighed. 'I wish, although I'd have to buy a ticket first and I keep forgetting. No, this is from my landlord, and it's not good news.'

Lulu tutted. 'Don't tell me they're putting your rent up again? By heck, they've got a brass neck. At least Dick Turpin wore a mask. You want to go to that Citizens Advice place, love. Find out your rights.'

'I wish it *was* just a rent increase,' Holly admitted, feeling tearful suddenly. 'The fact is they want me out, Lulu. I'm being evicted.'

Lulu gaped at her. 'You what? They can't do that!'

'They can.' Holly brought out the envelope from her coat pocket and handed it to her friend. 'It's all there. Proper official forms and everything. I've got two months to find somewhere, so there you go. Happy New Year.'

Lulu scanned the pages in her hand, tutting and muttering as she did so. 'This can't be right,' she said, handing it all back to Holly after a few moments. 'Surely you have rights? There must be a law against it.'

'There's no law to say they can't evict me,' Holly assured her. 'Or *seek possession* as they so nicely put it. They've complied with all the rules, as far as I can see, and they've given me enough notice, so there's nothing to stop them.'

'But you've done nowt wrong!'

'It doesn't matter. They don't have to have a reason. This is a no-fault notice. In other words, I've done nothing to warrant being evicted but tough luck anyway. As the letter says, they're planning to sell it instead of renting it out. They've very kindly offered me first refusal.'

Lulu frowned. 'Could you buy it?'

Holly laughed. 'As if! Even though it's a dump and probably not worth much, it's still more than I could afford. I'd never get a mortgage on my wage. Well, not one that big anyway. I'm stuffed, that's the truth of it.'

She folded the documents up and put them back in the envelope, then shoved the whole thing inside her pocket again.

'It's my own fault,' she admitted wearily. 'If I'd just listened to my common sense and asked Nell about renting the flat above Spill the Beans...'

Lulu stared at her. 'I didn't know you were planning to do that.'

'No, well, I didn't want to say anything to you. I didn't want you to think I was abandoning you.'

'Abandoning me!' Lulu snorted. 'It's only down the road, love. You could be here and back in ten minutes. Why didn't you ask her?'

'Because I was worried she'd say no and then it would make things awkward between us. She'd been adamant she didn't want any more tenants in there, so I thought it was unlikely she'd agree and not worth the hassle. But then Lewis got in there first didn't he?'

'Lewis? The gardener fella that Dr Sawdon was on about? Didn't realise he lived nearby.'

'Well he does.'

'Not his fault. Nell put an advert in Maudie's window. I saw it meself.'

'But I didn't. And she put an advert in *The Whitby*

Gazette too, which is where Lewis saw it. Serves me right for only ever reading trashy magazines.'

'I'm sorry, love. If I'd known you'd been considering the flat I'd have tipped you off about the advert, but I never thought.' Lulu sighed. 'Well, this is all a bit of a mess isn't it? And only about five weeks until Christmas too.'

'I know. Well, at least I won't have to look for that new Christmas tree now,' Holly said, forcing a laugh. 'Told you my old one was falling to bits didn't I? No point shopping for another if I'm going to be sleeping in a cardboard box. There's a silver lining to everything.' *Who said my glass is always half empty? Jonathan's friends can stick that in their pipe and smoke it.*

'Cardboard box my eye,' Lulu said, waving a hand dismissively. 'Stands to reason you'll be moving in here with me. Obviously.'

Holly's mouth fell open. 'Oh, golly, Lulu, I wasn't hinting at that, honestly.'

'Wouldn't matter if you were,' Lulu assured her. 'Come on now, love, where else are you going to go? This is practically your second home any road, and you know I'd love to have you. I've got three spare bedrooms up there, and you can put your own bed in one 'cos you know I've only got one single bed in the smallest and the others are empty. You can store whatever else you need to keep in the other two bedrooms, so you won't even have to pay storage charges. I know it's a bit shabby upstairs, but you're welcome to decorate it how you like, and it's warm and dry. No damp here. Not like that hovel you live in.

Now, since that's sorted, I reckon it's biscuit time.'

Holly shook her head, stunned at how fast Lulu was moving. 'But—but—I can't just land on you like this! This is your home. You won't want me hanging around all the time.'

'Who says I won't?' Lulu demanded. 'You're the granddaughter I never had after all. Who better to move in than you?' Her eyes narrowed suddenly. 'Unless you don't want to? I understand that living with an old woman isn't as much fun as having your own place...'

'Oh, Lulu, don't be daft. You know I hate that house next door, and I love coming round here to be with you. You're not some old woman. You're practically my gran, you know that. I'd love to move in here, I just don't want you to feel obliged to ask, that's all.'

Lulu let out a shout of laughter. 'And when have I ever done anything if I haven't wanted to do it, might I ask? Come on, love, you know me better than that. I reckon it will be fun. Fancy me having a housemate at my age. I'll feel ten years younger by Christmas, I reckon. Blimey, what's that for?' she squealed, as Holly threw her arms around her and hugged her tightly.

'You know what that's for,' Holly said, feeling a lump of emotion in her throat. 'It's for being the kindest, most lovely neighbour anyone could ever have.'

'Housemate,' Lulu corrected her, her eyes glistening with tears. 'And don't be so daft. Go and fetch them biscuits and let's celebrate.'

For the first time in a long time, the smile on Holly's

face was genuine. At last she really did have something to feel happy about.

***

'I've never heard anything so stupid.'

How did Holly know Jonathan was going to say that? They were walking along the pier at Whitby, clutching cups of coffee in a bid to keep warm while she wondered vaguely why they were braving the icy blasts coming from the North Sea instead of being tucked up all warm and cosy in Jonathan's flat.

It hadn't been her idea to go for a walk, but he'd told her the flat was a bit of a mess and he didn't want her to see it until he'd had a chance to clean up.

'Why would I care about that?' she'd said, trying to reassure him that she wasn't the type of girlfriend who would inspect his home for dust. 'Besides, if you like I could help you tidy up. I don't mind.'

'Of course you can't do that,' he'd replied immediately. 'What do you take me for? No, we'll go for a drive into town and take a walk along the seafront. Blow away the cobwebs.'

And the hangover too no doubt Holly thought, although she said nothing. It was quite clear to her from his bleary, red-rimmed eyes, stubbled chin, and the way he kept massaging his temples, that he'd been out drinking last night. She didn't ask where he'd gone, or who he'd been drinking with. She didn't want to know—not that she thought for a minute that he'd tell her the truth anyway. Which said a lot really.

They'd been walking for about twenty-five minutes and Holly's fingers were numb with cold, her cheeks were tingling, and she was beginning to think she was about to die of frostbite. She'd tentatively asked Jonathan if maybe they should just brave the untidy flat anyway, which was when he'd rushed her over to the nearest street vendor who was brave enough to be out in this weather and bought them both coffees. He'd then persuaded her to follow him onto the pier, which in Holly's opinion was sheer madness.

The wind whipped around them, and her hair kept smacking her in the face. There were only two other people on the pier, and they were well wrapped up in thick parkas, scarves, and woolly hats. They sat, hunched together on a bench, looking miserable. Holly couldn't help wondering what they were doing there, since they clearly weren't enjoying themselves.

Even the seagulls seemed subdued. Usually they swooped around searching for food, dive-bombing passers-by in a threatening manner. Today they marched up and down, looking for all the world as if they were simply trying to keep warm. Holly wouldn't have been at all surprised to see them cupping their beaks with their wings and blowing into them; or to find a group of shivering seagulls gathered round a campfire, sharing mugs of soup, and squawking depressing songs of hardship and woe to each other.

Of course, she didn't tell Jonathan any of that. He already thought she was insane and whenever she confessed to him about the pictures she saw in her head he would knit his eyebrows together, tut loudly and start talking about something else.

So instead of telling him about the seagull soap opera that was developing in her mind, Holly finally told him about the eviction notice, or rather the notice to quit from her landlord, and about Lulu's wonderful offer for Holly to move in with her. Which didn't quite have the effect she'd expected.

Instead of being pleased that things had resolved themselves so well and so easily, he'd looked dumbfounded that she would even consider such a move, which was when he told her he'd never heard anything so daft.

There was a sort of inevitability about it all, Holly realised suddenly. Nothing ran smoothly when Jonathan got involved, and what had seemed perfectly logical and acceptable to her was always bound to seem stupid and out of the question to Jonathan. Maybe that was why she hadn't mentioned any of it to him during the week. Honestly, even though she hadn't seen him, she could have texted him at any time to break the news, but even though they'd had a couple of short conversations she'd not said a word. The truth was, she knew deep down that he would pour scorn on the idea, and she didn't want him to. Just for once she wanted him to agree with her that it was a marvellous solution. Fat chance.

'But it makes sense,' Holly protested, feeling an unexpected surge of anger towards him. 'I won't have far to move, I'll still be close to work, and Lulu and I have always got on so well. Plus, she's got loads of room and—'

'It will never work,' he told her firmly. 'How can you seriously want to live with an old woman who's nearly ninety? Come on, Holly, be sensible. You'll end up just being her carer, and don't you realise that's exactly why she wants you to move in?'

'Of course it's not the reason!' Holly was stung on Lulu's behalf. 'She's not like that.' *And even if it were true, I'd be happy to care for her.*

'You're so naive,' he said, sounding cross. 'And where does this leave me, eh? You tell me that!'

'What do you mean, where does it leave you?'

'Oh, come on. You can't expect me to stay the night at the old woman's place can you? Let's face it if you move in there our nights of passion are over. You don't drive, and I'm buggered if I'm driving over from Whitby every night after work to pick you up and bring you back to my place, then take you back again later or first thing in the morning so you can get to work on time.'

'Well, I'm sure Lulu wouldn't mind if you stayed.'

'Of course she'd mind! That generation always gets hung up on stuff like that. Besides, even if she said it was okay, I'd not be able to—you know—with her just across the landing. I mean, talk about off-putting.'

'I don't know what else to suggest,' Holly murmured, her anxiety deepening. She supposed he had a point. She didn't think Lulu would kick up a fuss about him staying with her because she was as broad-minded as anyone, but Holly had the distinct impression that she wasn't Jonathan's biggest fan, so things would feel a little awkward. And he was right, it would be inhibiting, having her so close when he stayed over. Holly would feel uncomfortable enough, so how could she expect Jonathan to be okay with it?

'You can't move in there,' he said, sounding as if the decision was made. 'Simple as that. You'll have to find somewhere else.'

'But where? And how am I going to afford it?' She felt a growing sense of panic.

'Well let's face it, if you move in with your neighbour we may as well end it. There's just no way it could ever work.'

Holly clutched the coffee cup and stared at him, eyes wide with fear. 'You don't mean that?'

'What choice do we have? How could we ever make it work? Come on, be sensible. Unless of course...' He rubbed his chin, seeming to think things over.

'Unless what?'

'Well, I suppose you could always move into mine,' he said thoughtfully. 'There'd have to be a lot of compromises, obviously, but it might work.'

Holly's heart leapt as it sank in that Jonathan wanted her to live with him. 'Are you serious?'

He rolled his eyes. 'No, I just said it for fun. What do you think?'

It wasn't the most romantic way of asking her to move in with him. Holly's excitement dampened a little and then the realities began to hit her. How would she get to work every morning? Buses weren't the most reliable at that time of day, and she had to be at the surgery by eight. And then there was Lulu. She'd be so far away from her. What if she needed Holly one night and she wasn't around? Besides, Holly would miss her.

Reluctantly, she shook her head. 'I don't think it's an option. I'm sorry.'

Jonathan looked astonished. 'What do you mean, it isn't an option? I thought you'd be over the moon to move in with me.'

Cautiously she explained her misgivings to him. He wasn't very happy, even though he had to concede that the work situation was tricky.

'I suppose I could run you in every morning,' he said, sounding reluctant, 'although it might be a bit of a bugger during the bad weather. If the snow comes it's a nightmare getting down to Bramblewick from up here. You might be able to get time off though, or at least be allowed to be late.'

'But that would hardly be fair on Anna, and they'd have to call poor Joan in,' she pointed out.

Jonathan flopped down onto the nearest bench, slopping a bit of his coffee onto his jeans, which only seemed to make him grumpier. 'Fine. Well, if you'd rather move in with an old woman that's up to you. I guess we're over then.'

'No! I mean, I didn't say that it was definitely out of the question.' Holly's stomach lurched in fear as she contemplated a future without Jonathan in it. Who else would ever want someone like her? Who else would put up with her forgetfulness, her stupidity, her total lack of common sense? Not to mention her fat thighs and appalling dress sense. 'Maybe,' she ventured hesitantly, 'we could get a new place together? Somewhere a bit closer to Bramblewick?'

'And what about my job?' he demanded. Jonathan was a mechanic, who worked in a garage on the outskirts of Whitby. 'There's no way I'm moving further away from work. Why the hell should I? It's you that needs to move, not me. I'm happy where I am, thank you very much.'

Holly sighed, knowing he was right.

They sat in silence, sipping coffee and watching the waves pounding onto the beach below them.

'The way I see it,' he said eventually, 'you have two options. Move in with me, or we finish it now. There's no other way around it. I can't make the decision for you; it has to be your choice.'

Tears pricked Holly's eyes as she contemplated the difficult decision she had to make. She couldn't bear the thought of losing Jonathan, but then again she really didn't want to move away from Lulu, and she knew the commute to work would be difficult, if not impossible.

'Can I have some time to think it over?' she asked. 'There's no rush. The landlord's given me two months to move out anyway.'

He was clearly annoyed that she wasn't desperate to accept his offer to move in with him, and Holly could understand why. It was hardly flattering was it? But what could she do? There was so much to consider, and she had to be realistic.

'I suppose so, if you really need time,' he said, sounding even more bitter than the coffee. He drained his cup and dropped it in the nearest bin. 'Right, well I've had enough of freezing my nuts off out here. I'm going home to sort the flat out. Are you ready to go?'

Holly stared at him. 'Where to?'

He sighed in obvious exasperation. 'The bus station. Are. You. Ready. To. Go?'

Was he serious? Was he actually expecting her to get a bus back to Bramblewick, when she'd come all the way on two buses to see him and they'd spent less than an hour together? She felt sick and there was a growing feeling of unease that she couldn't ignore. Why wouldn't he let her go back to the flat? And why did he not want to spend the full day with her, as they'd originally planned?

'Yes, I suppose so.' At least he'd parked his car at the harbour car park, so he'd be walking practically the whole way to the bus station with her. They'd get another ten minutes or so together, and beggars couldn't be choosers.

They turned their backs to the wind and made their way towards the car park and the station.

As they parted company Holly waited for him to put his arms around her, to kiss her goodbye. Instead he took his car keys from his pocket and twirled them around in his hand, looking impatient.

'When you've finally decided what it is you want, perhaps you'd be good enough to let me know,' he muttered, sounding angry.

'It's not like that!' Holly protested.

'I think it is,' he said. 'How do you expect me to react? You've made me feel like an idiot, Holly. Here I am asking my girlfriend to move in with me, and what does she do? Does she squeal with excitement and rush home to pack her bags? Oh, no, not *my* girlfriend. *My* girlfriend tells me that she'll have to think about it because, after all, she'd miss an eighty-odd-year-old woman so much that maybe it would be easier all round if we just broke up.'

Holly gave him a pleading look. 'That's not what I said at all! Why are you being like this?'

'Why am *I* being like this?' He gave a mirthless laugh and shook his head. 'You know what, Holls? It's time you had a good look at yourself and the way you treat me, because I'm getting a bit fed up with feeling second best all the time. If it's not that old bat it's all your mates. I'm always last in the queue aren't I? Well, maybe it *would* be better if we broke up. Maybe I should find someone who actually cares about me and about my feelings, instead of always putting everyone else's feelings first. See you around, Holly.'

She grabbed his arm as he began to walk away. 'Jonathan, wait!'

He wrenched free of her grasp. 'Seriously, go home and think it over. I've said all I have to say.'

'Jonathan, please.' She couldn't let him go like this. She had an awful feeling that if she did she'd never see him again. 'Look, I'll give it some serious thought, I promise. It's not that I don't want to live with you. I do! Of course I do. It's just the whole getting to work thing that's the problem, but I'll check bus timetables and see what I can do, okay? Please...'

He eyed her steadily for a moment then shrugged. 'Okay, you do that. You know where I am when you've made your mind up.'

He strode away without a backward glance and

Holly stared after him, her heart thumping with fear. What could she do? She didn't see a way of getting to work on time, and besides, whatever she said, Lulu was a major consideration in all this. She couldn't just leave her behind. But it seemed it was either her or Jonathan. How could Holly possibly choose?

***

'Look, Holly, it's really none of my business, and I'm the last one to tell you what you should do.' Rachel hesitated, a cup of tea halfway to her lips as she clearly considered her next words. She sipped her drink, placed her cup back on the table and took a deep breath. 'But if you really want to know I think you'd be a bloody fool to move in with Jonathan, so there you go.'

Holly didn't quite know how to reply to that, she was so taken aback. She looked over at Anna for support, but she was studiously avoiding her gaze, munching on an apple, and staring out of the window as if there was something stunning to look at, rather than the surgery car park.

Holly had been quiet all day, and Anna had pounced on her as they sat down for dinner in the kitchenette. Connor had promised to call in at their home, Chestnut House, before going on his visits, so she didn't have to go home and let Chester out. Finding herself free for once she'd taken the opportunity to eat lunch with Holly and grill her for information.

'I know something's wrong,' she'd insisted. 'You've

not been yourself for—well, let's go with days shall we? We've all noticed, haven't we, Rachel?'

Rachel, who'd joined them and had been flicking through a bridal magazine while drinking tomato soup from a large mug, glanced up and gave Holly a sympathetic look.

'We're just worried about you, Holls,' she said. 'If you've got something on your mind we really wish you'd share it with us. We'd love to help.'

'There's nothing you can do to help,' Holly told them. 'This is something I've got to figure out for myself.'

'Well, why don't you tell us what it is, and maybe we can look at it with fresh eyes and give you our input?'

Holly hadn't wanted to tell them at first. Thinking about it, how awful did it sound that she couldn't choose between her boyfriend and her dearest friend? But the fact was, she really didn't know what to do for the best. Half regretting it even as she began to speak, she confided in them that she'd been issued with a notice to quit, and that both Lulu and Jonathan had offered her a home, but that she was being forced to decide between them and she just couldn't.

They'd both been silent for a few moments then had exchanged glances. Anna picked up her apple as Rachel suddenly tutted and said, 'Well, it's not that hard is it?'

Excuse me, Holly thought indignantly, *but it's extremely hard! If it wasn't I wouldn't have bothered telling you all about it, would I?*

'It's a big deal, Jonathan asking me to move in with him. I can't just throw that back in his face can I? Not without a good reason.'

'You need a good reason? I can give you plenty,' Rachel said, in a tone that said she'd love to do just that.

Anna leaned forward and gave Holly a conciliatory smile. 'What Rachel means is, it's obvious that Louisa needs you the most. She's not the type to come right out and ask for help is she? But think about it, Holly. She's so used to having you next door, and she's probably grown to depend on you. If you move all the way to Whitby what's she going to do?'

'Her arthritis must be so painful,' Rachel added. 'I know she struggles with even the most basic tasks these days. Not that she ever complains of course. But without you, how do you think she's going to manage?'

'Yes, that had occurred to me thanks.'

Of course it had. It preyed on her mind the whole time. How could she abandon Lulu like that? Even so, it didn't explain Rachel's insistence that she'd be a bloody fool to move in with Jonathan.

'And then there's the distance.' Anna took up the baton. 'It's two buses from Bramblewick to Whitby, and while that's all very well and good in the summer, imagine doing it in the winter. I don't even think there are buses that would get you to work on time. So what would you do? Get a taxi? It would cost a fortune and eat away at your wages. It doesn't even make sense.'

'I know, I know.' Holly gave a big sigh, realising she was right. Living in Whitby wasn't doable. Even if she learned to drive it would be ages before she'd be able to drive herself to work. Not that she could afford a car anyway. And that was always supposing she ever passed her test, which wasn't guaranteed. Far from it.

Rachel pushed her sandwich box away, looking angry. 'What right has Jonathan got to give you that ultimatum? I mean, how dare he!'

'Okay, Rach,' Anna soothed, putting her hand on Rachel's arm.

'It wasn't an ultimatum,' Holly snapped, furious on Jonathan's behalf. 'He just can't see how we can make it work if I move in with Lulu, that's all, and he's got a point hasn't he?'

'Oh, really? And what point is that?'

'Seriously? Isn't it obvious? For a start, he's worried that I'll end up being Lulu's carer.'

'And are *you* worried about that?'

She eyed Holly steadily as she swallowed nervously. 'Well, no, of course not. Lulu's like my gran. I already help her out as much as I can, and I'd be happy to—'

'So that's one problem ticked off. Next?'

Holly glared at her. 'How's he supposed to come over and see me when he's been working all day? I can't expect him to come all the way here from Whitby. It's hardly fair is it?'

'Yet he expects you to do the same? He's not bothered that you'd have to get yourself up at the crack of dawn to make your way to the surgery, then get two buses back after a long day at work. How is *that* fair?'

Holly blushed, not really having an answer to that one. She had a point after all.

'There's—there's the other thing too,' she mumbled.

'What other thing?' Anna sounded intrigued.

Holly blushed even harder, wishing she'd not

opened her mouth. 'You know.'

They looked at each other then back at her, clearly baffled.

'What are we talking about here?' Anna asked, clearly at a loss.

Holly sighed. Her and her big mouth. 'Sex,' she whispered, looking around as if she were about to be arrested for uttering the word in public.

Rachel raised an eyebrow. 'What about it?'

'Well, how can we...I mean, in Lulu's house, with her across the landing! Ugh!'

Rachel smirked. 'Oh dear. You and Jonathan will just have to abstain won't you?'

'I see your problem,' Anna said hastily, 'but you must weigh it up against all the other things. It can't be the most important consideration. I mean, there are...ways and means.'

'And wheres,' Rachel added, giggling. 'One of our barns is empty if you're desperate.'

'Very funny.' Holly dropped her sandwich, half-eaten, back into its box. 'I don't know what to do.'

'You must have an instinct,' Anna said. 'Surely, deep down, you know the answer?'

Holly did, but if she followed her instincts that would be the end of her and Jonathan, and she just couldn't face losing him. He was all she had. The only one who loved her just as she was, who understood, who made allowances for her. Without him life would be meaningless. Who else would ever want her? She'd be alone forever. It didn't bear thinking about.

'Well,' Rachel said, pushing back her chair as she got

to her feet, 'we can't tell you what to do, as much as we'd love to. But I'm surprised at you, Holly, I really am. I would have thought the choice would be a foregone conclusion. Just shows how wrong you can be about people.'

Holly watched, aghast, as she headed out into the corridor, leaving her with Anna, who shifted uncomfortably and said, 'She didn't mean that, Holly. She's just—'

The door swung open, and Rachel marched back in, walked straight up to Holly, and put her arms around her.

'Sorry, Holls. That was mean and I shouldn't have been so horrible. I just want you to be happy, and I think if you do move in with Jonathan you'll feel so guilty and so worried about Louisa that you won't be able to settle anyway. Plus, the commute is going to be a nightmare for you. I worry about you. You know that don't you? But I'm sorry. Like I said, I shouldn't have been so horrible.' She hugged her tightly and then rushed back into the corridor.

Holly turned to Anna, her mouth open in shock. 'What was that about?'

'Like she said,' she replied gently, 'she's worried about you. We all are. We all just want the best for you, Holly. I really hope you know that.'

She sounded genuine. Rachel had sounded genuine too. Could Jonathan possibly have misheard them that night at the party? Maybe they'd been laughing at someone else? Or maybe they'd been laughing at something else entirely, and he'd got the wrong end of the stick? It really wasn't like them to be mean-spirited about anyone, after all, and Lewis had said...

Lewis. For a moment Holly had an overwhelming urge to seek him out and ask his advice. He would know what to do. But that was ridiculous. He barely knew her; he hardly knew Jonathan and had never even met Lulu. How could he possibly tell Holly what was best? Yet she could almost hear those deep, sexy, posh tones, pointing out that Lulu was an old lady in her late eighties, who'd already had a venous leg ulcer once, had problems with her circulation, and suffered badly from osteoarthritis. She was often in pain, struggled with movement, and had difficulty sleeping.

But then there was Jonathan, telling her that if they didn't live together they might as well call it quits. He would never stay over at Lulu's, and since Holly didn't drive it was so much harder for her to get to Whitby, to his place. She couldn't see a solution. How could she possibly please them both?

Chapter 8

It had been a busy week at Kearton Hall, and as December crept closer it didn't look like things were about to ease up. The Hall was a hive of activity. Visitor numbers were well up on the early autumn figures, and the wreath-making workshops were a huge success, each one fully booked. The Hall itself was beautifully decorated for the festive season, and bookings were rolling in for the four special Christmas dinner evenings which were to be held in the Great Hall.

The tills at reception, in the gift shop, and the café were jingling, the staff were rushed off their feet, the grounds were swarming with rosy-cheeked tourists, and spirits were high.

It was, thought Lewis, a wonderful place to work. Having worked on his own for quite a while it made a refreshing change, as did having the regular income. The estate was generous with its employees, and it was a nice feeling, having money in his bank account for once, especially at this time of year.

That feeling had lasted all of two days, until he'd realised he needed two new tyres for his van. That had pretty much eaten up all the spare cash he'd earmarked for Christmas treats.

It was a good job he wasn't much of a spender he thought, as he wandered down Castle Street towards Helmston Market Place, hands tucked into his coat pockets, his breath forming wispy clouds before him as he walked along the frosty pavements. He supposed he didn't really need the van any longer, and maybe he ought to sell it and buy something smaller and cheaper to run.

There was a part of him, however, that was forever cautious. You just never knew how things would pan out, and if he ever wanted to do some freelance gardening jobs the van would be needed. Besides, a bit tatty and old it might be, but it was reliable. For what he could afford to spend on a new car it would probably break down every five minutes. Best to err on the side of caution.

He decided that, since he'd had to go into Helmston for the tyres, he might as well have a wander around. After all, it was his day off and why hurry back to the flat? Not that he minded being alone there. He was really enjoying living above Spill the Beans, and his life was ticking along just fine. In fact he hadn't felt so contented for many years. After living with two scruffy, noisy flatmates, it was a pleasure to have a place all to himself, and he was certainly in no danger of getting lonely. He had invitations coming out of his ears.

Just last night he'd had dinner with Bernie and Darcey at The Gatehouse. He'd really taken to Bernie who was a blunt, no-nonsense Yorkshireman. Darcey was much younger than Bernie, and on the surface, they seemed to have little in common. She was university educated, had a love for history and heritage and a flair for business and accounts, and read widely judging by the bookshelves in their home. Bernie, on the other hand, openly admitted that he'd barely picked up a book since leaving school at fifteen and was devoted to the outdoor life. Yet somehow they got on so well, and it was obvious that their marriage was a successful one. Lewis had really enjoyed himself at dinner and had promised to go again.

He'd already received an invitation to the staff New Year's Eve party. Sir William and Lady Boden-Kean would be in attendance, which wasn't as inhibiting as it sounded, since they were a young couple and fun to be around. They insisted the staff call them Will and Lexi, which he was cool with, though he knew some of the older, longer-serving staff members struggled with it. Will's cousin, who was the events manager, and his wife were also going, and since Nat was a pretty lively character the party promised to be anything but stuffy. It was going to be quite an event, and Lewis was really looking forward to it.

Nell and Riley MacDonald, meanwhile, had already cooked for him at their home, The Ducklings, and assured him he'd be very welcome to go there for Christmas lunch.

'Honestly, we'd love to have you,' Nell told him. 'We've got Anna and Connor and their two kids coming, so one more won't make any difference, and we don't want you sitting in that flat by yourself.'

Lewis had thanked them profusely but told them he couldn't give them an answer just yet, as he'd previously been invited to Christmas lunch by Abbie and Jackson at The Gables.

'Thanks though. I'll let you know what's happening when I know myself.'

It was a nice dilemma to have, but he hadn't made up his mind whether to go to The Ducklings, to The Gables, or to just stay at home and have a bit of peace and quiet for once. You could, he supposed, have too much of a good thing, and he didn't buy into all that, *no one should be alone at Christmas* stuff. That rather depended on the company in his opinion. Sometimes it was infinitely preferable to be by yourself. Anyway, it wasn't December until tomorrow. He had plenty of time to decide.

Being Saturday, the market was in full swing, and the stalls were crammed with festive goods. Lewis thought he might as well have a meander around them all, see if anything caught his fancy. Having been paid at the end of November he'd already taken care of the rent and his other regular bills. After drawing out what was left, he'd shoved a couple of hundred pounds in his bedside drawer back at the flat, which would take care of his food shopping for the month.

He'd brought the rest of his money with him but had spent most of it on the tyres. He was sure he had enough money left for Christmas cards though. Lewis realised he had loads of them to buy, not least for all his old customers. They were miles cheaper at the market than the local card shops, and those tyres had cost him a small fortune.

The smells from the various food stalls reminded

him that he'd not yet had lunch. There was a van selling roast pork sandwiches, parked beside a small stall selling roast chestnuts. He closed his eyes and sighed with pleasure as the various scents mingled together and he tried to separate them in his mind. Fried onions from the burger van, sage and onion stuffing from the pork sandwich man, even sizzling bacon from a van selling all day breakfasts and bacon butties. The only problem was which to choose.

In the end he went for the roast pork sandwich with stuffing, gravy, apple sauce and crackling. It was a meal in itself and took him ages to eat as he wandered around the market, eyeing up Christmas decorations, feeling grateful that he wouldn't have to buy all new baubles and lights for his tree, since his former flatmates had informed him that his were tatty, and they didn't want them.

Well maybe they *were* tatty, but they'd done the job and they'd have to do it again for another year. He'd been delighted to be told by Bernie that he could have a tree for nothing, and that he was to help himself to holly and mistletoe. They had tons of the stuff in the grounds, so he would definitely use some to make his flat look nice and festive. It would save him a fortune and look much better than all the glittery, tinselly stuff on sale here.

Popping the last bit of sandwich into his mouth—with some regret, it had to be said—he wiped his fingers on the paper napkin that had come with it and looked around for a waste bin. There was one over by the pub, so he headed over and dropped the empty container into it, his fingers brushing against someone's hand as they dropped in a similar container. Great minds, he thought, a ready smile on his face as he glanced up. The smile froze on his face and his stomach turned over alarmingly, causing a none-too-pleasant reaction with the roast pork sandwich.

If there was any consolation to be had, it was that Holly looked as shocked as he felt. They stared at each other unblinkingly for a moment, as if they'd been caught in some terrible act that rendered them speechless. Then Lewis gathered his wits and shook his head, breaking the spell.

'Holly, hi. Fancy seeing you here.' He groaned inwardly. How crass did that sound? Why shouldn't she be here for one thing, and for another... *really*? He might as well have asked her if she came here often. Oh, the shame of it.

She adjusted her woolly pom pom hat and gave him an embarrassed smile. 'Fancy. I was—er—I just...' She glanced over at the bin and her face flushed.

He couldn't help but smile. 'Roast pork sandwich?'

She gave him a guilty look. "Fraid so.'

'With stuffing and apple sauce?'

She bit her lip and nodded.

He tutted, shaking his head in mock consternation. 'Gravy and crackling?'

'Oh, stop it!' She started to laugh, and he laughed too. 'I feel bad enough as it is.'

'What for? I've just eaten the very same thing!'

'But you're—' She shut up and hitched her bag up, looking sheepish.

'I'm what? Go on, you can say it.' Like he hadn't already guessed.

'You don't need to lose weight,' she pointed out. 'You're allowed to eat stuff like that.'

'You don't need to lose weight either,' he told her firmly. 'And there's no law in the land that says we can't enjoy a hot roast pork sandwich at a Christmas market. In fact,' he added, 'I think it might be the law that we have to.'

She laughed again and shook her head. 'You are daft.'

His heart leapt at the sound of her laughter. She looked like a different person, he thought, standing there in that adorable red duffle coat and a grey woolly pom pom hat. Her eyes were sparkling with amusement, and there was no trace of anxiety in them for once. Even her voice sounded different—lighter. He noticed her cheeks were pink with the cold and she was slightly hunched as if protecting herself from the weather. She needed warming up. He pushed away the image that thought conjured up, alarmed at how it made him feel. There were other ways to warm her up!

'I don't suppose...' He glanced over her shoulder in the direction of the wide passageway that led from the market to Castle Street. Was this such a good idea? But then, she'd probably refuse anyway. Her beloved Jonathan was probably lurking somewhere, so she'd make some polite excuse and hurry away. Now that he'd started he had to ask the question.

'What?' she prodded, as she pulled her hat further down on her head and held her gloved hands to her face, as if to warm herself up a little.

That decided him. 'I don't suppose you fancy a hot drink to warm us up and wash away that sandwich? Somewhere where there's heating preferably.'

To his surprise and delight she nodded eagerly. 'Oh, I'd love that. I'm about to freeze up, honestly. What about The Castle Keep Café?'

Since that was the place he'd thought of too, it seemed like a good omen.

'Great. Let's go then.'

They walked down the passageway, and Holly asked him what he was doing in Helmston. He told her about the tyres, and she commiserated about the unwelcome expenditure right before Christmas, which was gratifying. The Castle Keep Café was just across the road, right by the entrance gates to Helmston Castle and, to their relief, they could see an empty table in front of the window.

'Brilliant. Let's get in there quickly before someone grabs it!'

They waited impatiently for a break in the traffic, then raced across the road. Lewis held open the café door for Holly, who gave him a surprised but grateful smile. It was lovely and warm inside, and they both gave audible sighs of pleasure as the heat began to permeate their frozen bodies.

A waitress was passing by, and she grinned at them. 'Bless you, you look nithered. Go and take a seat and I'll be with you in a jiffy.'

Lewis led Holly over to the one vacant table and they sat down, spending the next few minutes unwinding scarves, removing gloves and hats and muttering things like, 'Ooh, that's better.'

Finally feeling brave enough to attempt it, they took off their coats and hung them over the backs of their chairs.

Lewis leaned back and closed his eyes. 'Bliss.'

'I know! I can't believe how much the temperature's dropped today.'

Neither could Lewis. He was glad he'd got his greenhouses sorted and had taken necessary steps to protect his plants.

'So, what would you like to drink?' He picked up the menu and scanned it, thinking it was a bit pricey for a simple café. He mentally totted up what he'd spent that day and tried to fathom out how much he had left. Eventually he rummaged in his coat pocket and discreetly pulled out a handful of change, trying to count it under the table so that Holly wouldn't see it.

'I think I'll have the white hot chocolate with a shot of caramel,' she announced, putting the menu down.

He glanced up and saw her frowning at him. His face grew hot with embarrassment.

'Are you okay?' She sounded puzzled and he gulped.

'Yeah, fine. White hot chocolate with caramel?' He pulled a face. 'Wow, that sounds sweet!'

'I know but I just fancy it.' She beamed at him then leaned forward, trying to see what he was doing.

He closed his fist tightly around the money, but evidently not quickly enough.

'I can pay for these,' she told him softly.

Lewis was horrified. 'Certainly not! What sort of

man invites a lady for a drink then makes her pay?'

She flushed slightly. 'So I'm a lady am I?'

He shoved the money back in his pocket and ran a hand through his hair, remembering too late that it always stuck up at the front when he did that. He frantically tried to flatten it and hoped she hadn't noticed. 'Of course you are. What a thing to say. Right, white hot chocolate with a shot of caramel it is.'

'Honestly, I don't mind paying,' she told him, her voice sounding urgent. 'At least let me pay for my own.'

'Definitely not.'

'But if you haven't got much money...'

He tried to look puzzled, as if he didn't understand her comment, then laughed in what he hoped was a convincing manner. 'Oh, you mean the change? No, no, I was just seeing if I had enough on me to pay in cash. If not I'd have just paid by card, but no worries, I have enough I think.'

God he really hoped he had, because his debit card would be declined for sure, and he didn't possess a credit card.

'Right, loveys, are you ready to order?' The waitress, having delivered two plates of scampi and chips to some customers at the next table, arrived by their sides and whipped a notebook and pencil from her apron pocket.

'Just a white hot chocolate with a shot of caramel and a cup of tea please,' Lewis said. He'd quickly calculated that he should have enough for both drinks. He'd have killed for a hot chocolate, but he was about twenty pence short for that, so tea would have to do.

He really wished he hadn't bought that sandwich. The Christmas cards would have to wait. Maybe he could get them cheap at the supermarket when he did his food shop tomorrow. He mentally crossed his fingers that Holly wouldn't decide she'd quite like another drink, because that really would be embarrassing.

The waitress returned a few minutes later with their drinks and Holly's eyes widened. 'Oh, wow! Look at that!'

Lewis looked. The hot chocolate was in a large mug and was topped with a huge mountain of whipped cream and tiny little marshmallows. It even had white chocolate flakes sprinkled on top. He glanced down at his boring cup of tea and sighed inwardly. Oh well, if she was enjoying herself what did it matter?

Holly set to work, scooping the cream up on her long-handled spoon and picking off the marshmallows one by one. It was quite pleasurable to watch her. He'd never known anyone look so blissful over a drink before.

'So, what are you doing here anyway?' he asked. 'Christmas shopping?' *And where's your git of a boyfriend?*

'Lulu—she's my neighbour—needed her prescription, and I thought I'd make an afternoon of it. Jonathan's got to work you see. Overtime. So I thought I'd do some shopping at the market, try to get into the Christmas spirit.'

He heard the dejected tone in her voice and saw the light dim in her eyes. He hated to see the change in her. He wished he'd never asked her now.

'If you need a tree,' he told her, desperate to put the

smile back on her face, 'I'm your man.'

Or I could be... Oh, God! What was *wrong* with him? She was totally obsessed with that slimeball Jonathan. He was on a hiding to nothing here, so why was he being so stupid about it?

'I can get you a big discount,' he said hastily. 'Or if you want holly and mistletoe I can get you loads of that for free. All legal of course.' To his dismay the offer of free foliage didn't seem to cheer her up. 'Of course, not everyone wants all that green stuff in their house. I expect you've already got loads of Christmas decorations anyway.'

Holly's head was bowed over her mug of hot chocolate. She carefully laid her spoon down on the saucer and he heard her sniff quietly. Oh God, what had he said now?

'Are you okay?'

She wiped her cheek and looked up, her eyes bright with unshed tears. 'Sorry. I'm being stupid. You must be so sick of me looking so miserable. Everyone else is. I don't know what's wrong with me lately, really I don't. I never used to be like this.'

'Don't be silly.' He reached into his pocket and brought out a tissue. 'Here. It's clean, promise.'

She gave what was a cross between a laugh and a splutter and took the tissue with thanks. Dabbing her eyes she said, 'And now I suppose my mascara's run and I look like a raccoon?'

'Not at all. You look perfect.' He blushed fiercely and took a gulp of his tea. Okay, so she did look perfect, but he didn't have to say so did he?

She pushed the tissue into her bag and sat up straight. 'I'm okay now, honestly. What were you saying?'

He hesitated, wondering whether it was safe to continue with the conversation. 'Er, I was saying about the Christmas tree and—oh hell!'

Her eyes filled with tears again and she stared at him in horror. 'Sorry, sorry. I don't know what's the matter with me today.'

'Actually,' he said gently, 'I think you probably do.' *Leave her alone. Don't push her. It's her business, not yours.* He braced himself and plunged on regardless. 'Want to talk about it?' *Nice work, idiot! Do you never listen to a word I say?*

'Not really,' she sniffed. 'It's all boring anyway, and why should you care what's going on in my stupid little life?'

He could never tell her why, not in a million years.

'I'm sure it's not a stupid little life,' he murmured, staring at his tea, and thinking that he'd not felt this awkward for years. He was completely out of his depth here, and he'd grown accustomed to an easy life. He'd made damn sure there were no complications. His life was stress-free, easy, uncomplicated. Just how he liked it. He'd had enough games to last a lifetime, and yet here he was, getting all entangled with someone whose own life, far from being boring, looked like a complete car crash. He should walk away now. Hell he should run and run fast. 'And if I didn't care I wouldn't have asked, would I?' *I hate you, Lewis Palmer. You're a total prat.*

She didn't seem to have picked up on his unease, nor his admission that he cared about her, thank goodness. She picked up her spoon and stirred what was left of the cream into the hot chocolate. The marshmallows had long gone. 'It was just when you talked about Christmas, and the tree and everything. Thing is, I don't know where I'll be at Christmas. I'm being evicted you see.'

Of all the things he'd expected to hear that was the last thing he'd thought of. His mind began to race. Well, she could sleep in his bed. He'd take the sofa obviously. It would be a bit cramped, but they'd manage. She could stay there as long as she wanted. He'd never see her out on the street.

Then rational thought took over. She had loads of friends in the village. None of them would see her on the street. He knew Abbie would welcome her at The Gables and he was pretty sure Nell would invite her to stay at The Ducklings. And besides, what about her boyfriend? Surely he'd put a roof over her head? The thought depressed him immensely, and he sipped his tea as he mulled over the prospect of someone as vulnerable as Holly being tied even closer to Jonathan. She'd be like a fly in a spider's web, he thought gloomily. She'd have no chance.

'Why are you being evicted?' he managed eventually. 'If it's a problem with rent—'

'No, nothing like that,' she assured him. 'It's what they call a no-fault eviction. The landlord wants to sell up you see, and as long as he gives me enough notice and has put my deposit into a certain scheme thingy that protects it, well, there's nothing to stop him chucking me out whenever he wants. And he wants. So that's that.'

'How long have you lived there?'

'All my life.'

He gasped. 'All your life? Seriously?'

She nodded. 'My mum and dad rented it first, then when they split up and moved in with other partners, the man who owned it at the time let me take over the tenancy. He was lovely, but when he died his kids sold it to a company and they've really not been great landlords.'

'I'm so sorry. It must be awful, losing your childhood home like that.'

She tilted her head to one side, considering. She looked so cute his heart seemed to leap up into his throat. 'Not really to be honest. It wasn't that much of a happy home, what with mum and dad rowing all the time. And it's a dump. It needs loads doing to it. It's riddled with damp and the bathroom and kitchen are ancient. I'll be glad to be out of there if I'm honest.'

He frowned, puzzled. 'Okay, so what's the problem? Surely one of your friends can put you up until you find somewhere else?'

She picked up the mug and cradled it in both hands but made no attempt to drink from it. His heart went out to her.

'Oh, I'm not short of offers,' she told him. Her eyes clouded over with misery again. 'That's the problem really.'

'It is?'

'Thing is, Lulu, my next-door neighbour, offered to give me one of her spare bedrooms for as long as I want it. She's lovely, Lulu. Honestly, she's like the grandmother I never knew, and she's been there for me all my life. I love her to bits, I really do. And she's got loads of room at her place, so I wouldn't be in the way. Far from it. She's got really bad arthritis you see,' she explained. 'She struggles to do some things and her mobility's reduced. She's in a lot of pain, but she never complains. It would be great to be so close to her all the time. I go round there as much as I can but it's not the same as being under the same roof is it? And she'd never bother me if she was struggling, but if I was living there, well, I'd pick up on her difficulties much quicker wouldn't I? It would be so much better for both of us.'

'Then what's the problem?'

She stared at him, her mouth opening and closing as if she was trying to force the words out but couldn't quite bring herself to do it.

A coldness crept over Lewis. 'It's your boyfriend isn't it? It's Jonathan.'

She nodded and finally gulped down a huge mouthful of hot chocolate. Lewis suspected it was more like lukewarm chocolate now.

'I really don't know why I'm telling you all this,' she gabbled. 'Honestly, I'm sure you've got better things to do with your time then listen to me banging on about stuff you couldn't give tuppence for.'

'I asked, didn't I?' he said. 'I'm listening. I'm a captive audience. Go on, tell your Uncle Lewis all about it.'

Great, like that wasn't a creepy image to put in her mind!

'Well, the thing is, Jonathan doesn't think that it's a good idea to move in with Lulu.'

I'll bet he doesn't, Lewis thought grimly. 'Oh, why not?'

'He's worried that I'll just end up being Lulu's carer,' she began. 'He thinks that's why she asked me in the first place.'

'Do you think that?'

She shook her head. 'No. Lulu's not like that. She's proud and stubborn. If anything, she hides how much she needs help. She'd never play games like that.'

'So, are *you* worried about becoming her carer?'

'Not at all. She's very independent, and she wouldn't expect me to run around after her. But the thing is, if she needed me to do anything for her I'd happily do it. Like I said, she's the gran I never knew, and I'd do anything for her. If it turned out that she needed me more than I expected, well, so what? I'd do whatever I could to help, of course I would. I don't know why Jonathan doesn't understand that.'

'Hmm. It's a mystery.' He daren't say any more, though lord knows he was longing to.

'Well, anyway, Jonathan asked me to move in with him instead.'

'Right. And you don't want to upset either of them by choosing the other?'

'It's worse than that,' she admitted. 'Jonathan says—he says if I move in with Lulu then we're finished.'

Lewis gaped at her. 'Are you kidding?' From his point of view, it was the best thing that could happen to her, but he could see why it would be a dilemma for her. She was in love with this prat after all. Or at least, she thought she was.

She shook her head. 'I wish I was,' she said. 'I mean,

I can see what he means in a way. He says that it's too far for him to visit me after work—he lives in Whitby you see—and he wouldn't feel comfortable staying over at Lulu's with her being just across the landing and us so close by. So, as he sees it we'd never get to see each other or be alone together, and therefore there's no point in continuing with our relationship. So the obvious solution, as far as he's concerned, is for me to move in with him.'

'But what about your job? He won't come all the way to Bramblewick to visit you, yet he'd expect you to travel there and back from Whitby every day?'

She gazed at him in dumb misery.

Lewis took a steadying breath. No point in telling her what he really thought. It would only put her on her guard, make her defensive. He couldn't stand to listen her making excuses for that git. 'So what is your instinct telling you?'

'I can't lose Jonathan,' she said, her eyes filling with tears again.

Lewis felt sick with disappointment and with despair that she was so obsessed with someone who clearly wasn't deserving of her affections.

'Is Jonathan really that important to you? Please,' he said quickly, aware that he was breaking his own code, 'don't go on the defensive. It's just, as an outsider, I can see that he's not making you that happy.'

'It's my fault,' she whispered. 'You don't understand. He didn't used to be like this. He was so charming and lovely when we met, so kind. He couldn't do enough for me, and he made me feel really special, loved. But I messed it all up. He puts up with such a lot from me. If I could just be better—if I could just sort myself out, be less stupid, less selfish—than I know things would be really good between us again. I just...' She shook her head, seeming dazed.

'Just what?'

'I just can't seem to do it right. I can't seem to... be *enough*.'

Lewis held his breath, feeling his heart thumping in his chest. There was so much he wanted to say to her, so much she needed to understand.

'I'd do anything to make him happy,' she continued. 'No one else would be so understanding when I get it all wrong. Who else would put up with me the way I am? But, the thing is, I just don't see how I can do the commute to work. Especially in the winter when the snows come and I can't even drive, and Jonathan says it would be too far for him to pick me up and I have to be at work for eight anyway and the buses wouldn't get me there on time...'

'Hey, hey, breathe.' Lewis reached over and put his hand over hers. An electric shock ran through him, and he pulled it away hastily.

'Sorry,' she murmured. 'I just don't know what to do for the best.'

He studied her for a moment, fighting the temptation to tell her exactly what she should do. But it wasn't down to him, he knew that. Besides, he wasn't Jonathan. He wasn't going to tell her what was best for her.

'What would Lulu tell you to do?' he asked suddenly.

Holly blinked in evident surprise. Her head tilted to one side in that endearing manner again, and he wondered how he'd got himself into this situation. He was thirty-four years old and had managed to evade romantic entanglements all this time. Oh, he'd had dates of course. He wasn't a priest after all. But he'd never got involved and had no intention of doing so. He'd always made that very clear from the outset to any girl he took out. He wasn't looking for love or commitment, or marriage, or any of that stuff. He'd finally got his life just as he liked it, and he had no intention of ever letting his peace of mind be threatened again. How on earth had this woman chipped away at all those defences and lodged herself into his heart, his mind, his very soul?

He shivered and wasn't sure if was from terror or delight. It felt good to feel this way about someone; to care, to feel excited when he saw her, to think about her even when she wasn't around. But it was scary as hell too. As if it wasn't bad enough that Holly was already in a relationship with another man, she was also in a dangerous trap. This boyfriend of hers was using her emotions against her, turning her vulnerability and low self-esteem into a weapon. He'd been here before and he'd been helpless to change things. How could he stand by and watch it happen all over again?

'She'd tell me to do what was best for me,' Holly said slowly.

'So she wouldn't tell you to move in with her?'

'No, definitely not. She'd say it was up to me. There'd be no pressure at all.'

They gazed at each other, and Lewis raised an eyebrow. Did she see the significance of what she'd just said? 'Holly, would you do me a huge favour?'

She was on her guard instantly. 'What sort of favour?'

He knew he was taking a huge risk, but he had to do it. She needed someone to stand up for her, be her ally. Someone who knew what they were dealing with, the way he did.

'This is going to sound crazy, I know, but... do you think you could keep a diary for me?'

Her mouth dropped open. 'A diary?'

'I know. I said it sounds crazy, but honestly, trust me on this. Do you think, for me, that you could keep a record of everything that happens between you and Jonathan?'

She gave a nervous laugh, clearly confused and worried by his request. 'Why would I do that?'

He shrugged, trying to sound as if it wasn't anywhere near as serious as it truly was. 'You say you get confused, that it all becomes twisted in your mind when you have conversations with him. Well, this would make it all clear to you. You'd know exactly what was said.'

'But—but—' she stared at him for a moment then shook her head. 'That's awful! Like spying on him.'

'It's not about him,' he said, knowing he was lying, but only partly. It was after all as much about her and protecting her sanity. 'You need clarity and to be confident that you're saying what you think you're saying. It's pretty obvious to me that you're no longer sure of yourself. This way you'd have no room for doubt. You'd be clear what you said wouldn't you?' *And, vitally, what Jonathan said.*

Holly lowered her gaze. 'I think—'

They both jumped as there was a loud bang on the window next to them. Lewis looked up quickly, just in time to catch a flash of black leather and a Manchester United scarf.

'Jonathan!' Holly's eyes widened and Lewis heard the dread in her voice.

Then the man himself was standing by their table, hands in pockets, glaring down at them both.

'Well, well, well. Isn't this a cosy little scene?'

Holly had gone deathly white, which was the only reason that Lewis decided he had to explain himself to that loathsome creature.

'It's not what it looks like,' he said calmly, though he longed to grab hold of that so-called man's lapels and slam him against the wall. 'Holly and I bumped into each other in the market, and since we were both freezing cold we thought we'd nip in here and grab a hot drink to warm us up.'

'Yeah, and I'm supposed to believe that am I?' Jonathan sneered. 'No wonder you were dragging your heels about moving in with me, Holls. You sure it was that old bat next door who asked you to move in, and not Blondie here?'

'Jonathan!' Holly sounded appalled. 'Nothing's going on! I rang you last night didn't I? I begged you to let me go to your flat so we could talk, and you said I couldn't because you were working overtime all day today. If I was planning on meeting Lewis I wouldn't have asked to see you, would I?'

'Yeah, well, I *was* working overtime, but I never said all day. You weren't listening properly as usual. Finished at twelve, like I said I would, and I thought I'd come and see you, and since Helmston's on the way to Bramblewick, I thought I'd stop and get you something nice as a treat. Got a right shock, didn't I, when I saw my girlfriend sitting in the window of a bloody café with her so-called friend.'

'He's not my so-called friend,' Holly protested. 'He *is* my friend.'

'That's me,' Lewis said. 'Strictly friends.'

He glanced out of the window and his eyes narrowed. There was a young woman standing across the road, staring at them. If looks could kill they'd all be dead by now. Her expression changed as she saw him staring back at her and she turned, rushing through the passageway towards the market. He frowned. Where did he know her from? He was sure he recognised that face, that scowl...

Light dawned and he turned back to Jonathan, who was standing beside the table wearing a martyred expression while poor Holly tried to explain herself. He wanted so much to announce what a coincidence it was that he'd just seen the girl Jonathan had taken out into the garden at the party. He'd love to see him squirm his way through some sort of denial, he really would.

He had no doubt that Jonathan had lied to Holly about working overtime. He'd clearly been in Helmston, spending the day with—Gina was it? If only he and Holly hadn't been sitting at the window table, Jonathan would never have spotted them. Now he had Holly at a disadvantage, even though Lewis was positive that he was the one in the wrong. But if he mentioned it know he just knew that Jonathan would find a way to wriggle off the hook. Holly would buy his story, whatever it was, but at the back of her mind it would be another doubt, another fear for her to wrestle with. He couldn't do it to her.

Instead he sighed heavily and got to his feet. 'If you'll excuse me, I think it's time I headed home.'

'We can agree on that much, mate,' Jonathan muttered.

Holly looked stricken. 'I'm ever so sorry about this, Lewis,' she said. 'Thank you for the hot chocolate.'

He smiled at her, determined to reassure her that nothing Jonathan said or did would stop them being friends.

'No worries, it was a pleasure. See you around, Holly.'

As he headed towards the door he heard Jonathan demand, 'What did he mean, *see you around*? Have you two made another date, or what?'

Lewis couldn't get out of the café fast enough. If he stayed much longer he wouldn't be responsible for his actions, and that really wouldn't help Holly, even though he suspected it would do him the world of good.

***

Holly stared out of the window, her fingers tightly wrapped around the strap of her bag, her jaw clenched rigid with tension. Beside her Jonathan drove in stony silence.

He was angry. She always knew he was angry when he was driving because he became much more aggressive on the roads, speeding up, tailgating, slamming on his brakes at the last minute instead of slowing down steadily, yelling abuse at other drivers, and launching onto a roundabout with barely a glance to his right.

It was pointless to tell him to slow down because that would only make him worse. She'd asked him to wait while she fastened her seatbelt when they first got in the car, but he hadn't. He'd roared out of the car park while she was still struggling to loosen the belt and she'd been terrified that he'd have to brake suddenly, and she'd hurtle through the windscreen.

How can he say he loves me when he's so happy to take risks with my life? But even as the question formed she reassured herself that he just didn't realise what he was doing, that he hadn't understood the risk, and of course if he had he would never have been so reckless.

They finally arrived back at Holly's house, and she waited, not sure if he intended to drive off again or not.

'Well, are you getting out or what?' he demanded.

She cringed, unclicking her seatbelt. 'Are you coming in?'

'Is there any point?'

She fiddled nervously with the zip on her bag. 'I think so.'

He drummed his fingers on the steering wheel then turned off the engine. 'Sod it,' he said, snatching the keys from the ignition. 'Let's have this out once and for all.'

Holly almost wished she hadn't said anything. Maybe it would have been better if she'd just got out of the car, said thank you for the lift and hurried indoors. When he was like this there was no reasoning with him.

Reluctantly she climbed out of the car and slammed the door shut, then followed him meekly down the garden path. She stole a glance at Cuckoo Nest Cottage and thought about Lulu's medication in her bag. She'd pop over later as soon as Jonathan had left. Always supposing he wasn't staying over. She couldn't imagine he would be somehow.

Her fingers shook slightly as she unlocked the front door, and she stepped aside to let him in. He barged past her and headed straight into the living room, plonking himself down on the sofa, hands in his jacket pockets, legs spread, a belligerent expression on his face.

Holly dropped the bag on the armchair and slowly unbuttoned her duffle coat. 'Do you want a drink?'

'No, I don't want a drink,' he said moodily. 'You could bang the heating on though. It's like a fridge in here.'

'The heating is on,' she admitted. 'I left it on so it would be warm when I got home.' She put her hand to the nearest radiator and nodded. 'It's on. It's just that this house is so draughty and—'

'Not like my place then,' he told her. 'Warm as toast

in there.' He linked his hands behind his head and smirked. 'You'll find that out when you move in. It will be a new experience for you, being warm.'

Holly swallowed. 'The thing is, Jonathan,' she began, sinking into the armchair and clasping her hands together, 'the thing is, about that...'

He narrowed his eyes. 'What about it?'

'I think, on balance, that I need to accept Lulu's offer.' She reared back as he sat bolt upright, his eyebrows knitted together in anger.

'You what?'

'It's just work really,' she explained desperately. 'The commute. If I could drive it would be different, but there's no way I'd be able to get to work on time, what with needing two buses and coming all the way from Whitby. And if it's bad weather I might not get in at all, and—'

'So quit your job and get another.'

She stared at him, appalled. 'I can't do that!'

'Why not? You said you used to work at the chemist's in Helmston before you got the job at the surgery. So if you can do it once you can do it again. There are chemists in Whitby, you know. There are doctors in Whitby, too, funnily enough. You never know, there might be a job going somewhere, and if not there are plenty of shops around. I'm sure you could find something.'

'But I love my job,' she said, her voice small. She realised that she did too. Despite the awkwardness with Anna and Rachel at the moment, she was happy at Bramblewick Surgery. She loved the interaction with the patients and the doctors were so friendly, and they had such laughs together in the office. Or they used to...

'It's just a ten-a-penny job,' he told her patiently. 'It's not like you've had to train for it like I did to be a mechanic is it?'

Offended, Holly folded her arms. 'I've done loads of training! First aid, confidentiality, system training, fire training—'

'Yeah, yeah, but I mean proper training.'

'We're training all the time,' she protested. 'We're always having to update our knowledge and we have to do tests every year. It's a lot more involved than you think.'

He smirked. 'Yeah, sure it is. But it's not like it's hard is it? I mean if you can do it anyone can. Anyway, my point is, there are other jobs. You'd probably earn more in a factory, come to think of it. Or doing a night shift in a supermarket. There are plenty of pubs you could work in too, so you're not going to be out of work for long. Your job's no excuse.'

Holly shook her head. 'It's not just my job.'

'Ah! Now we're getting to it,' he said. 'Go on, let me guess. The old woman next door needs you.'

'Well she does!' Holly cried. 'You know she has medical problems, Jonathan. I can't just leave her all alone.'

'So why isn't she in a home if she's that bad?' he demanded. 'Why should it be your responsibility? You're not even family.'

'Lulu *is* my family!' Holly couldn't believe he was

suggesting that Lulu go into a home. 'And she'll never have to go into a home as long as she's got me. I'm moving in with her as soon as possible to make sure she's okay. It—it seems silly to wait until my notice expires. I might as well be at Cuckoo Nest Cottage where I can keep an eye on her, and where it's warm and dry.'

They glared at each other as Holly's heart hammered against her ribs. Was he going to end it after all?

Suddenly, Jonathan shook his head and leaned back in the sofa again. He gave her a resigned smile. Holly watched him, feeling slightly unnerved. What was he up to?

'Okay, Holls,' he said at last. 'You win. Just wish you'd make your mind up. I wouldn't have redecorated the bedroom if you hadn't said you'd move in with me.'

Holly frowned, puzzled. 'But I never said I would move in with you,' she said. 'I said I'd think about it.'

Jonathan's mouth fell open. 'Are you serious? For crying out loud, here we go again.' He sighed. 'Honestly, Holly, your memory. Yeah, you said you needed to think about it *at first*, but then you said yes, remember?'

'No,' she said, feeling dazed. 'I don't.'

'At the car park,' he said. 'You said you didn't know what to do and needed time, so I started walking away and you grabbed my arm to stop me.'

Holly remembered doing that, but that proved nothing surely? 'And?'

'What do you mean, *and*?' Jonathan sounded appalled. 'Are you seriously telling me that you remember stopping me from leaving but you don't remember telling me that you'd made your mind up and you were going to move in with me?'

'I *didn't* say that!' Holly shook her head, her mind whirling. She hadn't, she knew she hadn't. Had she? And in that split second, she was no longer sure. Jonathan was looking at her with real concern, as if he was worried about her mental health.

'Jeez, Holls, do you really think I'd have gone to all that trouble to redecorate the bedroom if you hadn't said yes to moving in?' He rubbed his chin, considering her. 'You know what? I'm seriously beginning to worry about you. Maybe you should see one of them doctors at your work. I think you might have dementia or something. Something's not right, that's for sure.'

'But I would have remembered if I'd said that...' But would she? She seemed to have been making so many mistakes lately, getting things wrong, forgetting things. After all, wasn't that the reason she'd turned down the phlebotomy job? She just couldn't trust herself any longer. And he was right, there was no way he'd have spent money, not to mention time, redecorating if he hadn't needed to. Jonathan hated painting and wallpapering. She *must* have said yes.

'I'm so sorry,' she mumbled. 'I honestly forgot. I don't know what to say.'

His expression changed. He gave her a sympathetic smile and jumped up. 'Aw, it's all right, love, don't worry yourself.' He perched on the arm of her chair and pulled her into a hug. 'You can't help it. You've obviously got a lot on your plate, what with the eviction notice and running around after the old lady. No wonder you're so forgetful. Hey, chin up. How about I order us a takeaway for our tea, eh?'

She looked at him tearfully. 'You're staying?'

'Well, I'll stay for tea,' he said. 'Got to go home after that though, 'cos I'm going out for a drink with Josh from work.'

'Oh, right.' She bit her lip, but she knew she had no right to protest. Not when he'd spent precious free time redecorating for her when there'd been absolutely no need to do so. 'So, you and me...?'

He frowned. 'What about you and me?'

'Are we still together? Only you said if I moved in with Lulu we were finished.'

He cupped her face and gave her a long kiss on the lips. 'Does that answer that question?' he asked her.

She smiled. 'I guess it does.'

'Well then, stop being so daft. As if I'd finish with you over that! You take things so seriously, love. Blimey, if I can put up with you ignoring me when we're out with your friends and flirting with Blondie, I'm sure I can put up with you living miles away from me with some old woman.'

Holly reared back. 'I don't ignore you! And I wasn't flirting!'

He held up his hands. 'Hey, let's not get into this again tonight, okay? Honestly, I can't cope with any more rows, Holls. I'm a nervous wreck as it is. If it's not one thing it's another. I just want a quiet life, is that too much to ask? Please, no more drama okay?'

Holly's heart thudded as she tried to process how

things had become so twisted in Jonathan's favour, but she was muddled, and could feel a headache coming on.

'Okay?' Jonathan repeated.

She nodded. 'I think I have a headache,' she told him.

'I'll get you some paracetamol and then I'll put the kettle on,' he said, dropping a kiss on the top of her head as he got to his feet. 'You just relax. Let me take care of you. I love you, Holls, you know that don't you?'

'Yes, yes of course I know that,' she murmured, as he ruffled her hair and wandered into the kitchen.

She leaned back and closed her eyes. Everything seemed so confused in her mind and she was just too tired to think it all through. The main thing was she still had Jonathan, even though she'd let him down yet again and had caused him so much bother. She was so lucky he was the forgiving type. No one else would ever put up with her.

Her thoughts strayed to her afternoon with Lewis, and she opened her eyes again as she remembered his strange request that he record every conversation she had with Jonathan. It was unthinkable, a betrayal, and yet...

She bit her lip as an unforgivable thought occurred to her. If she'd recorded their conversation in Whitby she would be certain that she'd agreed to move in with him. Or that she hadn't. Was it wrong to be so deceitful? And yet, surely it was as much for Jonathan's good as her own if she started to feel more certain of herself, to be able to check on everything she'd said to him? It could only help. Her gaze slid over to her bag and she reached inside it and took out her phone. It wouldn't take a moment to start recording, and she could write it all down later. In future she would keep her diary with her so that she could make notes, as her phone's memory wasn't great, but for now it was a solution wasn't it? And she wouldn't reread what she'd written, unless she was really, really uncertain about something.

'Here's that paracetamol,' Jonathan said, strolling back into the living room a moment later, a glass of water in one hand and a box of tablets in the other. 'Take those and you'll soon be yourself again. No more silly arguments tonight, okay?'

Holly smiled at him and put her phone on the table next to her armchair. She reached for the water and the paracetamol. 'Thank you,' she told him gratefully.

'No bother. Now, let's have a look for those takeaway menus shall we?'

He rummaged through the drawer in the sideboard, muttering to himself about whether he fancied pizza or Indian. Holly eyed the phone nervously, but there was nothing to reveal that the recording was in progress. She swallowed the paracetamol and sat back, reassuring herself that she'd done nothing wrong. She didn't have to listen to it. It was just for her own peace of mind if she ever needed it, that was all.

***

Lewis hesitated before knocking on the front door,

uncertain suddenly whether he was doing the right thing. It had seemed so clear when he set off for The Gables, but now that he was here he wasn't sure. It seemed like a horrible invasion of Holly's privacy, and anyway Abbie might not know anything, or even want to share it with him if she did. Maybe he should forget about it and go home.

He half turned away, but as he did the front door opened and Isla stood there. She looked surprised but her face broke into a smile.

'Hiya, Lewis! Fancy seeing you here.' She grinned. 'Are you coming in or what?'

He noted the beret on her head, the scarf around her neck, the thick padded coat.

'You're going out.'

'Wow, you ought to be on University Challenge you're so brainy.' She nudged him. '*I'm* going out, yeah, but Mum's not. She's in the kitchen. Go on through.'

Reluctantly he nodded and stepped into the hallway, where he was immediately pounced on by an ecstatic black Labrador and an excited Cavalier.

'See you later, Lewis,' Isla said. 'Bye, Mum! Bye, Rachel!'

She'd slammed the door shut behind her before Lewis had even registered that Rachel was in the house too. He wondered for a moment if he could sneak out of there without Abbie ever knowing, but even as the thought crossed his mind the kitchen door opened and there she was.

'I thought I heard Isla talking to someone,' she said, a welcoming smile on her face. 'Don't just stand there,' she called over her shoulder as she went back into the kitchen, both dogs following her, tails wagging furiously. 'Come on in. Isn't it cold? I've got the heating turned right up today. I'll put the kettle on. Another cuppa, Rachel? Look who's here.'

Rachel looked pleased to see him. 'Hiya, Lewis. Nice to see you again.'

'Were you looking for Jackson?' Abbie asked, turning to him after switching on the kettle. 'Only he's not here. He'll be here later though. Isla and her friend are catching the bus to Helmston to do some Christmas shopping and he's going to give them a lift back. Was it urgent?'

Lewis reddened as he pulled up a chair and sat opposite Rachel at the table. 'Er, I didn't come here to see Jackson actually. It was you I wanted to talk to.'

Rachel held up her hands. 'I get the feeling this is a private matter. I'll get my coat.'

'No, no, honestly. Don't go on my account. It's not private. Well, that is, it is private, but not about me. I wanted to—I need to ask your advice. Both of you really.'

They exchanged surprised glances and Abbie sat next to Rachel and stared at him in anticipation. 'Ooh, sounds intriguing. What is it you need advice about?'

'It's really awkward,' he said, rubbing the back of his neck under his scarf. He was getting hot. He unwound the scarf and dropped it on his knee. 'I don't even know if I should be saying anything but I'm worried.'

'About what? Is there something wrong with the flat? Because Nell wouldn't mind you telling her if something needs doing you know.'

'No, no, the flat's fine. It's—' he looked from one to the other and blurted out, 'it's about Holly.'

'Ah.' This time they gave each other knowing looks. 'What's Jonathan done this time?'

'Emotionally he's tied her up in knots, and not for the first time obviously. Look, I know it's none of my business, but the thing is I have a vested interest in this.'

Abbie raised an eyebrow. 'You do?'

Rachel squealed. 'You and Holly?'

Now his face scorched. He reached down and patted the dogs, who had gathered at his feet and were staring up at him in adoration. 'No, no. What I mean is, I've come across men like Jonathan before, and I know what they can do. How they can change people. I was wondering how much Holly's changed? You said something at the party about what Jonathan's done to her. What *has* he done to her?'

Rachel blew out her cheeks. 'Where to start? You wouldn't recognise her. I sometimes wonder if I dreamed what she was like before.'

Abbie nodded. 'I think she'd already started dating him when I joined the practice, but she's altered so much even in the year I've been here.'

'But in what way?'

Abbie got up to make the drinks and Rachel sat back in her chair, considering. 'Holly was the loud, lively one. Whenever we went out anywhere she was the first up on the dance floor. She used to love doing karaoke apparently. I only saw her sing once and she was bloody awful at it, but she didn't care. She was so happy up on that stage with the microphone, giggling away. Not a trace of embarrassment.'

'Holly was always really straightforward,' Abbie mused. 'She used to say what she thought. Not in a cruel way,' she added hastily. 'Just, there were no games, no pretences. She wasn't afraid to give her opinion.'

'She never seemed afraid of anything,' Rachel said wistfully. 'Holly hasn't had the easiest life. She had a rough childhood with parents who hated each other and didn't seem to think much of her either apparently. Then they left and she's lived on her own ever since, and that house she lives in is a real dump. She's never had any money to speak of, and the only person she ever relied on was Louisa Drake next door. They've known each other all Holly's life, and she really trusts her. But you know what? Despite it all, Holls always had a smile on her face. She made everyone else around her feel better about everything. She brought an optimism with her.'

Abbie put mugs of tea on the table as Rachel wiped away a tear. 'You okay, Rach?'

Rachel sniffed. 'Yeah, yeah. Just, I'd kind of forgotten what she was like back then. She's so different now it's untrue.'

Lewis nodded his thanks at Abbie as he contemplated what he'd just been told. It was as he feared.

'The thing is,' Rachel continued, 'I feel partly responsible.'

Abbie sat down, clearly surprised. 'Why on earth would you feel responsible? You didn't bring them together!'

'No, but I sussed him out from the start. Earlier than any of you.' She looked over at Lewis. 'My ex-husband abused me for years,' she explained. 'Physically and mentally.'

'I'm sorry,' he murmured. 'I didn't mean to cause you any pain.'

'You haven't. He did.' Rachel tutted impatiently. 'Oh, I said I would never let him get to me again and I won't. But the mental abuse, in a way, was worse than the physical abuse. It stays with you for such a long time, in here.' She tapped her temple. 'You feel worn down, worthless, and that feeling just doesn't go away, no matter how many times other people tell you you're marvellous, or even how much they love you.' She sighed. 'Xander's very understanding, thank goodness, but sometimes I still hear Grant's voice in my head, telling me I'm useless, stupid, a waste of space. So you see, I should have acted on my suspicions earlier, warned her off, made her listen. Perhaps I could have saved her all this.'

'I never knew you felt like this,' Abbie said sadly. 'You really shouldn't, you know.'

'She wouldn't have listened,' Lewis said calmly. 'All that would have happened is that she'd have fallen out with you, and then she'd have been even more isolated than she already is.'

'Isolated?' Abbie's eyes widened. 'She's not isolated. She has us, all of us. We all love her.'

He shook his head. 'It won't feel like that to her. I'll bet you anything you like that he's making her believe you don't really want her around. That you see her as a joke.' He paused, considering, but he decided they ought to know. 'In fact, I have evidence of it. Holly told me herself that Jonathan had heard us mocking her, making fun of the dress she was wearing at the party. I told her no one had said anything other than how stunning she looked, but how much she believed me I don't know.'

Rachel's eyes filled with tears again. 'Oh, my God! No wonder she's been so funny with us at work.'

'I'm only telling you this because I think you need to understand what we're dealing with here,' he told them. 'Please don't say anything to her about it. She needs to believe she can trust me.'

Abbie's eyes narrowed. 'Am I missing something here, Lewis? Just, you only met Holly a short while ago and you seem to be very involved with her already.'

Rachel gave a weak smile. 'Told you, he likes her don't you?'

'I do like her,' he said. 'But I also have some experience of gaslighting. I can't just stand by and watch it happen all over again. Believe me, I tried not to get involved, but I feel I have a responsibility.' Well, it wasn't a lie was it? He saw no reason to admit just how much he really liked Holly. Besides, it was irrelevant.

'Gaslighting?' Abbie leaned forward, curious. 'Is that what Jonathan's doing?'

'Absolutely. He's a narcissist and he's gaslighting her.'

'I think you're right,' Rachel agreed sadly.

'Forgive me,' Abbie said, 'I've heard the term, obviously, but I'm not entirely clear what we're talking about here. Could you clarify?'

Lewis nodded. 'It's a form of emotional abuse—'

'And a very effective one,' Rachel added, with a shudder. 'It makes you question your sanity, honestly.' She tutted. 'Sorry, Lewis. Carry on.'

He smiled. 'No worries. As you say, the abusive partner's actions make the victim doubt their sanity, their actual reality. By denying things which the victim knows to be true, by playing mind games, dismissing their opinions and doubts, and refusing to give them a voice, the gaslighter leaves them totally confused, anxious and increasingly depressed.'

'And it's all about power,' Rachel added. 'The abuser wants to control his victim. And the really scary thing is, by the time he's convinced her that she can't trust herself, that she's remembering things incorrectly and everything that's happening is her fault, it's even more likely that she'll stay with him, because who else would put up with someone like her?'

'You say *her*,' Abbie said. 'I'm presuming that men are victims of this sort of abuse, too?'

'Yes, and women can be the abusers, of course.' Rachel turned to Lewis, her eyes full of sympathy. 'You say you have experience of this?' she asked gently.

Lewis stared into his cup of tea, seeing his childhood spread out before him. He suppressed a shudder. 'My father was like Jonathan,' he said eventually. 'He destroyed my mother. She was a shell of a woman, always afraid to voice an opinion, permanently trying to appease him. The only time I ever saw her smile was when he was away working. Weekends and holidays were a nightmare. Then he sent me off to boarding school as a weekly boarder, so I only saw her when he was around. For a while I even forgot she could laugh.'

Rachel reached over and squeezed his hand. 'I'm so sorry.'

Abbie blinked away tears. 'Aw, Lewis. Bless you.'

He shook himself and sat up straight, smiling as Alby the Labrador rested his head on his lap and gazed up at him mournfully. 'I'm fine, honestly. It was a long time ago. He did it to me too, as I think you've guessed. Parents can gaslight their children, just as much as their spouses. He used to twist everything I said, confuse me, make me believe everything was my fault. It took me years to figure out what was going on, and I don't think my mum ever did. Even when she was dying she was worrying about my father. Desperate that he didn't get too stressed, that her illness didn't cause him any inconvenience.'

He realised that his tone had turned bitter and tried to pull himself together. He took a sip of tea. 'I've read everything I could about people like him, and the way they operate,' he explained. 'Partly for my own protection, and partly so I would recognise it if I ever saw anyone else being treated that way. I just wanted to make sure really. I wanted to get an idea of how Holly used to be.'

'Different,' Rachel said softly. 'She used to be very different.'

'She sounds like my mother when she met my

father. I don't remember her being like that, but my aunt told me she used to be lively and outgoing. Everyone loved her, my aunt said. She was so popular, and people wanted to be around her. Yet I remember hearing her crying one night as my dad stood over her and told her that no one liked her, that the reason no one came to the house any more was because she got on everyone's nerves. Even then I knew that it was my dad who'd driven people away, not her. My own friends stopped coming to the house and they told me it was because of him. But then, he could be extremely charming too. People I'd never met before came up to me at my mum's funeral and told me how much he'd adored her, and how lucky she'd been to have such a wonderful husband, and how fortunate I was to have such a brilliant father. I wanted to scream at them.'

'It's like they can't bear the other person's happiness,' Rachel mused. 'They take someone who's happy and kind and loving and they stamp on them. They want to squeeze out all that joy, all that hope. They want the other person to feel as wretched and worthless as they feel inside.'

'Do you think that's how Jonathan really feels?' Abbie said, surprised.

'I don't care whether he does or he doesn't,' Rachel admitted. 'But I do know that he's destroying Holly, and I can't bear it.'

'But what can we do?' Abbie said. 'She won't hear a word against him. You know how she always defends him. It's become almost impossible to talk to her.'

'He's clever,' Lewis said. 'And what he wants more

than anything is for Holly to be isolated from all her friends. If he can drive a wedge between you and her she'll be even more dependent on him, and it will be easier for him to convince her of anything he wants her to believe. She'll have no fight left in her. But if Jonathan is clever, we must be even more so. We can't let him have what he wants.'

'So no matter how Holly pushes away from us, we have to make sure she knows we love her,' Abbie said, gathering Willow the pretty Cavalier into her arms and cuddling her fiercely.

'And keep talking to her, no matter how much she tries to back away.' Rachel cradled her tea, her eyes steely with determination.

'And let her know that we're on her side.' Abbie turned to Rachel. 'We must let the others know. No more letting things slide. Operation Holly is a go.'

'Remember,' Lewis added, 'we need to keep reassuring her that she's not stupid, that we value her opinion, that she's far from worthless. She needs to know how very special she is.'

Because she really was and, somehow, he was going to make sure she remembered that.

Chapter 9

The move into Lulu's was painless. A lot of Holly's furniture was old tat, left over from her parents' marriage. It had definitely seen better days, and it certainly had no sentimental value, so she decided to get rid of it. She mentioned it at work, and to her surprise Rachel told her that Xander would collect it and take it to the tip for her.

'We've got the van now,' she explained. 'Had to, what with animal feed and whatnot, so it won't be any bother.'

'But are you sure he won't mind?' Holly asked, uncertain.

Rachel had laughed at the thought. 'Why on earth would he? You know he thinks the world of you, Holls.'

He did? It was news to Holly, but she was touched by the offer and thanked Rachel profusely.

So with that arranged she had only the bedroom furniture, which Holly had bought from her catalogue, a lamp, a bright and cheerful seaside print, a couple of ornaments, some DVDs, her TV, clothes, makeup and a few personal bits and bobs to take to Cuckoo Nest Cottage.

On moving day Ash and Jackson turned up

unexpectedly and carried the bedroom furniture upstairs while Xander was at the tip. Izzy arrived not long after and helped her gather her smaller possessions, and together they transferred them to Lulu's place, just as Nell popped by, on a break from Spill the Beans. She brought with her a celebration sponge cake and a huge *Welcome to Your New Home* card, signed by all her friends, even Gracie, Rachel's son Sam, and all three of Abbie's children, including three-year-old Poppy, who'd managed a colourful scribble.

Holly was moved to tears by their efforts. 'I don't know what to say,' she kept repeating, until Nell laughed and hugged her and said, 'You daft ha'porth, you don't have to say anything. You know how much we all love you, right?'

Holly noticed tears in Nell's eyes, and her own filled up immediately. 'Oh, heck,' she muttered. 'You've set me off now.'

'Right pair you are,' Lulu said, tutting, though her own eyes looked suspiciously bright. 'I'd best put the kettle on since we've got a house full.'

'Not for me,' Nell said, sounding regretful. 'I've got to get back to the shop. Chloe's on her own and it's packed in there.' She gave Holly another hug. 'Hope you'll be very happy here, Holls,' she whispered.

'Thank you.' Holly blinked away the tears as Nell smiled and left for work.

Izzy and Lulu began making drinks for everyone, and Xander, who'd just arrived back from the tip, admired the cake which led Ash to suggest that, just maybe, Holly would like to cut it?

'By heck, he's not backwards in coming forwards is he?' Lulu demanded, but Holly laughed and cut everyone a large slice of cake.

She couldn't remember feeling this optimistic for ages, and it was so lovely of her friends to help her out. She really hadn't expected it and had been worrying about getting everything moved all week. Jonathan had already arranged to be away that weekend at a football match with Josh, so he couldn't help, and she'd been reluctant to mention it to anyone at work, not wanting them to think she was incapable of doing anything for herself.

She'd finally broken it to Anna that she'd decided not to do the phlebotomy training and, although Anna had seemed understanding and had assured her it was fine and she didn't mind being the one to do it, guilt had eaten away at her all week. Anna had enough to do after all. She really felt she'd let her down, but she was too nervous to take on the job. The last thing she wanted was for the practice to be sued because of some stupid mistake she'd made. If Anna realised just how clumsy and stupid she was, she'd be thanking her for turning it down.

Anna herself dropped by during the afternoon, with Gracie and baby Eloise, and even Chester in tow. Holly hadn't seen the girls for some time she realised, as she noticed with shock how much they'd both changed over the last few months.

'Haven't they just?' Anna agreed, as Gracie accepted a slice of cake from Izzy, much to everyone's surprise; Gracie was quite choosy about what she ate and when, so no one had really expected her to accept. It felt like a small triumph really, but Holly could see a difference in Gracie. Now eleven years old she seemed to be blossoming. She hadn't had an easy time of it, as she was on the autism spectrum and had struggled to adapt to her new home and school, but today she seemed happy and confident.

'How's she doing at her new school?' she whispered to Anna, as Gracie told Chester, her mouth full of cake, that it was no use him begging for any, she couldn't give him cake as it was bad for him, and dogs had to maintain a healthy weight. Evidently her almost forensic study of dog care had paid off.

Anna placed Eloise on an eager Lulu's lap and sat down, a smile on her face. 'Really well. She's settled in much better than we expected. Loves her teacher and, of course, she's got a best friend now so that helps. Hallie's ever so good with her, so understanding. Plus, she loves Chester to bits. He can always cheer her up if she's had a down day.'

'Is she still doing her dance class?'

'Oh yes. She loves that. The highlight of her weekend. She's been there this morning.' Anna glanced around, looking thoughtful. 'Are you sure there's nothing you want doing, Holls? I feel a bit redundant. I'm ever so sorry I couldn't get here earlier, but Connor was at the surgery catching up on paperwork, and I had to take Gracie to Hatton-le-Dale for class, and the house was a tip. I thought I might as well get on with it while they were all out of the house and Eloise had a nap.'

'No worries,' Holly assured her. 'As you can see there's nothing to do really. Ash and Jackson got all my bedroom furniture in place for me, and I've made the bed, and Izzy put my painting up and set my ornaments and lamp out where I wanted them. Xander even took all my old stuff to the tip for me. Everyone's been ever so kind. I really can't thank you all enough.'

There were general mutterings of 'Don't be daft,' and 'It was nothing,' and 'You're welcome. Any time.'

Anna laughed. 'Well, I can see I'm surplus to requirements. Did you like your card?'

'Oh, I loved it,' Holly said, genuinely delighted. 'I can't believe you all signed it, even the little ones.'

'Except Eloise,' Anna said, nodding over at her daughter, who was staring in fascination at Lulu as the old lady pulled faces at her.

'Can't believe she's almost a year old,' Izzy mused. 'Time's flown by hasn't it?'

'It certainly has. We've been together nearly a whole year too,' Ash reminded her, squeezing her hand.

'And now we're getting married!' Izzy put her arm around him. 'Can't wait.'

'Me neither,' he assured her. 'One week to go. You *are* all coming I take it?' he asked, gazing round at them all.

'Well, I might not be able to,' Jackson told him. 'I'll have to see how I'm fixed.'

'Yeah, right. You'll be there, mate, if I have to drag you there. You're my best man, so you've got no excuse.'

'And since I'm your only bridesmaid, I suppose I'd

better cancel my other plans,' Anna teased. 'Not long now, Izz.'

'Golly, just one week! I'm getting really nervous now,' Izzy admitted.

'Just enjoy it, that's my advice,' Anna said. 'It flies by so fast.'

'It's going to be perfect,' Ash assured his fiancée. 'I mean, at the end of it all you'll have me! What more could you ask for?'

'Well, there is that,' Izzy said, laughing.

Holly laughed too. It was so long since she'd felt like this—like part of the circle. She experienced a strange sensation in the pit of her stomach and wondered briefly what it was, before it dawned on her. Happiness. She was happy.

There was a knock on the door and the bubble of joy inside her burst. What if it was Jonathan? Obviously, she'd love to see him, and it would be great if he'd decided not to go to the football match in order to come and see her instead, but what if he was in one of his less amiable moods? What if the match had been cancelled or he and Josh had missed their train?

He'd be in a vile mood. Particularly since so many of her friends were here. Jonathan always felt pushed out and neglected when they were around, for reasons she'd never fully understood. She'd never heard any of them being unfriendly towards him.

She realised she was holding her breath as Xander went to answer the door, and her stomach twisted itself into knots of anxiety.

Xander returned, bringing with him Lewis of all

people. Holly let out a breath and her stomach untwisted immediately.

'I hope I'm not intruding,' he said, glancing around at everyone then resting his gaze on her. 'I just thought I'd come over and wish you good luck in your new home. I brought you these from the Hall. Don't worry,' he added, smiling, 'I've got permission. I wouldn't dream of bringing you stolen flowers.'

'Oh!' She gasped in surprise as he handed her a beautiful bouquet of bright red and orange flowers, mixed with holly berries and spruce, all tied together with a red ribbon. 'Wow!'

'They're gorgeous, Lewis!' Anna beamed her approval at him. 'Are those anemones?' she asked, carefully stroking a delicate-looking white flower with a black centre.

'They are, as are the cherry red flowers. The orange ones are ranunculus. Do you like them? I thought they were a strikingly cheerful combination.'

'They're stunning!' Holly told him.

'And I love the way you've arranged them,' Anna added. 'Very professional.'

'Can't take credit for that I'm afraid. My friend Tanya turned them into a bouquet.'

Holly experienced a twist of jealousy so sharp it took all her strength not to change the expression on her face.

'Really? How kind of her. You must thank her for me.'

And who was this friend? He'd never mentioned her before. Though, why should he? He rarely talked about his private life, and she'd never asked. For all she knew he could be in a steady relationship, even engaged. What difference did it make anyway?

'I will. I *had* to include the holly berries of course. But I think it's quite an eye-catching assortment, don't you? All those bright, jolly tones.'

'It's a beautiful bouquet,' Izzy said. 'Is your friend a florist then?'

Lewis nodded. 'Yeah, she runs a little flower shop down Water's Edge in Kearton Bay. She supplies displays to the estate sometimes. She was dropping some off this morning and saw me gathering these together, which is when she offered.'

'Well,' Anna said, 'she's done a great job. What a lovely thing to do, Lewis.'

'If you take little 'un,' Lulu said, nodding at Holly, 'I'll find a vase and you can get them in water.'

'I'm sorry, Lulu, I haven't introduced you have I? This is Lewis, my, er—he lives in Nell's flat.'

'Aye, I've heard all about you,' Lulu told him, eyeing him steadily.

Lewis shook her hand. 'Pleased to meet you,' he told her. 'I've heard a lot about you too.'

The two of them smiled, seeming to approve of each other.

'Well, anyway, about the vase. I'll see to the flowers. The vase is under the sink isn't it?'

Holly jumped up so that no one would notice her blushes. Why Lewis's statement about his so-called friend had disturbed her so much she had no idea, and why was she so unnerved by Lulu's reaction to him?

She was much more thrilled he'd brought her a bouquet, or even that he'd come to wish her luck in her new home, than she ought to be.

'We'd better be getting back,' Izzy said, nudging Ash. 'You've got my tea to cook.'

Ash groaned in mock misery. 'I'm just a slave to you, aren't I?'

'Why else would I be marrying you?' she said, her eyes twinkling.

'Start as you mean to go on,' Anna advised. 'I made a big mistake with Connor. He only cooks once in a blue moon these days. I really should get tougher.' She winked at Holly, who was filling a vase with water. 'Need a hand with those, Holls?'

'No, I can manage fine thanks.'

'Right, well I think I'll get off too,' Anna announced, getting to her feet. 'Let me take Eloise off you, Louisa. I know she gets a bit heavy after a while, doesn't she?'

'She's a bonny bairn,' Lulu assured her, planting a kiss on the baby's cheek. Eloise rewarded her with a wide smile, revealing the beginnings of two teeth.

'I see Father Christmas has bin early to you,' Lulu said. 'Getting your two front teeth already, eh?'

'And her bottom ones are already through,' Anna confirmed. She lifted her daughter and gave her a cuddle. 'Connor was fretting, of course, because Gracie got hers earlier than Eloise and he kept checking to see if hers were coming. You'd have thought he was a vet, not a doctor. I told him, she's not Gracie. They're not going to do everything the same.'

'Gay-cee.'

'Ooh, she said your name, Gracie,' Izzy said.

Gracie picked up Chester's lead and slid her hand into the loop. 'She can't say it properly,' she informed them.

'Well, no, but she's making a very good attempt at it,' Ash pointed out. 'She must think a lot of you if she's trying to say your name,' he added encouragingly.

Gracie looked distinctly unimpressed. 'Are we going now?' she asked Anna.

Anna sighed. 'Yes, yes we're going.'

'We'll walk up with you,' Izzy said. She turned to Lewis. 'You haven't forgotten it's our wedding on Saturday? You will be there?'

'Of course,' he said. 'The Sea Star Hotel, right?'

Holly watched curiously as the others all smiled their approval. How funny that they'd accepted Lewis so easily. What was his secret, she wondered, thinking sadly that Jonathan was still very much on the edge of the group, and they never seemed that pleased to see him.

'Right! The service starts at one o'clock. I could give you directions to the hotel if you like?'

'No need,' Xander said. 'We'll give him a lift there. Why waste the petrol when we're all going to the same place?'

'That's very kind of you,' Lewis said. 'Thank you.'

'Not a problem. And now that's settled, do any of you want a lift home in the van now?' Xander offered, but they all declined, saying the walk would do them good.

There was a general exchange of hugs and *thank yous*

and *lovely to see yous*, then the door shut, and it seemed suddenly very quiet.

'I'm sorry,' Lewis said. 'I didn't know you had a house full. I expect you're tired out. I should probably go.'

Holly, who had gone back to arranging her flowers, spun round. 'Oh no, you don't have to go, does he, Lulu?'

'Course not. Only just got here, haven't you? What would you want to go already for? Don't be daft. Sit yourself down and let's have a cuppa.'

'Well, only if you're sure...'

'Course we're sure. Go into the room. May as well make yourself comfortable.'

'Would you like me to make the drinks?' Lewis offered politely.

Lulu shook her head. 'Well, you really are a proper young gentleman aren't you? But no, lovey, I'd best make it meself. It doesn't do to sit down too long. Seen these ankles?' she added, nodding down at her swollen legs. 'Aren't they a sight, eh? Got to keep moving as much as I can. I'm on me bum too often as it is, what with the arthritis.'

Holly lifted the vase. 'What do you think?'

'Made a cracking job of that,' Lulu said approvingly. 'Go and put them on the windowsill in the front room, love. Shift that old ornament. You can put it in a drawer or something. Them flowers deserve pride of place. Gorgeous they are, Lewis. You played a blinder there.'

Holly wasn't sure if she was imagining it or not, but it seemed to her that Lewis blushed a little. How sweet that Lulu's compliment had affected him so much.

She carried the vase carefully into the living room, with Lewis following her, after answering Lulu's questions about how he liked his tea. He looked around, seeming to approve of the large, cosy room, despite the ancient furniture and faded carpet.

'This is lovely,' he told her, his voice warm with admiration. 'I love that brick fireplace.'

'Yeah, it's a shame it's been blocked up,' Holly said with genuine regret. 'I keep telling Lulu she ought to open it up, get a real fire put in, but she always said it was too much palaver. Maybe she'll think again now I'm here.'

'It's much bigger than I expected,' he said, sounding thoroughly impressed.

Holly saw the room afresh, from his perspective. She was so familiar with the house that she'd stopped noticing how lovely it really was she supposed. But the living room, with its brick fireplace and thick beams, managed to retain a light and airy feel, thanks to the white walls and dual aspect. Large bay windows overlooked both the front and back gardens, letting in masses of natural light, and the house never felt gloomy or oppressive.

Lulu came in, carrying a tray of tea.

Lewis jumped up and took it from her, and she smiled her thanks before shuffling over to the sofa. 'By, you're a good lad,' she told him as he set the tray down. 'Yours is the one on the left, love. Mine's on the right and Holly's is in the middle.'

Lewis duly handed out the respective drinks before

settling down in an armchair. 'You have a lovely home, Mrs, er—'

'Drake but call me Lulu for God's sake. Mrs Drake's for when I fill in forms, and Louisa's me Sunday name.'

He smiled. 'Lulu it is.'

'And you're right,' she added. 'I do have a lovely home if I say so meself.'

'It's an odd name, though,' he mused. 'Cuckoo Nest Cottage. I mean, it's very charming, but cuckoos—'

'Don't build nests of their own,' she finished for him. 'Aye, well, there's a story behind that.'

'I rather thought there might be,' Lewis said, his eyes twinkling.

'All these years,' Holly said, sounding ashamed, 'and I never thought to ask. What *is* the story, Lulu?'

Lulu settled herself comfortably on the sofa and cradled her mug of tea.

'Well, since you ask I'll tell you. This cottage was bought by my husband John's grandfather. He bought it for his true love, who'd grown up in Bramblewick and had always loved it. Back then it didn't have a name, or if it did, it's long forgotten. Now, John's grandmother had been brought up by neighbours because her own parents had abandoned her. She never even got to meet them, honestly. There was some story that the mother had gone and got herself pregnant by some ne'er do well who was just passing through, and after she'd had the bairn she took off in search of him and never came back.

'How true that is no one knows, but the upshot of it was that this poor motherless and fatherless bairn was dumped on her neighbours, who already had four children of their own to care for. They weren't right pleased about it, but they did their Christian duty and took care of her. Mind, she was never made to feel welcome or part of the family, not like their own children, and she grew up feeling unloved and unwanted. A cuckoo in the nest, you might say.'

'Poor thing,' Holly murmured, her eyes bright with tears.

She looked over at Lewis, who gave her a soft smile of understanding. Holly hastily took a sip of tea and turned back to Lulu. 'Carry on.'

'Well, when she met John's grandad, she didn't think he'd look twice at her. He'd done quite well for himself you see, and if he was going to be interested in anyone, it would surely be her guardians' daughters, who were a much better prospect, obviously. She kept fobbing this poor chap off, insisting that he was just making a fool of her and didn't mean his declarations of love for her. Took him a good while to convince her that he was genuine, and to prove to her he meant it he bought the cottage that she loved so much. Just for her.

'When they were wed, he brought her back to the place on their wedding day and told her that from that moment on it would be known as Cuckoo Nest Cottage, because at last, the little cuckoo had her own little nest, and her young would always have a place to call their own and would never be homeless.'

She shook her head, a smile on her lips. 'My John always said his grandad called his grandma his Little Cuckoo until the day he died. What do you think to that then?'

Holly could barely speak. She stared at Lulu, emotion choking her.

'Well,' Lewis said at last, 'that's quite a story.'

'Oh, Lulu!' Holly gasped. 'That's lovely.' She gazed around the living room, her eyes blurry with tears. 'I always knew this place was special. It always felt like home to me, more than next door ever did.'

'Then it seems John's grandad were right. Cuckoo Nest Cottage still serves its purpose. Little cuckoos will always have a nest here, for as long as they need it.' She nodded in evident satisfaction and leaned back against the cushion, cradling her tea with a contented smile on her lips.

Lewis sank back in the armchair, gazing admiringly at the old, oak beams and brick fireplace. Evidently, Cuckoo Nest Cottage had won him over too.

Holly reached for her tea and blinked away the tears. She could well relate to Little Cuckoo. She'd grown up with her own parents, but they'd been too busy scoring points off each other to bother much with her. She'd simply seemed in the way. It was this cottage and Lulu herself that had kept her grounded, made her feel that she had somewhere to go and someone to turn to.

When she was in danger of becoming homeless, it was Cuckoo Nest Cottage that had become her shelter. Her nest. She was so glad she'd stood up to Jonathan. She'd been right about that at least, even if she seemed to be wrong about just about everything else.

She gave Lewis a sly glance. He was studying a painting on the wall with interest. She was glad he'd come over to see her, and how kind of him to bring her those lovely flowers.

Thank goodness Jonathan was away with Josh for the weekend. She'd been quite upset when he told her about the football match and revealed he couldn't, or wouldn't, cancel it to be with her on moving day. He really wouldn't have been happy to see Lewis there, and he'd have been furious about the bouquet. Things had turned out for the best, after all.

The next thing to think about, of course, was the wedding. She would keep everything crossed that Jonathan didn't object to Lewis being invited. She sighed inwardly, realising that the only thing she could do was keep as far away from Lewis as possible during the event. It would be best, for all their sakes.

Chapter 10

Lewis had thought long and hard that morning about whether he should attend Izzy's and Ash's wedding. After all he barely knew them, and he was smart enough to realise that they'd mainly invited him because they saw him as some sort of ally with the ongoing problem of Holly and Jonathan.

The trouble was if Jonathan went to the wedding—and it was by no means guaranteed that he'd turn up—then Lewis would have to stay well clear of Holly. Not because he wanted to, but because it would make her life a lot easier if he didn't give her boyfriend ammunition. Should he just stay at home?

But then that would be giving Jonathan exactly what he wanted, and the worst thing he could do was give in to those games. No he would go, but he would keep out of Holly's way for her own sake. He just hoped that she wouldn't take it personally.

He gave a short laugh as he fastened his tie. Take it personally? She probably wouldn't even notice. If Jonathan was by her side she wouldn't notice anyone else. Sad but true.

He shook his head ruefully and looked at his reflection in the mirror. Passable. He could have done with a new shirt really, but funds were tight. At least his suit was reasonably smart, if a little old-fashioned. He wore it so rarely that it didn't get chance to wear out. He stroked the tie, his mind straying to the Christmas he'd received it. One of the many presents from his mother, who'd always made it her mission to ensure he needed hours to open all his gifts. She loved nothing more than buying things for him, and mostly her presents were thoughtful and demonstrated how well she knew him. The tie had been an exception. He'd eyed it doubtfully when he'd pulled aside the wrapping paper and lifted it up, examining it with what he hoped was convincing enthusiasm.

'Great. Just what I needed. Thanks, Mum.'

He remembered her laughter. 'I know very well that you're horrified, but you never know when you'll need it. There are always occasions when a tie is necessary, and one day you'll thank me for buying you that one. When you're fastening it you can think of me and be glad I'm looking out for you.'

He smiled softly at his reflection, the tie still between his fingers. 'Thanks, Mum.'

He couldn't dwell on the past. Xander and Rachel were picking him up any minute now. He snatched up the wedding card he'd remembered to get from the local shop, Maudie's, at the last minute and quickly scribbled his message inside it. Then he sealed the envelope, stuck it in his inside jacket pocket and rushed downstairs, locking the door behind him.

Outside, the air was sharp with the cold, but it was a fairly bright day with no threat of rain in the blue washed sky.

The village was busy. There were only two Saturdays left before Christmas, including today, and people had a lot to do before the big day. Lewis could imagine that Helmston and Whitby, Oddborough and York would be heaving. He was quite glad to be getting out of the way. Starfish Sands was down the coast near Filey, and it was a quiet little resort. He was quite looking forward to the wedding, despite knowing few people and having to avoid Holly at all costs.

A Land Rover pulled up and the passenger window lowered. Rachel waved to him. 'Hey, you're on time! Brilliant. Get in, Lewis.'

He obliged, climbing into the back seat where he was greeted by a cheerful looking boy with freckles.

'Sam, this is Lewis,' Rachel said. 'Lewis, this is my son, Sam.'

Lewis held out his hand. 'Pleased to meet you, Sam.'

Sam looked impressed and duly shook his hand.

'Pleased to meet you, Lewis,' he said solemnly. 'You're Holly's friend, aren't you?'

Lewis cast a wary look at Rachel and Xander, who were clearly pretending not to have heard him. Xander put the car into gear, and they set off, with Rachel fiddling around with the radio.

'Er, I'm a friend of Holly's and Abbie's and Jackson's, and Nell's and Riley's...' He shrugged. 'And your mum and dad's too obviously.' He clapped his hand to his forehead. 'I mean, your mum and Xander's. Sorry.'

'Oh, it's okay,' Sam assured him. 'Xander's my dad

too, really. Especially when they get married.' He leaned forward and whispered. 'He's miles nicer than my real dad. I don't see him much anymore.'

'Ah.' Since Lewis knew something of Rachel's ordeal with her ex-husband he could well imagine that Xander was infinitely preferable to Sam's father but, after all it was nothing to do with him and the man was still Sam's dad when all was said and done, so he thought it best not to offer any reply to that. Instead he changed the subject, addressing them all.

'I've never been to The Sea Star Hotel, have you?'

'Never,' they admitted, although they'd all seen it from the outside, having visited Starfish Sands on occasion.

'It looks really nice though,' Rachel said. 'I hope it's everything Izzy and Ash want. They deserve their special day.'

'Ours soon,' Xander said, smiling at her. 'Not long to go.'

'Can't wait,' she murmured, smiling back.

Lewis felt a pang of envy at their obvious love for each other. How did it come so easily to some when others struggled for years to find it? Or never found it at all he thought, thinking of his mum. Then he remembered Rachel's history with Sam's dad and realised he wasn't being entirely fair. Love hadn't come that easily for her, had it? She'd had to go through a lot to find it. Maybe there was hope for him after all. And for Holly.

He hoped he could stick to his decision and keep away from her at the reception. It wouldn't do her any good if he gave that lout a reason to make her life a misery by spending too much time with her. And Jonathan's definition of too much time was any time at all. He mentally crossed his fingers that Jonathan wouldn't turn up. He was sure everyone but Holly would really appreciate his absence, and even she would have a much better time without him, even if she didn't fully acknowledge the fact to herself.

As the car turned into the long, winding lane that led to Starfish Sands, Lewis gave himself a lecture. He was going to enjoy the wedding and leave Holly and Jonathan to themselves this afternoon. Their relationship was between them. He'd done as much as he could. For once, he would mingle with the other guests, enjoy small talk, congratulate the bride and groom, and put every effort into convincing himself that he didn't care how Jonathan behaved, or that Holly would still infinitely prefer her boyfriend's company to anyone else's, including his own. Today there would be no agonising or worrying or wishing things could be different. Today he was going to have fun.

***

Something had upset Jonathan. Holly could see the dark look in his eyes and the downturn of his mouth as he drove towards Starfish Sands. She couldn't fathom it out. He'd turned up to Cuckoo Nest Cottage on time and had seemed in a cheerful mood, especially when she greeted him at the door and told him how handsome he looked. That had obviously pleased him.

He was wearing a smart navy suit, white shirt, and navy tie, and had clearly had a haircut too. She was so excited to see the smile on his face that she'd given him a huge hug and then done a twirl for him in the hallway, hoping for a compliment.

He'd puffed out his cheeks, stepped inside and said, 'Great, you're ready. I was worried you'd still be faffing with your makeup.'

Disappointment surged through her, but she pushed it aside. After all, he'd seen this dress before. She'd worn it several times in fact. There was no way she was making the same mistake she'd made at Abbie's party. Today all eyes would, quite rightly, be on Izzy. Besides, Jonathan wasn't one to gush. She should know that by now and stop wanting him to be something he wasn't. Love was all about compromise after all.

Lulu was in the kitchen as they walked through, and she nodded a greeting at Jonathan.

'You look very smart,' she told him, although there was a distinct lack of warmth in her tone. 'Cup of tea before you go?'

Holly glanced at Jonathan, but he shook his head. 'I'd really like to get off,' he said. 'Never know what the traffic will be like, especially on a Saturday.'

'In December?' Lulu's eyebrows shot up in disbelief, but Jonathan merely shrugged.

'He's right,' Holly said hastily. 'Lots of Christmas markets and events going on in the area at the moment, so the roads could be busy.' Although, they'd missed the heavy morning traffic and she couldn't imagine there'd be a problem. But she wasn't the driver.

Jonathan was, and he had more experience of these things. 'We'd better get off. I'll just get my bag.'

She turned toward the living room door and as she did, she heard Lulu groan.

'What is it?' she asked, seeing the expression on her face.

'Aw, love, sorry to have to tell you this but you've laddered your tights. See?'

Holly twisted round, just about managing to see the long snag down her left leg. Dammit!

Jonathan tutted. 'Might have known it would be too good to be true.'

'I'll just nip upstairs and change them,' she said. 'I won't be two minutes, honestly.'

'I'll believe that when I see it,' he said, but he gave her a good-natured grin and she beamed at him before rushing back into the hall and taking the stairs, two at a time.

When she came down Jonathan and Lulu were in the living room. Lulu was sitting in an armchair by the gas fire, remote in hand while she watched some cookery programme on the television. Jonathan's face was like thunder. He didn't like cookery programmes, but she couldn't imagine they annoyed him that much.

Before she could ask him what was wrong—not that she wanted to because who knew where that would lead—he jumped up and said, 'Thought you were never coming. Right, let's go shall we?'

Holly hurried over to Lulu and dropped a kiss on her cheek. 'Are you sure there's nothing you need before I leave?'

'Don't you worry about me,' Lulu assured her. 'I'll be fine. You have a smashing time at the wedding and give my regards and best wishes to Izzy and that fella of hers.'

'I will,' she promised. Izzy had invited Lulu, but Lulu had declined the invitation, saying she'd only get uncomfortable after an hour or two of sitting on hard hotel chairs, and it wouldn't be fair to expect anyone to run her back to Bramblewick, especially all the way from Starfish Sands. Izzy promised her a slice of wedding cake, and she assured them all that was good enough for her.

Holly felt guilty leaving her alone, but she did seem quite comfy watching television by the fire, and it was only for an afternoon really. She and Jonathan weren't attending the evening reception as he'd already accepted an invitation from one of the blokes at work to go to his stag do. He'd told Holly he didn't mind if she went to the event on her own, but it wouldn't be the same, so she decided an evening in with Lulu would be better.

Jonathan hooked his arm through hers and practically dragged her out of Cuckoo Nest Cottage. As they pulled into the car park at The Sea Star Hotel, Holly realised he hadn't spoken a word to her the entire journey. It was such a strange and sudden change of mood, and she couldn't think what had caused him to become so sullen when he'd seemed quite relaxed and happy earlier.

They managed to find a parking space easily enough, thank goodness, and Jonathan turned off the engine.

'Right, let's get this over with,' he muttered, unclipping his seat belt, and climbing out of the car before Holly even had chance to think about it.

Her heart sank. *Get this over with.* Is that how he saw her friends' wedding? She'd really hoped that, by now, he felt like part of the gang and would make some effort to enjoy the day, but clearly that wasn't the case. This was just Jonathan doing his duty and counting the hours until he could leave and rush off to his mate's stag do. She was immediately on edge and nervous and had everything crossed that he'd relax as the afternoon wore on and would start to enjoy himself.

As they reached the hotel, she couldn't help but smile. It was a fairly modern building, with lots of plate glass windows and chrome, but it wasn't ugly by any means. It was beautifully decorated for the season, with rows of fairy lights draped across the brickwork and a huge Christmas tree clearly visible in the downstairs window. Small conifers outside the hotel had also been decorated with fairy lights, and the whole place had a gorgeous festive, celebratory feel to it.

They walked up the steps into the lobby, where another Christmas tree stood, sparkling with lights in a multitude of colours. The staircase to the right of the reception desk had garlands illuminated with soft glowing amber lights, snaking all the way up the bannisters, and there was tinsel along the desk and a large Christmas wreath above the lift doors.

Holly realised that she and Jonathan were standing under a sprig of mistletoe, and she nudged him and pointed upwards.

He tutted. 'Talk about overkill. Gone a bit OTT with the Christmas decs, haven't they?'

'Doesn't this look gorgeous!'

Holly spun round hearing the exclamation and forced a smile as Abbie hurried over to hug her, holding an angelic looking Poppy's hand, while Bertie and Isla, both looking very smart, were gazing around them in obvious admiration.

What a shame Jonathan seemed unable to see the beauty in it all.

'Abbie, you look lovely. You all do,' Holly said truthfully, beaming at the children. Bertie tugged at his shirt collar, clearly unhappy about wearing it, but Isla did a little curtsy and admitted she'd chosen her own dress and it was the nicest one she'd ever owned.

'She looks so grown up, doesn't she?' Abbie said, shaking her head. 'Makes me feel very old. But yes, she does look lovely. Even Bertie's presentable for a change. Love your dress, Holly. You look great. Both of you,' she added, glancing over at Jonathan. 'It's been a heck of a hassle getting all the kids ready, I can tell you. I could really have done with Jackson's help, but he was at his flat. Ash stayed there with him last night, and from the phone conversation I had with him this morning it's hard to say who's the most nervous, groom or best man. I was worried sick we were going to be late, but we made it on time, thank goodness. Are Jackson and Ash here yet?'

'I don't know,' Holly admitted. 'We've only just got here ourselves.'

Abbie nodded over at Jonathan. 'All right?'

Jonathan shrugged. 'Fine. You?'

'Fine thanks.'

Niceties completed, they proceeded to ignore each other. Isla told Holly she loved her dress, which was more than Jonathan had done. Holly also realised, with some embarrassment, that he hadn't said anything complimentary to Abbie, or made any attempt at conversation or even eye contact with the kids. She blushed and sent a silent prayer that he would loosen up pretty sharpish. She couldn't face another afternoon of the silent treatment, and having to act as a buffer, yet again, between her boyfriend and her friends.

'Shall we go in then?' Abbie hooked her arm through Holly's, and they nodded, smiling, as the receptionist asked if they were there for the Uttridge/Clark wedding.

'Obviously.' Jonathan waved his hand over the buttonhole in his lapel and gave the poor woman an insolent stare. Holly could have gone through the floor with embarrassment.

'We are, yes,' Abbie said politely, giving the receptionist a warm smile. 'I hope we're not the last ones to arrive.'

The receptionist smiled back at her, pointedly ignoring Jonathan. 'At least you're here before the bride,' she said. 'That's always a bonus. If you'd like to go down the corridor to the left and turn right at the end, the wedding room is straight ahead of you. You won't be able to miss it.'

'Thank you very much,' Holly said, her voice dripping with gratitude, trying in her own way to make amends for Jonathan's rudeness.

'Right, gang. Let's go,' Abbie said cheerfully, shepherding her children in the direction of the wedding room. Jonathan and Holly followed behind them. Holly cast a wary glance at him. He had his hands in his pockets and his face was set. As they entered the wedding room, an usher directed them to their seats, and they saw a very pale and nervous looking Ash and Jackson sitting at the front. They smiled weakly and Abbie giggled.

'Bless them. They're terrified. Look at their little faces.'

Jonathan scowled and Holly's own smile died. What *was* the matter with him?

She soon found out. They'd no sooner taken their seats before she heard him mutter, 'Oh, look. What joy. Blondie's here. That's made *your* day then.'

Holly looked over to where Lewis was sitting a few rows in front to the right of them, next to Sam, Rachel and Xander. He looked very smart in a grey suit, and she realised she'd only ever seen him in jeans before. She felt a little flutter of appreciation but curbed the enthusiasm in her voice as she replied, 'Don't be silly. I've told you over and over again, he's just a friend.'

Jonathan slowly turned his head to face her and the expression of loathing on his face sent a sudden shock through her.

'Really? The sort of friend who sends you a massive bouquet of flowers for no reason, eh? Or maybe there *was* a reason.'

So that was it! He'd seen the flowers in the living

room and must have asked Lulu where they'd come from. She would have told him the truth because why wouldn't she? There was nothing to it after all.

'It was a moving in present,' Holly whispered. 'Nothing more.' *And more than you got me, come to think of it.*

He glared at her. 'They must have cost a fortune. You don't give someone flowers like that unless you're expecting something in return. Or you've already had it.'

Holly's eyes widened. What was that supposed to mean? A sudden and unexpected fury on Lewis's behalf coursed through her. He'd just been kind, and he didn't deserve this slur on his character.

'Maybe in your world, but most normal people don't think that way, thank goodness.'

Oh, why had she said that? Her stomach turned over with fear as his mouth dropped open and he stared at her. Then he gritted his teeth and turned away.

'So now I know where I stand,' he murmured, and there was that tone in his voice that she was so familiar with. She knew the wedding was ruined for her already. She would have to leave straight after the service, because he was going to make damn sure that it was too uncomfortable to stay.

Abbie leaned over. 'Make sure your phone's on silent,' she whispered. 'Don't want any embarrassing ringtones going off just as they exchange their vows do we?'

Holly reached into her bag for her phone, and as she did so her fingers brushed against her diary. She'd done as Lewis said and, after every meeting with Jonathan, she'd faithfully written down every word she could remember of their conversations, even though she hadn't so much as glanced at the entries. She wondered, with a chill, what she'd be writing in the diary that night.

Chapter 11

Lewis had an uncomfortable sensation that he was being watched all through the service. A small part of him hoped it was Holly looking at him, but he dismissed the idea almost immediately. She wouldn't dare even if she'd wanted to, and why would she want to? She'd only have eyes for her beloved Jonathan. He was being fanciful. Wishful thinking probably.

He turned his attention to the front of the room, where Izzy, looking radiant in an ivory lace dress, and Ash, clearly nervous but beaming with pride, exchanged their rings and vows to the cheers and obvious delight of their friends and families.

It was, he thought, the sort of wedding he'd have liked himself, if he'd ever contemplated getting married. Not too big or overwhelming, but with everyone there who mattered. Full of happy, smiling faces.

At the thought of that his gaze slid, almost involuntarily, to Holly and Jonathan. His heart sank. She looked worried sick, and his face bore his usual sullen expression. What had annoyed him this time? God, he loathed him. Jonathan reminded him so much of his father that it made him feel sick to look at him.

He reddened as Holly's gaze found him. She seemed uncertain how to react to him. Her brief smile quickly gave way to a look of anxiety, and she peered nervously at Jonathan before casting her eyes down to the order of service in her hand. Okay, he got the message. Don't give Jonathan any more ammunition. Well, he'd already realised that hadn't he? He had no intention of going anywhere near either of them, even though it was depressing to think that he'd be so close to her and wouldn't be able to so much as chat to her, for fear of sparking an argument.

He realised that Izzy and Ash were making their way back up the aisle to the strains of Ellie Goulding, and people were clapping and smiling, while Ash and Izzy grinned like the proverbial Cheshire cat and stole loving, excited glances at each other as they headed towards the exit.

'And just think,' Xander said, nudging him, 'we get to do this all over again in nine days. Hope you've got your tux cleaned.'

'Tux?'

'It's black tie,' Rachel said, stuffing the tissue she'd been using to dab away her tears inside her handbag. 'You did know that, right?'

'No, I didn't,' he admitted. 'Good job you mentioned it.'

'It's not a problem is it?' Xander asked. 'If you don't own one you can hire them cheaply enough.'

'No, of course not. No problem at all. As long as I know.' His heart sank. He barely had enough money left to cover his food bill for the rest of the month.

How was he going to afford to rent a tuxedo? Maybe he'd have to make up an excuse not to go to the wedding. He couldn't be the only bloke to turn up in an ordinary suit.

He glanced over at Jonathan and his eyes narrowed. No doubt he'd have a tuxedo. If he didn't own one already, he'd persuade Holly to buy him one. She could wear any old rag as far as Jonathan was concerned, so long as he got what he wanted. She'd still look beautiful, he thought wistfully.

'Are you taking root here?' Xander said, grinning. 'Everyone's leaving in case you hadn't noticed.'

'Oh, sorry.' Lewis hastily got to his feet and followed the crowds as they headed out of the wedding room and into the large dining room where the reception was to take place.

'Look at Jackson's face,' Rachel said, nodding over to where Jackson was taking his place at the top table, his face twisted with anxiety as he clutched the notes for his best man's speech tightly in his hand. 'This is going to be quite an ordeal for him.'

'He'll be fine once he gets going,' Lewis said confidently. 'Once he realises the crowd are behind him he'll just get on with it. Oh, looks like I'm on your table,' he added, noticing the name card set out before him. 'Sorry. You're stuck with me again.'

'Don't be daft.' Rachel laughed. 'It's a pleasure.'

There were several round tables set out around the room, each draped in thick white tablecloths, with burgundy napkins that matched Izzy's bouquet and Anna's matron-of-honour dress. There were beautiful centrepieces on each table of white flowers and burgundy candles, and a large Christmas tree stood in one corner, decorated in burgundy, white, green and gold.

Lewis was half relieved, half disappointed to discover that Holly was at another table. He found himself sitting with Rachel, Xander and Sam, Abbie, and Abbie's children, Bertie, Isla, and Poppy.

Holly, meanwhile, was with her beloved Jonathan, Connor, Gracie, Nell, Riley, and two people he didn't recognise. Holly's back was to him, so he couldn't even catch a glimpse of her face but told himself that was a good thing. He needed to concentrate on the reception and remember his promise to himself not to give Jonathan any ammunition. He couldn't bear to be the cause of any more upset for Holly.

Lewis wasn't really one for weddings, but he enjoyed this one. The speeches were got out of the way fairly quickly, and Abbie told him that Ash and Izzy had done that deliberately to help soothe not only Jackson's, but also Ash's nerves.

Abbie couldn't have clapped louder over Jackson's speech, which amused him more than the actual speech had done. Izzy's father made a very touching speech about how proud he and Izzy's mother were of their daughter, and how happy they were that she'd found someone so perfect for her.

Ash, hesitant and clearly overwhelmed by the occasion, basically told Izzy how much he loved her and how he couldn't believe his luck that she'd agreed to marry him. For a moment, it was as if they'd both forgotten there was anyone else in the room as they smiled at each other. Thankfully, Izzy's father had nudged them both back into awareness, and then, after all the speeches and toasts were over, Jackson announced he had a little surprise for the happy couple.

Izzy and Ash looked baffled as a large television was wheeled into the room and plugged in. As it flickered into life, their faces lit up as they realised what was happening. One after the other, the pupils in their classes appeared on screen, sending best wishes and lots of love to their favourite teachers. Sam, Bertie, and even Gracie spoke on camera, despite Gracie having left Bramblewick Primary the previous summer.

Sam and Bertie clearly found the whole thing very funny, but Gracie was extremely solemn, politely wishing her much-adored Ash and her mum's best friend a very happy wedding day. At the end of the short film, a wide shot of the playground appeared, with what looked like hundreds of children and at least a dozen staff members all standing together, holding up a huge banner which read, "Congratulations!" They all chorused, "Happy wedding day, Mr and Mrs Uttridge" and cheered, then the screen went blank again.

Lewis looked over to the top table where Izzy was openly crying and Ash was mopping her tears with a handkerchief, while blinking his own away quite furiously. There was loud whooping from the guests at a couple of the tables and Abbie told him they were teaching colleagues who'd organised the whole thing, along with Jackson, and had massively struggled to get it done without Ash or Izzy getting wind of it.

'That's so lovely,' Rachel said, looking suspiciously dewy-eyed herself. 'You never said a word, Sam!'

'We were threatened with death,' he told her.

Abbie burst out laughing. 'You ought to be an actor like Xander,' she said. 'Talk about over-dramatic.'

He grinned. 'Well, they made us promise to keep quiet and said it would ruin everything if we blabbed, so it's the same thing really.'

'I didn't have to keep quiet,' Bertie said smugly. 'Mum already knew about it, 'cos Jackson told her.'

'That's not fair!' Sam said crossly.

'No, it's not,' Rachel said, narrowing her eyes at Abbie. 'Can't believe you didn't tell me about it. Call yourself a friend!'

'We wanted it to be a surprise for everyone here, not just Ash and Izzy. It wouldn't have been half so emotional in this room if most people knew about it would it?'

'Not really,' Rachel admitted. 'Golly, that really was a tear-jerker.'

'Hmm,' Xander said, 'but now that's out of the way, is there any chance of some food? I'm starving.'

Luckily, at that very moment, it was announced that the buffet was open, and everyone abandoned their tables with undue haste and rushed to the long table at the side of the room, where a delicious looking spread awaited them.

The food, Lewis decided ten minutes later as he stared in wonder at the feast before him, was always the best part about a wedding. He was on basic rations at home for the foreseeable, having had to pay so much for his new tyres, so it would be a relief to pile up his plate and stuff his face for once with some real culinary delights.

There were so many things on offer too. It was far from the standard party buffet. He tried to decide between the roast beef with mustard and herb crust, the slow roast pork belly, sticky ribs, crackling and cider apple sauce, or the fillet of salmon with parsley and basil pesto and tomato salsa. It was impossible to decide. Just as he reached for one thing, his eyes drifted to another, and he changed his mind again. If he didn't get a move on there'd be nothing left. But it was such a big decision. Not only did he have the main courses to consider, but all the bowls of different salads and other accompaniments too, and that was before he even looked at the desserts. His mouth watered as he gazed at lemon meringue pie, raspberry pavlova, and lime cheesecake. How was he supposed to choose between them?

'Do what I'm doing,' Nell advised, as if she'd read his mind, 'have a bit of everything.'

He laughed, but a quick glance at her plate revealed she wasn't joking.

'Why not?' he said cheerfully and proceeded to load his plate with all his favourites. It wasn't as if they were on rations after all. There was plenty to go around. He dreaded to think what it all must have cost. If he ever got married, he'd have to ask people to bring a packed lunch.

It was as if the thought of his own mythical marriage drew him to her. He turned around and there was

Holly, her eyes wide as she clutched two plates full of food.

'Oh, hi,' he said, in what he hoped was a casual voice.

'Lewis, hi.' She gave him a brief smile. 'Enjoying yourself?'

'Great. Food's lovely isn't it?' He nodded, with some embarrassment, towards his own private feast. 'As you can tell.'

Her smile widened, became genuine. Her eyes twinkled. 'A man after my own heart.'

He somehow managed to keep his tone even as he replied, 'Oh, absolutely.' *You have no idea.*

'Well, er, I'd better go and take Jonathan his food,' she said, sounding unenthusiastic.

'Of course. Has he hurt himself or something?' Lewis hoped he didn't sound too pleased about the possibility.

'Hurt himself?'

'Well, sending you to get his food.'

'Oh, oh I see. No.' She looked deeply uncomfortable. 'His phone rang so he asked me to get something for him while he took the call.' She glanced over to where Jonathan was sitting alone at the table, leaning back in his chair, phone clutched to his ear. Lewis followed her gaze and narrowed his eyes, wondering just who Jonathan was talking to. Judging by the unsavoury gleam in his eyes and the smirk on his lips, it wasn't one of his workmates. Holly seemed to be wondering too he thought, noting the anxious look that crossed her face.

'I'd better take this to him,' she said. 'Enjoy your meal, Lewis.'

'Yeah, yeah, you too.'

He watched her hurry away and sighed, feeling thoroughly depressed.

'Don't worry, we fully intend to stick by her side all afternoon.' Anna, looking beautiful in her long, burgundy silk dress, murmured in his ear. 'We won't let Jonathan keep her away from us.'

'I'm glad,' he said, 'but I can't go near I'm afraid.'

'Why not?'

'Because Jonathan's got a thing about me, and he makes her life a misery if we talk to each other. I can't give him ammunition against her, so I'll have to leave the small talk to you lot this afternoon, unfortunately.'

She surveyed him sadly. 'That is unfortunate,' she said at last. 'You seem to have become her best friend within weeks of meeting her.'

He laughed uneasily. 'I wouldn't say that,' he said.

'I would. It's funny really how some relationships are like that.' Anna squeezed his arm, her eyes warm with sympathy. 'You'd better go and eat that food, Lewis. It's getting cold.'

'Right. Absolutely. Speak to you later.'

'You will,' she told him. 'Now, I'd better decide what to eat or everyone will have beaten me to it.'

***

'All right, babe. See you soon, okay?' Jonathan's eyes narrowed as he saw Holly approaching and he muttered into his phone, 'Yeah, you too. Laters.'

A wave of nausea washed over Holly, and she dumped the two plates on the table, her appetite suddenly vanished. 'Who was that?'

Jonathan seemed to recover his composure in record speed. He sat up straight, stuffed his phone in his jacket pocket and reached for a plate without even asking which one was his.

'Eh? Oh, Josh from work.' He picked up a fork and prodded at the belly pork. 'What's this? Didn't you get me no chicken legs? No vol au vents? Where's the pork pie for crying out loud?'

'It's not that sort of buffet,' she told him. 'So, you were talking to Josh?'

Jonathan scowled as he examined the contents of his plate. 'I was looking forward to a cold buffet,' he grumbled. 'Not this sort of crap.'

'There are cold dishes as well,' she told him. 'If you want some, go and get them.'

'Charming.' He scooped some food onto his fork and began to chew, still scowling. Evidently though, he quickly decided that the belly pork wasn't as bad as he'd suspected, as he shovelled more into his mouth with indecent haste.

'Do you always call Josh babe?' Holly hadn't meant to ask the question but she was trembling with anxiety and dread and—yes—anger. Did he think she was a complete idiot? She'd heard what he'd said on the phone, and it was obvious he was lying to her. She wasn't going to let him get away with it. Not this time.

Jonathan made a big deal of chewing his food,

taking his time to answer her. She wondered if his mind was working frantically to come up with an excuse, or if he had one ready-made.

'Babe?' he said at last, spluttering with laughter. 'What are you on about now?'

'I heard you,' she said coldly. 'You said, "All right, babe". Do you always talk to Josh like that?'

'Babe!' He repeated, his voice heavy with scorn. 'You're not right in the head, you. As if I'd say that. I said, *mate*. You wanna get your hearing checked.'

'There's nothing wrong with my hearing.' Holly sank into her chair, fearing her legs would give way beneath her if she didn't. She was scared stiff to push the subject, but she was also tired, so very tired, of the doubts and the confusion. She just wanted him to be honest with her. 'I heard you say, babe. And it makes me wonder if all these supposed nights out with the boys from work really happened, or if you've been seeing another woman.'

Jonathan pushed his plate away and folded his arms. 'Oh, here we go again. You and your twisted mind. You want locking up. There's something wrong with you, up here.' He tapped his temple, glaring at her with contempt. 'I'm sick of this. Sick of putting up with you and your accusations. Paranoid, that's what you are. Paranoid.'

'Well,' she said, her resolve wavering and her eyes, to her dismay, filling with tears, 'it wouldn't be the first time would it? What about Ruth?'

'Oh, not this again!' He shook his head. 'For the last time, there was nothing going on between me and

Ruth. It was all in your head. We've been over and over this and you still bring it up.'

'But the letter she sent me—'

'I told you a million times, she was just some girl with a crush. Lived in a fantasy land. Barmy like you.' He pulled the plate back and loaded a potato onto his fork. 'Eat your meal. It's getting cold,' he instructed her, his mouth full of food.

Holly wrinkled her nose in disgust. 'I'm not hungry.'

'Fine. I'll have yours then.'

Before she could stop him he'd tipped the contents of her plate onto his own, then he slammed the empty plate down on the table in front of her. 'Problem solved.'

Holly flinched, but she wasn't about to give up. 'What did you mean, "See you soon"?'

'Oh for—' Jonathan tugged at his tie in exasperation. 'Will you give it a rest?'

'I heard you say, "See you soon",' she persisted. 'See who soon? Not Josh. You don't call Josh babe, and I know you said babe, no matter how much you deny it.' She shook her head, feeling dazed and grief-stricken. 'There's someone else isn't there? All these phone calls, and the overtime you keep working, and not letting me in your flat that day, and going all week without seeing me. It's happening again.'

'What are you on about, happening again?'

'It's just like when you were seeing Ruth.'

His eyes darkened and he leaned towards her, his voice low and heavy with fury. 'I've told you, there was nothing going on with me and Ruth. It was all in your head, and hers. What a pair. Both of you, twisted and warped. Seeing things that weren't there. Making it all up in your heads. Why do I even put up with you? We had all this out back then. I even took you to Majorca, didn't I?'

'You took me to Majorca to shut me up,' she said tearfully. 'You didn't want me to talk about it and you thought a holiday would be enough to make me forget it.'

'I didn't want you to talk about it because it never happened,' he snarled. 'You've got a screw loose, honestly. If you're going to keep bringing the past up, what's the point? We may as well forget it. I've had it. Stuff your belly pork. Why don't you eat it? That's what you do best, isn't it? Stuffing your face. Go ahead. Add a bit more lard to those thighs. God, no wonder no one else wants anything to do with you.'

He scraped back his chair and stood.

'What are you doing?' she said, her voice hoarse with unshed tears.

'I'm leaving this poxy wedding, that's what I'm doing,' he told her. 'I've had enough. I'm done. I'm off to see Josh as it happens. Make of that what you like.'

'You can't leave,' she gasped. 'What will I tell people?'

He bent down and muttered in her ear, his voice loaded with what sounded horrifically like hatred.

'Tell them I'm off to meet my bit on the side. Who knows, maybe I am. Then again, maybe it's *you* that's the bit on the side. Ever thought of that?'

He straightened, a smirk on his face as she stared up

at him, terrified. Then he turned and stormed out of the dining room without a backward glance.

Holly couldn't move. She sat, frozen to the spot as a million thoughts, each one worse than the last, swirled around in her brain. The buzz of conversation around her dimmed. All she could hear was the blood pounding in her head, as the photograph of her life crashed to the floor of her mind, the glass in the frame shattering into pieces, shards of glass scattering everywhere, too sharp for her to even try to pick them up.

She felt cold, icy cold, despite the central heating in the hotel dining room. She realised she was shivering and tried to stop herself. People mustn't notice. They mustn't see. She needed to pull herself together, fast.

'Tea.'

She looked up, still dazed, as Lewis dropped into the seat next to her and handed her the cup. 'Wh—what?'

'Tea. Sweet and hot. It will warm you up and calm you down. Always does the trick.' He guided her fingers into the cup handle. 'Go on, drink it up. Then we'll talk.'

'I—I can't.'

'Yes, Holly. You can.' His tone was kind but firm. Holly realised that tears were rolling down her cheeks and, as Lewis reached over and wiped them away, fresh ones spilled over onto his fingers.

He produced a clean tissue and mopped them up. 'It's okay, it's clean.'

She remembered him saying that to her once before and closed her eyes, all too aware of the crushing futility of it all. The endless cycle of fear and dread and confusion.

'I'm sorry,' she murmured.

'Nothing to be sorry for,' he assured her. 'Come on, drink your tea. Lulu told me it makes everything better, so it must be true.'

She gave a half laugh, knowing it was just the sort of thing that Lulu would say, and obeyed him. The tea was sweeter than she usually drank it, but she didn't care. It was warming and comforting, and she needed that. She managed to empty the entire cup while Lewis sat patiently waiting, saying nothing. She realised, as she slowly came back to life, that some of her friends were watching her, anxious expressions on their faces. When she looked directly at them, they smiled sympathetically then looked away. Evidently they'd decided to leave it all to Lewis.

'Did you draw the short straw?' she asked wearily.

Lewis frowned, clearly not sure what she meant. 'Sorry?'

She nodded over to where Rachel, Xander, Nell and Riley were huddled together. 'I'm guessing you all thought I needed talking to and one of you had to take on the job. Seems you got landed with me.'

'Wow,' he said softly, 'you really do have a low opinion of yourself don't you? They all care about you, that's all. We saw Jonathan storming out and realised you would need someone to talk to. We didn't want to overwhelm you, so we thought just one of us should come over.'

'And they picked you.'

'I volunteered.'

'Really?' Her voice wavered as uncertainty knocked her off balance again. 'Why?'

He didn't reply for what felt like forever. 'I saw the conversation you two were having. Seemed very bitter. I wanted to come over but...'

'But what?'

They gazed at each other, and Holly had the strongest feeling that he was trying to tell her something just by the look in his eyes. It was so intense it quite took her breath away. A thought probed her mind, prodding at her, forcing her to think the unthinkable.

For a moment, she was alive to a whole world of possibilities and her heart lifted unexpectedly. Then she realised she was being stupid, grasping at straws. She was twisting things again, mixing things up, getting confused. Misreading situations as she so often did. She lowered her gaze and put the empty teacup on the table.

'I'm all right now, thank you.'

He seemed at a loss for words. Not daring to look at him directly she saw, through the corner of her eye, that he'd leaned back in his chair. Slumped might be a more accurate description. Evidently, she'd even worn *him* out. Disappointed him somehow, although she wasn't sure how. She owed him something, some sort of explanation at the very least.

'He was talking to someone on the phone,' she murmured, almost reluctantly. 'He called them, babe. He denies it of course,' she added hastily. 'I don't know. Maybe I was wrong. Maybe he did say mate. I just can't be sure—not about anything.'

'Have you been keeping the diary?' he asked gently.

She hesitated, then nodded. 'Yes. I write in it every time I have a conversation with him, like you told me.'

'And has it made things any clearer?'

She finally looked him in the eye. 'I haven't read it back,' she admitted. 'I just quickly write what I need to write, then I close the diary. I never look at the other entries.'

He sighed, shaking his head slightly. 'And why do you think that is?'

'Because—I don't know.' Because it seemed disloyal to Jonathan? Underhand? Sneaky? Or because it made her seem as paranoid as he insisted she was? Or because she was afraid of what she'd find written down? Any of those really. Maybe all of them.

'I want to go home,' she said, overcome with exhaustion. 'I really don't feel like partying, and I don't want to spoil Izzy's big day.'

'If that's what you want,' he told her, 'then that's fine. They'll understand.'

She looked around helplessly. 'I haven't got a lift home,' she realised suddenly. 'And I haven't brought any money with me for a taxi.'

'It's not a problem. I'll get us a taxi.'

'Us?'

He smiled. 'I'm ready for home too. I've eaten my body weight in roast beef, and I'm too tired to stay much longer. Home sounds like a good idea to me.'

Holly realised he was being kind. He hadn't had time to eat that much she thought. She remembered him scrabbling around for money in The Castle Keep Café.

Whatever he'd said, she had a feeling he was far from flush with cash.

'You shouldn't have to pay for a taxi,' she said. 'Tell you what, you order one and I'll pay them when we get back to Cuckoo Nest Cottage.'

He raised an eyebrow. 'Am I going back to Cuckoo Nest Cottage?'

She reddened. 'No, of course not, not if you don't want to. I just thought—well, Lulu would be pleased to see you. And I owe you a cup of tea at the very least.' *And I can feed you up, since you're going to be missing out on all this food because of me.*

The smile lit up his face, and she thought again how attractive he was, if not conventionally handsome. He had the kindest eyes, and there was something so comforting about him. She always felt totally safe and relaxed in his company. It was a wonderful feeling.

His hand folded over hers and her heart thudded with a sudden and most unexpected joy.

'I'll make that phone call,' he said, his deep, sexy voice sending pulses of delight through her and adding immeasurably to her confusion. 'Let's go home.'

***

Despite her fears, Izzy and Ash had been lovely and very understanding when Holly bid them farewell. She'd kissed them both and explained she really had to get home to check on Lulu, but that she'd thoroughly enjoyed their beautiful wedding, and wished them loads of happiness.

Lewis, who'd hovered by her side throughout the little speech, gave them both brief handshakes and thanked them for the invitation, assuring them that he'd really enjoyed himself. Izzy had laughed and pulled him into a hug, telling him that it was their pleasure and thanking him for coming.

'And thanks so much,' she added in a whisper, 'for looking after Holly. Take care of her, won't you?'

He nodded, not daring to speak in case Holly heard him. She was watching them closely enough as it was, and he didn't want her to think there was some sort of conspiracy or plot.

Ash clapped him on the back, and they waved as Holly and Lewis climbed into the taxi.

'Poor Izz will be freezing,' Holly observed, watching through the rear window as the happy couple finally turned away and went back into the hotel. 'She didn't have to come out to say goodbye. That dress was no protection against the cold at all.'

Lewis remembered the night of Abbie's party when Holly had stood outside in the garden in that thin, twenties-style dress. He remembered wrapping his jacket around her, wanting to protect her even then. He would give anything to tell her how he felt, to make her believe that Jonathan wasn't good for her, that she could do so much better. That, if she'd only let him, he would love her and take care of her for the rest of her life.

But watching the anxiety return as she leaned back in her seat and stared ahead of her, her forehead furrowed, thinking goodness knows what, he knew he couldn't possibly do it. Holly's life was a mass of contradictions and confusion.

Right now she was lost in a fog, masterfully created by a narcissist who had worked hard to trap her. The last thing she needed was another complication, more to worry and obsess about. She needed clarity and a hand to hold that would guide her out of the fog. She needed a friend she could trust. He had to put his feelings to one side and be that friend. No pressure on her, nothing to take away her focus on getting free from Jonathan's grip. She had to learn to be herself again, and to put all her faith in her own thoughts and actions. She couldn't simply switch from total dependence on one man to another. She had to remember who she was, and that she could always rely on her own instincts and abilities.

As tough as it was to acknowledge, he had to step back and give her space.

'I'm sorry,' she said quietly. 'I'm such a screw-up, aren't I? I don't know why everything goes so wrong for me all the time.'

It didn't take a genius to figure it out he thought, but he merely shook his head.

'You're no different to anyone else. Hey, you think you've got problems? I've just found out that I've got to wear a tuxedo for Rachel's and Xander's wedding. Where am I going to get one of those, for goodness' sake?'

She smiled. 'You could hire one?'

'I could,' he acknowledged, 'if I had more than a twenty pence piece and a button in my wallet.'

This time her smile was wider. 'Oh heck! Honestly, they won't mind if you don't wear a tux. Just wear the suit you're wearing now. You look—you look really good in it.'

'Do I?' He swallowed, the unexpected compliment knocking him for six.

She nodded shyly but didn't reply. They didn't speak much on the way home after that. Lewis was lost in his own thoughts, and he thought Holly probably had a lot on her mind, too.

When they reached the sign for Bramblewick, Lewis experienced a sudden surge of contentment. This village seemed like home already. He'd made some great friends and he was happy there.

It was a strange feeling to belong. He'd never really felt that before. Home, despite being the one place he could be with his mum, had also meant being with his father. And he'd hated boarding school with a passion. He'd enjoyed himself at college, but that whole experience was tainted by the memory of his mother's diagnosis and the beginning of her wretched illness.

He'd been torn between finishing his studies, which was what he knew his mother wanted for him despite his father's opposition, and wanting to be at home, to spend every spare moment with her. In the end, college hadn't been the great experience he'd hoped for. As for the flat share—that had been born out of necessity, not want. His flatmates were just that. They weren't really friends and they had little in common.

No, this was the first time he felt as if he had a home, with a flat he liked in a village he'd been welcomed to, and a job he loved with people who seemed to really like him. Life, he thought wistfully, was almost perfect. If he didn't have to worry about Holly...

'It's the one on the left,' Holly said suddenly, leaning forward to speak to the driver. 'Just past the terrace, by the bridge.'

The driver nodded and within a few moments they'd arrived at Cuckoo Nest Cottage.

'Can you wait there a moment?' Holly asked the driver. 'I'll just nip inside and get my purse.'

'And I'll linger here,' Lewis said, grinning. 'Just to prove she's not going to do a runner.'

The driver nodded. 'Aye, well, you can joke about it, but it does happen you know. You'd be amazed.'

Holly dashed indoors while Lewis nodded politely and made appropriate noises as the driver proceeded to tell him some hair-raising stories about just how rude and deceitful some people could be. When she returned he didn't notice Holly's expression at first, but he heard the panic in her voice as she thrust a note at the driver and told him to keep the change.

'What is it?' he asked, clambering out of the car as the driver, after expressing his gratitude for the large tip, set off for his next pick-up.

'It's Lulu,' Holly said, her voice sounding shaky. 'She's been stuck in that chair all afternoon. She's—she's in a bit of a state, Lewis. Could you help me with her?'

'Of course.' He strode purposefully into the cottage as Holly ran in front.

Lulu was sitting in the chair where they'd left her,

and judging by her face she'd been crying, which was alarming in itself. He couldn't imagine Lulu was much of a one for crying.

Concerned and anxious, he crouched down in front of her and took hold of one of her hands.

'Are you all right? Does it hurt anywhere?'

She shook her head and her eyes filled with tears. 'I couldn't get up,' she whispered. 'Bloody legs and back wouldn't have it, and my arms wouldn't hold me so I couldn't pull myself up. Too painful. I was stuck here and—and...' Her voice trailed off and she bowed her head, clearly distraught.

Lewis frowned. 'And what?'

Holly nudged him and he followed her tearful gaze and understood. Poor Lulu. Clearly, she'd desperately needed the toilet but hadn't been able to manage it. She must be mortified. Not that she had anything to be ashamed of, but he knew she was a proud woman. He hadn't known her long but that much was obvious.

'Right,' he said briskly. 'I'm going to lift you up, Lulu. Is that okay?'

'You don't want to be lifting a lump like me,' she told him. 'Last thing we need is for your back to go.'

'I think I can manage, don't worry,' he reassured her. Gently he scooped her up.

'Do you want to go upstairs, Lulu?' Holly asked. 'You can get out of those clothes, and I'll run you a nice warm bath. What do you think?'

'That'd be grand,' Lulu admitted.

'Right, that's sorted then.'

Holly hurried ahead of him as Lewis carried Lulu

upstairs. He gently deposited her in her bedroom and eyed her anxiously.

'How do you feel?'

'Like a blooming invalid,' she admitted gloomily. 'And a bit daft an' all. Fancy getting stuck in a chair!'

'Nothing daft about it,' Holly said. 'Now, I'll go and run that bath for you, then I'll help you into it. Give me a shout when you're finished, and I'll come and help you back out.' She turned to Lewis, and he saw the anxiety in her eyes, despite the cheerfulness of her tone. 'Think I'll hang around in my bedroom while she's in the bath just in case she needs me.'

The fact that Lulu didn't immediately protest that she wouldn't need anyone was confirmation enough that Holly was right to be worried.

Lewis nodded. 'I'll go downstairs and make us all a hot chocolate. How does that sound?'

'That would be lovely,' Holly said, smiling at him with obvious gratitude.

'Aye, I could do with cheering up,' Lulu confirmed.

'Right, I'll leave you to it.'

He headed downstairs, leaving Holly to deal with Lulu's bath. Before he heated the milk for the hot chocolate, he busied himself cleaning the armchair. Finally straightening up, he glanced around the living room. He really did love this place, he thought. It was so cosy and had such a good feel to it. Even so, there was something missing...

He went back into the kitchen and tipped the bowl of water and disinfectant down the sink, then put a pan of milk on the hob. As he made the mugs of hot chocolate, his mind turned over the obvious problems that Lulu was facing. Something would have to be done, no doubt about it. She was clearly struggling, and everyday life must be extremely difficult for her. She needed help. Fast.

He was just stirring the hot chocolates when Holly entered the kitchen.

He looked up and smiled at her. 'How is she?'

'Just getting dressed. I think she feels a lot better now she's clean and dry. I'll go up and help her back downstairs when she's ready. It was a heck of a struggle getting her in and out of the bath though. She'd never have managed it alone. Mm, those hot chocolates smell gorgeous. Thanks ever so much for all your help. I don't know.' She wrinkled her nose and shook her head slightly. 'What with my meltdown and then Lulu's predicament, you've really had your work cut out for you today, haven't you? Bet you never expected all this when you set off to a simple wedding earlier.'

'Well, no,' he admitted. 'But it's not a problem.'

'You're a real knight in shining armour,' she told him.

He handed her a mug of hot chocolate, determined not to pay any attention to the way she was making him feel.

'The thing is,' he said, recognising that he had to bring the conversation back to more important matters, 'it can't go on like this can it? Lulu needs help, and we must find a way to get her that help.'

'You mean, put her in a home?' Holly sounded appalled as she stared at him.

He frowned, unsure why she would make that assumption. 'Of course not. Why would you think that?'

She lowered her gaze, examining the froth on her drink for several moments before she answered. 'I just—I just thought that's what you might be insinuating.'

'Well, it's not. It would probably kill her to leave Cuckoo Nest Cottage,' he said. 'No, I'm talking about ways to help her stay here in comfort. There must be lots of things we could do to make this place more suitable and comfortable for her. A stairlift, for example. And a walk-in bath would help.'

Holly nodded. 'It would, but it's all very pricey isn't it?'

'There must be grants available surely?'

'If there are, Lulu wouldn't apply for them. She's way too proud. Besides, that would be admitting she can't cope, and as far as she's concerned that's the start of a slippery slope. She has a deep-seated fear that if social services get wind that she's struggling they'll want to put her in a nursing home, and she doesn't want to do anything to draw attention to herself.'

'But that's crazy!' Lewis laughed. 'That wouldn't happen. It's not a crime to get old, and there's no shame in admitting you need help.'

'Try telling Lulu that,' she said ruefully. Her gaze lifted to the ceiling as they heard a muffled knock. 'She's ready. You take her drink through to the living room and I'll go and help her downstairs.'

'Give me a yell if you need any extra help,' he told

her. 'I've cleaned the armchair, by the way. It just needs to dry out. I was thinking, do you want me to bring a Christmas tree and some holly and mistletoe? I can get them from the estate, and it would lift her spirits, I'm sure. I'll give you a hand decorating it all. Be nice to have a bit of Christmas cheer for her.' He lifted the two mugs and turned to the living room door. 'What?' he added as she raised an eyebrow.

She shook her head. 'Nothing. I think that's a brilliant idea, that's all. I'll go and get Lulu.'

As she headed upstairs, he mentally shrugged and carried the drinks into the living room. Pride or not, he mused, as he placed them on the coffee table, Lulu needed help. She would either have to accept that help or—well, there was no alternative was there? Why should she suffer this way if something could be done about it? And something *could* be done about it, he realised. He just had to get her to agree to it.

Chapter 12

If Holly was being honest, she hadn't given Jonathan much thought lately, which made a very welcome change. Normally, she'd have been going over and over their conversation, but apart from writing it all down in the diary as soon as she went to bed that Saturday night as she'd promised Lewis she would, she'd managed to push him out of her mind.

The problem of Lulu and what to do to make life better for her was far more pressing. She realised, with some surprise and not inconsiderable relief, that she was far more important to her than Jonathan and his latest tantrum. It felt wonderful not stressing about him for once. Of course, it still niggled at the back of her mind, but as long as she could keep it there she could cope.

She hadn't realised until now how exhausting Jonathan was, nor how much of her time thinking about him took up. She fell asleep after the wedding thinking about Lulu, and even more so about Lewis's kindness and his complete understanding of her predicament.

His attitude was in sharp contrast to Jonathan's feelings about Lulu, a fact that was brought home to

Holly at lunchtime on Thursday when, to her surprise, Jonathan rang. She really hadn't expected to hear from him. He'd been completely silent all week and usually she'd have been ringing him and texting him all day to say she was sorry and to try to make amends. She hadn't even attempted to contact him. Maybe that was what prompted him to get in touch.

She was sitting at her desk sipping coffee, while Rachel—whose patient hadn't turned up, meaning she had five minutes to spare—stood next to her, nibbling a shortbread biscuit. They'd been discussing Rachel's forthcoming wedding and how worrying the weather forecast was.

Anna had popped round from reception every time she had a free moment to offer reassurance and, kindly, neither of them had made any reference to Jonathan, or Holly's early departure from Izzy's wedding all week. Whenever they'd talked about the event, they'd discussed the lovely hotel, and Izzy's beautiful dress, and how delicious the food had been, and what a shame that Izzy and Ash were both at work today instead of on honeymoon.

They were booked on a flight to Spain with Izzy's mum and dad straight after Rachel's and Xander's wedding, and were spending Christmas and New Year over there, before going on to the Algarve for a week, just the two of them, before work resumed.

Rachel was just laughingly announcing that she'd probably end up wearing wellingtons under her wedding dress when Holly's phone began to ring. They both glanced down at the screen. Holly had left it on her desk so she wouldn't miss a call from Lulu, having made her promise to ring if she needed her.

Holly had already been home for dinner, which Lulu had tutted about, though she hadn't complained when Holly made them both tomato soup. There was no way Holly wanted her stuck in a chair all afternoon again, and she'd practically clamped Lulu's mobile phone, which she never used and hated with a passion, in her hand before she left.

Holly's heart had leapt as her phone rang, and it had landed with a thump somewhere in the pit of her stomach when she saw Jonathan's name on the screen. She glanced up at Rachel and saw she'd wrinkled her nose in obvious distaste, but quickly straightened her face when she saw her looking.

'Hope he's about to apologise,' Rachel said.

Anna peered round the office door. 'Next patient's arrived, Rachel.'

'Perfect timing,' she said. She squeezed Holly's shoulder. 'Don't take anything less than a grovelling apology,' she told her firmly.

As if!

Holly gave her a weak smile then lifted the phone with some reluctance.

'Hello, Jonathan.'

'Oh, so you're alive then!'

She sighed. Yeah, he sounded really contrite. 'I'm alive. Why shouldn't I be?'

'I just wondered since I've not heard a word from you.'

'I didn't think you'd want to hear a word from me,

since I annoy you so much.' She was aware that her tone was quite sharp and wondered fleetingly if she was pushing her luck but, truthfully she was feeling quite annoyed with him and didn't have the energy to worry about what he thought of her. There were more important things to think about.

'Charming. So, not a word of apology then. Might have known.'

'Are you serious? Why would I apologise to you? You're the one—'

'Look, if you're going to start twisting everything and making me out to be the bad one again, I might as well hang up now.'

Holly's pulse quickened and the first flutterings of panic stirred, but she forced herself to stay calm. 'Maybe you should then.'

There was a moment's silence as she steadied her breathing and told herself she had every right to speak to him that way. He'd ruined her friends' wedding for her, and if it hadn't been for Lewis...

'You take the cake,' he said grumpily, but she detected another tone to his voice, and she could tell he was taken aback by her attitude. The sudden rush of power was a liberating sensation. 'You and your mates push me out, make me feel like an outsider, then you accuse me of God knows what with God knows who, and yet somehow I'm the one in the wrong. Unbelievable. And you don't even bother to ring me either. You don't even sound like you care.'

'I've got other things on my mind,' she told him, feeling a bit brutal.

'Oh? Like Blondie, I suppose.'

'Like Lulu, and the fact that she spent the whole of Saturday afternoon stuck in her chair because she was in too much pain to stand up,' Holly said, her voice cracking as she relived Lulu's ordeal. She must have tried everything to stand up. She'd have been absolutely mortified by what had happened, bless her.

He tutted. 'That's bad,' he said grudgingly. 'Sorry to hear that.'

She closed her eyes, grateful to know there was some sympathy there.

'But it's like I've told you a million times, babe. She needs to go in a home. No other way around it.'

'She's not going in a home! She'd hate it.'

'Beggars can't be choosers, babe. I'm only thinking of what's best for her.'

Holly opened her mouth to speak, but an image of Lewis frowning over a mug of hot chocolate as he tried to think what they could do to make Lulu's life easier flashed before her eyes, and she realised suddenly that she was too disappointed with Jonathan to talk about it any longer.

'I must go. Work's really busy.' She ended the call and sat back in her chair, her heart pounding as she realised what she'd done. He'd be furious! She wrapped her arms around herself, trying to stop the shaking and calm the panic-stricken voice that was thundering in her head, demanding to know what she was playing at.

Yet, for the first time, there was also a nagging belief that she'd been right not to engage with him any longer. Jonathan would never understand how much she loved

Lulu, and the very fact that, after all this time, he still didn't comprehend how much she meant to her said a lot. Lewis understood already and she barely knew him.

It seemed to Holly at that moment that Lewis understood her better than she understood herself. She wasn't sure how that had happened, or where his wisdom came from, but it was partly reassuring and partly unnerving to realise that he'd learned more about her in a few weeks than her own boyfriend had in a year and a half.

Determined not to let Jonathan dominate her entire afternoon for a change, she concentrated on her job and got on with working through a pile of repeat prescription requests, in between answering the phone, booking appointments, photocopying, and a thousand other tasks that needed doing. It was always busy at the surgery, but the week leading up to Christmas was manic. The surgery was only closed for two days—Christmas Day and Boxing Day—but people tended to panic and even those who were notorious for not taking their medication regularly would demand their prescription early, "cos of it being Christmas". Anyone would think they were shut for weeks. If only!

After a hectic afternoon, Holly thankfully switched off the computer at six and hurried into the cloakroom for her coat.

'Crikey, you're in a rush,' Anna said, laughing as she almost collided with her on her way out.

'Sorry. I want to get back for Lulu, make sure she's okay.'

She patted Holly's arm. 'Of course. Give her my

love, won't you? And if there's anything she needs, anything we can do, just let us know.'

'Will do. Thanks, Anna. See you tomorrow.'

Holly was relieved, upon arriving home, to find Lulu in the kitchen making tea, a huge smile on her face.

'You look cheerful,' she said, dropping a kiss on her cheek. 'What's brightened you up?' She jumped, her gaze fixing on the ceiling as she heard a distinct thumping sound coming from above. 'What the heck—?'

'Don't fret, it's nowt to worry about,' Lulu assured her, taking milk from the fridge. 'That's Lewis up there.'

'What on earth's he doing?' Holly asked, unwrapping the scarf from around her neck as she realised she was overheating in the warmth of the kitchen.

'He's in the loft. Getting our Christmas decs down. Look in the living room, you won't believe your eyes.'

Holly hurried through and stopped dead, staring in delight at the beautiful tree that stood in the corner of the room, just waiting to be adorned with all Lulu's precious baubles and maybe some of her own too.

'We had to move the furniture round a bit to fit it in,' Lulu said, behind her, 'but it was worth it. Mind you, when I say we, I mean he. Did it all himself. And look at the holly and mistletoe he's brought us too. Even a Christmas wreath for the front door. Isn't it gorgeous?'

She pointed to a truly spectacular Christmas wreath that was lying on the table. It looked beautiful, and much better than the ones Holly had seen in the shops.

'Wow,' she said. 'That's so good of him. But it must have cost him a fortune, whatever he says.'

'Not at all.'

That familiar voice that always sent tingles through her made her spin round in delight. Lewis held a rather battered cardboard box, which she recognised as the one she'd struggled to put back in the loft for Lulu last January.

'I promise you,' he said, 'it cost me nothing. Freebies from the estate, even the wreath. They've been running wreath-making classes at the Hall,' he explained, 'and the estate manager's wife has been making them alongside the students, so she has a glut of them. She said I could have one for my flat, but I don't really need one. Thought it would be just the job for the front door of Cuckoo Nest Cottage though. Seems to fit, somehow, don't you think?'

Holly picked the large, evergreen wreath up, stroking the tartan bow and smiling at the berries and pine cones. 'Are those feathers?' she asked, surprised.

'Yes, from pheasants on the estate. She's had us collecting all sorts for her classes,' he said, grinning. 'They're a great money-spinner though, so I can't blame her.'

'It's ever so kind of you, Lewis,' Holly told him.

'I said that,' Lulu said. 'Our guardian angel, aren't you, love? He's staying for tea, any road, so I'm cooking and no arguments.'

'Oh, but Lulu—'

'What did I just say? Go and get your shower and get your PJs on, like you usually do after work. I'll start the tea and Lewis can crack on with putting the lights on the tree. That's always supposing they still work,' she mused.

Holly blushed. Fancy telling Lewis that she got her PJs on straight after work! It was true, but he didn't need to know did he?

He was grinning at her, and she grinned back.

'She's such a grass.'

'Never mind. You haven't seen me in my Sonic the Hedgehog pyjamas.'

'You never wear Sonic the Hedgehog pyjamas!'

His eyes twinkled most disarmingly. 'That's for me to know and...' He shrugged, as Holly's face scorched even hotter and the end of the sentence, *And for you to find out* hovered unsaid between them. She tried to drag her gaze away from his but found it surprisingly difficult to break contact.

'Well, I'm getting on with our tea, even if you two just want to stand here like you've taken root,' Lulu said, shuffling between them and snapping Holly out of her dreamlike state. 'Nowt fancy, mind, so don't be getting your hopes up. Sausage, chips, and beans okay for you? We don't bother much on a weekday.'

'Sounds wonderful,' Lewis told her, though Holly couldn't help thinking as his posh, chocolatey tones soothed her ears, that he must be used to finer fare than that.

'Well go and get showered and changed then,' Lulu said, pushing her gently in the direction of the hall. 'You've got about half an hour, maximum. Here, take your cuppa upstairs with you.'

Holly didn't dare look at Lewis again as she took the mug from her and rushed upstairs. She showered in record time and then pulled open the middle drawer in the chest in her bedroom, wondering which pyjamas she could risk showing Lewis. She was tempted to get dressed in normal day clothes, but Lulu had made such a point of the whole pyjama issue that she knew it would look odd if she didn't do her usual thing.

She'd have to be choosy about which ones she wore though. She wouldn't show him some of them for all the money in the world. What would he think to a grown woman wearing Frozen PJs? It was almost as silly as a grown man wearing Sonic the Hedgehog PJs, she thought, grinning to myself. Did he really wear those, or was he just saying that to make her feel less stupid? She tried to picture him in them but couldn't help imagining him taking them off again. Her skin burned and she tutted impatiently, wondering when she'd become so lustful.

She dismissed three pairs of pyjamas as being too childish, but she did have one pair that were appropriate. Not particularly appealing, but appropriate. Plain turquoise fleecy PJs. No logos, and no embarrassing affiliation to fairy tales or cartoon characters. They would do.

She pulled them on, then stepped into her fluffy white slippers. She found her comb and untangled her hair, then peered at herself in the mirror. She looked about twelve she thought gloomily, but she could hardly reapply makeup could she? That would look so obvious after a shower. Like she'd just put makeup on for his benefit. Ridiculous.

Sighing, she shut the bedroom door after her and

went downstairs. Lulu looked up from the cooker and Holly saw the grim set of her mouth.

'What's up?' she asked, surprised to see Lulu's mood had plunged so quickly. 'You're not in pain are you?'

'Not like you're thinking,' she said. She nodded at the living room door. 'You'd best go and see for yourself.'

Nervously Holly pushed open the door and her own mood plummeted, while her adrenaline levels soared. Jonathan was standing, hands in pockets, legs apart, face like thunder, watching as Lewis finished winding the fairy lights around the Christmas tree. Lewis seemed to be paying no attention to him whatsoever, although how he could ignore that menacing stance was beyond Holly.

They both looked at her as she walked into the room. Lewis gave her a reassuring smile while Jonathan's eyebrows knitted together, and he glared meaningfully at her pyjamas.

'Getting ready for bed are you?' he growled.

'I've just had a shower,' she explained. 'You know I always put my PJs on after a shower.'

Lewis cleared his throat. 'I'll just test these, see if they work.'

'I can do that,' Jonathan said. 'You get yourself off home. I can take over from here.'

'Er, Lewis is staying for tea,' Holly said hesitantly. 'Lulu invited him as a thank you for bringing the tree and the other stuff round. Perhaps,' she added, somewhat reluctantly, 'you'd like to stay for tea too?'

'I've already had my tea,' he said. 'I just thought I'd

come over here and check the—Lulu—was okay. You had me worried earlier, thinking about what happened to her.'

'Well,' she said, not able to look at Lewis, 'as you can see, she's okay at the moment.'

'So, it was a big fuss about nothing then?'

'Not at all,' Lewis said, plugging the lights into the socket. 'It's about finding practical solutions to make her living conditions comfortable, and we're looking into that.' He flicked the switch and the tree immediately shone with hundreds of twinkling, warm lights. 'Smashing,' he said. 'Looks good doesn't it?'

'Oh, it does,' she breathed. She turned the main light off, so the effect was even more beautiful. 'Lulu,' she called, 'come and look at this.'

Lulu shuffled in, her face breaking into a wide smile as she gazed at the tree. 'Aw, that's lovely,' she said. 'It's years since we had a real Christmas tree here. So much nicer than that artificial one in the loft. By heck, lad,' she added, shaking her head at Lewis, 'you've no idea how much you've cheered me up. What with the tree and... everything else.'

He shrugged. 'It's my pleasure.'

Jonathan dropped onto the sofa, looking none too pleased about the situation. 'Meant to say, babe,' he said, as if the tree didn't even exist, 'I thought I'd stay over tonight. That's all right with you isn't it?' he asked Lulu. 'Only, Holls said it wouldn't be a problem and it's been a while.'

Holly was too embarrassed to reply. She gave him a horrified look then slowly turned her head to check

Lulu's reaction. It was the first time she'd seen her lost for words.

'Anyway,' Lewis said, switching off the lights and plunging them into darkness. 'I must get off home. I'm sure I can leave you all to decorate the tree now the lights are in place.'

'But you're staying for tea, lad!' Lulu had finally recovered her voice at least. She turned the main light on again and Holly saw the unhappiness in her face and realised she'd already grown very fond of Lewis.

'I really do have to go home. I have some things to do, and I'd forgotten all about them.' He sounded thoroughly unconvincing, and Holly watched miserably as he reached for the jacket he'd left on the chair arm and shrugged himself into it. 'I'm sure Jonathan can find room for it.'

Jonathan said nothing but his eyes never left Lewis as he zipped up his jacket and headed for the door. Holly gave Jonathan a despairing glance, then followed Lewis and Lulu to the front door.

'I'm so sorry,' she whispered to him as he stepped out into the cold darkness.

'What for?' he asked. 'You haven't done anything wrong.'

'No, but...' she gave him a desperate look, trying to make him understand.

He touched her arm, and his voice was kind. 'Holly, it doesn't matter, don't worry okay? I promise, everything's fine.' He dropped a light kiss on Lulu's cheek. 'So, tomorrow, about one o'clock?'

She patted his face. 'I'll be ready, love.'

'See you tomorrow then. Bye, Lulu. Bye, Holly. Take care.'

Lulu pulled Holly into a hug as they watched him heading down the garden path.

'What's this about tomorrow?' Holly asked, as they finally closed the front door on him.

She tapped the side of her nose. 'Going out for the afternoon. He's got a half day booked at work and he's taking me into York. What do you think about that?'

'York! Whatever for?' Was it ridiculous that she felt a pang of jealousy? Of Lulu, of all people!

'You'll find out,' she said, smiling. 'By, he's a good 'un, that one. They broke the mould when they made him you know.'

They winced as Jonathan called, 'Any chance of a cup of tea, babe?'

'Hmm,' Lulu muttered, 'and that one's pretty unique an' all, thank God.'

'Oh, Lulu.' But she couldn't mount her usual defence of Jonathan this time. The thing was, she had no inclination or energy to do so. Who would have believed that possible?

Chapter 13

'What's with you and them blooming sweets?' Lulu demanded, giving Lewis a puzzled look as he popped another pear drop in his mouth.

He grinned as he pushed the crumpled paper bag further back on the dashboard. 'I started eating them to stop me from lighting up a cigarette,' he explained. 'Don't ask me why I stuck with pear drops because I have no idea, but it seems to be working. Are you sure you don't want one?'

She pulled a face. 'No, ta. If they were sherbet lemons now, that would be a different matter. Can't be doing with pear drops. Still, if it's stopped you smoking that's a good thing.' She settled back in her seat and gave him a thoughtful look. 'I can imagine you with a cig in your hand. You're just the type.'

He raised an eyebrow. 'And what type is that exactly?'

'Well, you know.' She shrugged. 'All sophisticated and posh, like. The type what makes smoking look cool.'

He laughed. 'Nothing cool about smoking,' he assured her. 'I don't know why I ever started.'

'Aye, well, we all have our vices.'

'Oh? And what's your vice, Lulu?'

She winked. 'That would be telling. You're far too young to know.'

'Lulu!'

She squealed with laughter at his shocked expression, and he smiled to himself, knowing it had given her a great deal of pleasure to believe she'd caused such a reaction. He had to admit he'd had a lovely afternoon with her. She was great company and had made him laugh so many times that he'd almost forgotten the purpose of their trip to York. Almost.

She would never have managed to get in his van, but Bernie had very kindly lent him his car for the day, so Lulu had travelled in style—something she wouldn't have done, bouncing around in his old Transit.

She'd told him she hadn't been to York for years and was looking forward to it, and her face had lit up when she saw the stalls and fairy lights of the Christmas market.

Unfortunately, she hadn't been able to explore as much as she wanted. She was in too much pain, so Lewis had taken her into a café for tea and cake.

Lulu was quite glad to get out of the cold, he suspected. They sat sipping hot drinks and watching shoppers hurrying past the windows.

'You know it's forecast snow?' Lulu told him. 'Weatherman warned us on the telly last night. Mind, I could've told them that days ago. I know the signs. My joints have been throbbing like the very devil.'

'Speaking of which,' Lewis said, 'drink up and let's get to our next stop.'

Lulu had been almost overcome when she saw what was on offer at the store he'd taken her to and couldn't quite believe it was all happening.

'But are you sure, love? Look at the price of everything. I dunno, it seems like such a massive expense.'

'But worth every penny,' he assured her cheerfully. 'It will change your life, Lulu, and it will make staying at Cuckoo Nest Cottage not only possible, but relatively easy. Put it this way, if you don't agree to all this you may have no choice but to go into a home before much longer.'

Her eyebrows knitted together. 'Is that blackmail, young man?'

He hooked his arm through hers and smiled at her. 'As if! It's merely stating a fact. You know as well as I do that you can't carry on like this much longer.'

'I know...' She sighed. 'It's just—'

'Look, there's no pressure,' he promised her. 'This is entirely your decision. I just hope you'll consider what you've seen today and think about the other day when Holly wasn't around, and you couldn't get yourself out of your chair. That's not much of a life in my humble opinion, and if you can change it for the better well, why wouldn't you?'

'I know, I know. Just, all that money...'

'You've got the money sitting in your bank account anyway. You can either leave it there or spend it making your life a lot easier.' He threw in his last bargaining chip. 'It would take a lot of the worry away from Holly too. Make her life better, not just yours.'

She peered up at him, clearly seeing through his strategy, but he was relieved to see she had a twinkle in her eyes. 'Well played, lad, well played. Go on then. Not like I haven't already given the debit card a good bashing today, is it?'

'You've made the right choice,' he told her, gesturing to the sales assistant that they needed help.

Half an hour or so later, they headed back to the car park, stopping on the way at a card shop, so he and Lulu could buy a wedding card for Rachel and Xander.

'We can stay a bit longer if you like,' he offered. 'If you need to do any last-minute gift shopping or anything.'

'Done it all,' she informed him smugly. 'I do it online.'

He gaped at her, stunned. 'Online?'

She nudged him knowingly. 'That's took the wind out of your sales hasn't it? Never expected an old fogey like me to be online did you?'

'Well, no,' he admitted. 'Not that I think you're an old fogey,' he added hastily. 'I just never imagined you having the internet. I didn't even know you had a computer.'

'Holly gave me an old laptop a couple of years ago,' she told him. 'I said to her, what flipping use is that to me? But she insisted that I have a go. Said it would open up the world to me. Well, it was around that time that me legs and me arthritis had got really bad, and I was stuck indoors a lot more than I used to be, so I thought, why not? I had the internet thingy fixed up and I'll tell you now, I don't know what all the fuss is about. They go on about it being hard to learn to use a computer. Is it heckers like! Took me less than a day to have it all up and running. Holly did try to get me to go on that Tweeter thing, and Facebooks or summat, but I'm not interested in that malarkey. But it's bin a godsend for dealing with me pension, and the bank, and getting me shopping delivered. Maudie's is a nice little shop, and very handy to have nearby, but it's a bit on the pricey side, and there's not the choice you get in a supermarket. I get it delivered once a fortnight and I did all me Christmas shopping weeks ago. Can't beat it.'

'Well, I never did,' he said, amazed.

'Oh, there's life in the old dog yet, mate,' she said, looking very pleased with herself. 'I reckon I'm as good at it all as young Holly.'

'I didn't expect that,' he said. 'Especially since you don't even like your mobile phone.'

'Oh, I can't be doing with those things,' she said dismissively. 'Why do I want to talk to people on one of those? If they've got owt to say to me they can come and see me and tell me in person. And as for the tiny screens! How the heck am I supposed to read anything on those? No, I like my nice big laptop screen. I get meself all settled in bed at night, and I go on there and pay me bills and do me shopping and listen to a few ballads before I go to sleep.'

'You're full of surprises,' he told her.

'Aye, well,' she gave him a knowing look, 'I'm not the only one am I?'

They'd reached Bramblewick and Lewis pulled up outside Cuckoo Nest Cottage.

'You'll come in for a cup of tea.' It wasn't a question, and he nodded in agreement as he opened the passenger door and carefully helped her out. She winced in pain, and he thought that, at least after today, things would start to improve for her. It wasn't a cure-all, obviously, but she would find life that bit easier. It was a good feeling to know that.

They walked down the path then Lulu stopped and sniffed the air. 'Can you smell that?' she asked.

He shook his head. 'What?'

'Snow. It's coming, lad. I can feel it.'

'Best get inside then,' he said, grinning.

'Oh, bugger.' She pulled a face. 'Just spotted you-know-who pulling up. Well, isn't that all we need?'

Lewis peered over his shoulder and tried to keep his expression neutral as Jonathan's car parked just behind Bernie's.

'He's keen, isn't he?' he murmured. 'It's only just gone half-past five. Holly won't even be home for half an hour.'

'Frightened to death he misses summat,' she grunted. 'Think you've scared him, love.'

'Me?'

'Competition.' She smirked at him as she put the key in the lock. 'He's never felt threatened before, but you've put a stop to his gallop. Reckon he's realised he's going to have to try a lot harder to keep her now.'

'What do you mean?' Lewis could feel his face heating up but couldn't pursue the conversation as Jonathan sauntered up behind them, a fixed smile on his face that didn't fool him and, he suspected, wouldn't fool Lulu either.

'Now then. We meet again.'

Lewis wondered how one harmless greeting could irritate him so much. It was strange, but he had the strongest desire to punch Jonathan in the mouth.

'We do,' was all he could manage.

Lulu pushed open the front door. 'She's not back from work yet, you know.'

'Oh, I know. Thought it would be a nice surprise for her to find me here when she gets back.'

'Oh, did you?' Lulu's tone of voice clearly expressed her doubts on that matter, but she said no more, hobbling awkwardly into the kitchen.

'Sit down,' Lewis told her immediately. 'I'll make the tea. Go and get your legs up and rest a while.'

'Had a nice trip out?' Jonathan queried.

'Fine thanks.' Lewis didn't even look at him, his gaze fixed on Lulu who was, he realised, looking worn out and clearly in pain. 'Here, I'll take your coat.'

'You're a good lad,' she told him, taking her coat off with some difficulty, then shuffling into the living room, calling out to him how glad she was that she'd left the central heating on, and the room was so warm and cosy. 'And it looks even cosier, with the tree up and decorated,' she added. 'Wait 'til you see it.'

Jonathan leaned back against the worktop, watching as Lewis took Lulu's coat into the hall to hang up, then filled the kettle with water.

'Oh, course, you haven't seen it all done yet have you? Me and Holls had a great time last night, putting all the decs on. Looks great if I do say so myself.'

'I'm glad.'

'Yeah, it was a smashing evening. Enjoyed myself so much I thought we'd do it again tonight.' He smirked at Lewis. 'If you know what I mean.'

Lewis could guess what he meant all right, and he felt a bit sick at the thought. 'Tea?'

'Nah, I'll wait until Holls gets home,' he said. He hesitated then asked, 'You bin invited for tea again tonight?'

'No. I'm just making Lulu this drink then I'm heading home.' He couldn't get away fast enough. He poured boiling water over a teabag and took milk from the fridge.

'Don't blame you. A whole afternoon in her company is more than enough for anyone, right?' Jonathan nodded at the living room door.

'Not at all. We've had a great time in York,' Lewis assured him coldly. 'She's marvellous company.'

Jonathan gave him a doubtful look. 'Is she? Well, it takes all sorts, I suppose.'

'Indeed.'

As Jonathan settled himself at the table, evidently waiting for Holly to come home and start making his tea, Lewis carried the drink through to the living room, where he found Lulu propped up on the sofa, legs on cushions, looking thoroughly fed up.

'Reckon I'm stuck with the bugger all evening,' she whispered, taking the cup from him. 'What does she see in him, eh, love? You tell me that.'

He shrugged, unable to give her an appropriate answer. 'I'm going home now,' he told her. 'Thanks for a really entertaining afternoon.'

'You're thanking me!' Her eyes widened and she reached out one gnarled, twisted hand and patted his cheek. 'It's me that's thanking you, love. What a day this has been, eh? Can't believe it. My angel.'

He straightened, smiling. 'Don't be silly. Just remember, the money's between me and you, okay? Our secret.'

She laughed. 'Oh, I won't say a word about that bit, although I wouldn't be surprised if me bank manager doesn't take out an ad in the Whitby Gazette. He'll be stunned. Never seen activity like that in my bank account before, I'll tell you. Even me debit card's probably gone dizzy with it all.'

Lewis dropped a kiss on her head and turned to leave. Jonathan stood in the doorway, arms folded.

'Very—illuminating.'

Lewis narrowed his eyes. 'Sorry?'

Jonathan flashed him a smile. 'The tree. Brightens up the room lovely, doesn't it?'

Lewis glanced round, noticing the now fully decorated tree. 'Looks great.'

'Hmm. Be seeing you, Lewis.'

Lewis pushed past him, not trusting himself to reply. He wished he knew exactly how much Jonathan had heard. He could make things very awkward for him if he put two and two together. Very awkward indeed.

***

Holly barely touched her tea, which was enough,

clearly, to put Lulu on her guard.

'All right, what's up with you?' she demanded, nodding meaningfully at the plate on Holly's lap, which was still more than half full. Her face softened suddenly, and she gave Holly a sympathetic smile. 'Is it the wedding on Monday? Nervous are you?'

Holly seized on Lulu's explanation gratefully. 'Yeah, a bit. Wouldn't you be?'

'Not if I looked like you I wouldn't, no.' Lulu prodded some mashed potato with her fork. 'You needn't worry, you know, you daft ha'porth. You're going to be the belle of the ball. You might even outshine the bride if you're not careful.'

'Hardly!' Holly laughed. 'Rachel will look amazing. She always does.' She sighed. 'They all will. I'm going to be the token fat bridesmaid.'

If she was looking for sympathy from Lulu, she was to be disappointed.

'Oh, what rubbish. Stop feeling sorry for yourself and get a grip. You know what your trouble is, young lady? You're self-obsessed.'

Holly was stung. 'Self-obsessed! Me?'

'Yes, you,' Lulu said brutally. 'You spend all your time worrying about yourself. About how you look, how you come across to other people, what everyone else thinks of you. You know, hard as this may be to understand, but tomorrow isn't about you, and it's Rachel they're all going to be looking at. Quite rightly too. So why don't you stop fussing about how you feel and how you're going to look, and start thinking about Rachel and what she's going to be facing the day after tomorrow, eh? All eyes on her, not to mention the worry of any of Xander's daft fans turning up to goggle at him. And look at that,' she added, nodding at the window. 'Talk about bad timing. If it settles they might not even make it to Kearton Hall.'

Holly glanced out of the window at the snowflakes that were falling with increasing speed. 'I think they're prepared,' she said. 'It's not like it wasn't forecast, is it?'

Lulu nodded. 'Even so, it's a tricky journey in bad weather,' she reminded her. 'Now that's something real to fret about, not like your mitherings.'

Holly tutted. 'Well, thanks very much. Sorry to get on your nerves.'

'That's all right,' Lulu said cheerily, 'as long as you pack it in now.'

Holly burst out laughing. 'Point taken. I'm done with this food though,' she said, staring down at the tray on her lap. How about you?'

'Aye, I've had enough, and enough is as good as a feast,' Lulu agreed.

Holly collected Lulu's tray and carried both into the kitchen. Secretly, she was quite relieved that Lulu had put all her recent quietness and anxiety down to the forthcoming wedding. Yes, it was a nerve-wracking prospect and no, she wasn't particularly looking forward to it, as much as she loved Rachel and Xander and wanted them to have the perfect day. But her main concern was Lulu herself, and just what Lewis was playing at.

It was Jonathan who'd raised the alarm. She'd got home from work last night to find Lulu humming little tunes to herself and looking remarkably cheerful, while Jonathan rolled his eyes and made it quite obvious that he was trying to listen to the news. He'd practically shot up from his chair when Holly walked into the living room and hadn't exactly been discreet about bundling her upstairs to the bedroom with indecent haste before she'd even had the chance to ask Lulu how her day in York had gone.

Holly had been wondering how she could reject him this time. The previous night she'd pleaded a headache but didn't think she could get away with that old chestnut again. It was an odd feeling, realising that she didn't want any physical contact with Jonathan. Usually she craved the closeness with him, the belief strong in the back of her mind that, somehow, they were forging a bond that would never be broken. Right now, something was making her feel that all she really needed from him was space, and she wasn't sure how that had happened or how to feel about it. Luckily, she didn't have to worry about it as it turned out that Jonathan had much more important things on his mind.

'I told you he was up to no good, didn't I? Mr Perfect! Hah! Not so perfect after all. I warned you he was too good to be true and I was right. You can't say I didn't tell you.'

'What are you talking about? Who's Mr Perfect?' Though, even as she said the words, Holly had a sudden sinking feeling she knew who this conversation was about.

'Blondie, who else?'

Holly groaned and sank onto the bed. 'What's he

supposed to have done now?'

'Not *supposed* to have done. *Has* done.' There was a gleam of triumph in Jonathan's eyes as he sat on the dressing table chair opposite her and faced her with all-too-obvious smugness.

'Okay then. What *has* he done?'

'Ripped Lulu off, that's what. Conned her out of her money. It's true!' he protested as she stared at him in disbelief. 'By hell, isn't it amazing how you always seem to believe the best in him and the worst in me. What does that tell you, eh?'

Holly didn't want to think about what that told her. Instead she concentrated on his accusations. 'What exactly do you mean? How has he ripped Lulu off? I don't think she's even got any money?'

'Well you know less than he does then. Although, by now you could be right. He's probably had it away with her entire savings.'

'Jonathan, you're not making sense. Can you just tell me what's going on?'

'All right.' He leaned back, folded his arms, and smirked at her. 'After they got back from York earlier, I heard him telling Lulu that it was between them—their secret.'

Holly wrinkled her nose. 'Is that all? Well, *it* could mean anything.'

'I haven't finished,' he growled. 'Give me a chance, will you? It was what Lulu said that was most interesting.'

Holly sighed, struggling to keep her patience with his dramatic, long-drawn-out way of telling her something that was probably banal, at best. 'And what was that?'

'She said she'd keep schtum, although her bank manager would probably be having a fit, because she'd never spent that much money in her life. Something like that anyway.'

Holly frowned. 'Are you sure about this?'

'Of course I'm sure! And I'll tell you something else, when he looked round and saw me listening, the blood drained from his face. Really didn't want me to know about it, I can tell you that much. So you tell me, just what has the old woman bin spending her money on, eh? And how come she's only started spending now when Blondie's in tow? She's not bin much of a one for splashing the cash 'til now, has she? Bit of a coincidence if you ask me.'

Holly hated to admit that he had a point, but she couldn't deny that Lulu was no big spender. In fact, Holly had always assumed that she had no money to spend. What had she been buying that cost so much money her bank manager would be alerted to the fact?

'Are you going to ask her about it?' he demanded. 'I'll back you up. I think we should know, don't you? If he's ripping her off then the police need to be told.'

'Steady on!' Holly pulled a face. 'For goodness' sake, we know nothing yet. Yes, I will ask her, but not tonight, and not while you're around. She won't tell me anything unless we're alone.'

He scowled. 'She may not tell you anything anyway. Seems to me like she's another one who believes every word Blondie says.'

'Lulu's far from gullible,' Holly had assured him, deciding to ignore his implication that she herself was also gullible, particularly when it came to Lewis. It just wasn't worth starting an argument about. Besides, she had bigger things to worry about. Like just what Lewis was up to, and what Lulu had been buying.

Holly didn't have long to wait to find out—at least about what Lulu had been buying. After she'd carried the tea through to the living room, she was alarmed when Lulu patted the sofa and told her to sit down as she had something huge to tell her.

'Gonna be some big changes around here, love. Life's about to get better, for both of us.'

Holly's stomach turned in dread. 'Oh? And what does that mean?'

'You know Lewis took me to York yesterday?'

'Of course.'

'Well, we went on a bit of a spending spree. Ooh, love, it was fantastic! And the upshot is, we'll be having a few deliveries after Christmas.'

'What sort of deliveries?' Holly dreaded to think. Lulu wasn't one for jewellery or new clothes. What on earth had she been buying?

'Well, me and Lewis went to a few of them specialist shops.'

Holly raised an eyebrow and Lulu let out a peal of laughter. 'Not them kind! I wish! No, you know the ones that sell stuff to make life easier for people like me, with mobility issues.'

'Oh, I see.' That sounded more hopeful. 'And?'

'Well, let me tell you, I'm feeling like a new woman

already and they haven't even arrived yet.'

'What haven't arrived yet?'

'My new mobility scooter, first off, so I can get around the village again. Won't that be fantastic?'

'Mobility scooter? Oh my goodness, that's amazing!'

'I know! And that's just the start. You know last week when I had my, er, little problem? Well, I'll never get stuck in a chair again, because I'm getting one of them chairs that lift you up and practically tip you out. They let me try a few in the shop, Holly, and you wouldn't believe how easy they are to get in and out of. Amazing! And then there's the electric bed.'

'Electric bed?' Holly was beginning to feel a little dazed. 'You're getting an electric bed?'

'I am. Just the job for my swollen legs. I can raise the end up, so my feet are higher than my heart, like the doctor says. By, it was comfy. I didn't want to get out of it when I tried it in the shop, but I did, and it was quite easy to do it too. I'm gonna have a lot of fun with that, I'll tell you. It's gonna make using my laptop a lot easier, an' all.'

'Crikey, Lulu, that's—it's a lot to take in,' Holly murmured thinking, *and a lot to buy in one shopping trip*, but Lulu clearly hadn't finished yet.

'Then they're coming to fit a walk-in bath for me—'

Holly gaped at her. 'A walk-in bath?'

'And the piece de resistance,' Lulu finished, making no attempt at a French pronunciation, 'is my stair lift. Now, what do you think of that little lot, eh?'

Holly couldn't speak. She opened her mouth but

closed it again, finding no words that seemed appropriate.

Lulu clasped her hand, looking suddenly worried. 'Now, love, I understand that it's not something a youngster like you wants in her home. Stair lifts do take up a bit of room, and I know the walk-in bath won't be to your taste. But it's a shower bath, and there's going to be a smashing shower fitted too. You like your showers, don't you? I know it's not ideal for you, but do you mind too much?'

'Of course I don't mind! This is your home, and anything that makes life easier for you is fine by me. It's just...' Holly bit her lip, not sure how to frame the question.

'Just what?'

'Well, it's an awful lot of money, Lulu, and I just worry that you've got yourself into a heap of debt.'

Lulu seemed to hesitate a moment before squeezing Holly's hand reassuringly. 'No need to worry, love. There are grants you can get, you know.'

'I know there are, but you've always said—'

'And I had some savings, so why not? Why struggle along when you can make life so much easier for yourself?'

'Well, exactly, but even so.'

'Now, you stop worrying. Have a look in me handbag. There are some brochures in there. You'll see the bath and everything else. I'd like your opinion on them.'

Holly obediently reached for Lulu's handbag, which was never far from her side. She pulled out a handful of leaflets and put them on her knee.

'That's the one I'm having,' Lulu told her, pointing at a photograph of a smart and stylish walk-in shower bath, with a rather swish, powerful shower overhead. 'What do you think? I tried to pick one that wouldn't say *old fogey*, for your sake.'

Holly laughed. 'Don't be daft. It's your bathroom, your choice. It's a lovely bath, Lulu. It will look great, and it will definitely make life so much easier for you.' She frowned suddenly. 'What's this?'

Lulu reached over and took the card from her hand. 'Oh, er—it's a solicitor's card. Nothing to worry about. Lewis took me to see a solicitor that's all. When you get to my age, there are things you need to sort out. You know how it is.'

Holly narrowed her eyes. 'Right. And did you get everything sorted?'

'We did, thank you very much. Now, that's enough chatting. Bit rubbish on a Saturday night now Strictly's finished, but there must be summat on. Can you pass me the remote, love, please?'

Holly reached for the remote control, her mind whirling. She'd had no idea Lulu had so much money in the bank, but it was clear that Lewis knew. He seemed to know a lot, which was worrying since he'd only just met her really. And why had he taken her to the solicitors? She'd never shown any inclination to visit one before.

She remembered Jonathan's warning and felt a sudden dread. Had he been right? Was Lewis up to something? He'd clearly wormed his way into Lulu's affections and had gained her trust to such an extent that he was party to more of her secrets than Holly herself. It hurt; she couldn't deny it. But it also unnerved her. What had he talked her into?

Holly wished suddenly that being a fat bridesmaid was all she had to worry about. Should she tackle Lewis? Demand to know what had gone on in York? She really had no idea what to do for the best.

Chapter 14

Monday, December 23rd had arrived at last. Holly was determined to put all her worries to one side for the day. It was Rachel's and Xander's wedding day, and nothing else mattered right now.

As the car crunched through the snow and turned through the gates of Kearton Hall, her tummy fluttered with a mixture of nerves and excitement, and Nell squealed in delight while Izzy and Anna grinned at each other.

'It's like a fairy tale,' Nell said. 'A Christmas wedding in a stately home, and it's snowing!'

'Good job we've all got these stoles,' Anna said. 'It's going to be freezing when we step outside.'

'These old houses are draughty too, aren't they?' Holly said. 'I hope they have central heating.'

'Are you sure I definitely haven't got lipstick on my teeth?' Izzy demanded for the third time.

Anna tutted. 'No, you haven't. What is it with you and lipstick today?'

'I'm wearing a new brand and I hadn't realised how smudgy it was. Wish I'd stuck to my old lippy.' She peered out of the back window. 'Rachel's car's not far behind. Wasn't she calm? Can't believe it. I thought she'd be a nervous wreck.'

'So did I,' Anna admitted.

'I would have been,' Nell said with a shudder. 'I don't know how any of you dealt with all this. I couldn't have done it. So glad me and Riley sneaked off to the registry office.' She gave a big sigh. 'Doesn't Rachel look beautiful though?'

'She really does.' Anna smiled at Izzy. 'We've had two absolutely gorgeous brides this month.'

'I don't think we look too bad either,' Nell pointed out. 'In fact, I think we look fantastic. Talk about glam.'

Holly looked at the three of them in their beautiful emerald green gowns, complete with faux fur stoles, and thought how gorgeous they looked. She really hoped she didn't stand out as the one who spoilt the image, although everyone had assured her she looked amazing, and no one had made any remarks about the dress being too tight or anything, much to her relief. She'd been delighted when it zipped up quite easily that afternoon, having kept her fingers tightly crossed that there'd be no unexpected clothing emergency to deal with.

So far, everything seemed to be running smoothly. Xander had broken with tradition and had a best woman instead of a best man. His agent Penny, he said, was the best friend he'd ever had, and he owed her everything. He'd insisted that he couldn't think of anyone he'd rather have at his side, and she'd been honoured to accept. She'd called Folly Farm earlier and told them that all was well and Xander would be leaving for Kearton Hall at any moment, so Rachel had no cause to worry.

Not that Rachel seemed worried anyway. Her son, Sam, was giving her away, and he seemed pretty calm, too. It was in sharp contrast to Rachel's mum, Janie, who seemed on the verge of passing out with nerves. She was full of *what ifs* and appeared certain of impending doom. Rachel had given her a gentle hug and told her to stop worrying.

'Honestly, Mum, it will be fine. What's the worst that can happen?'

As Holly heard a horrified gasp from Anna, she had a sudden feeling that they were about to find out.

Izzy craned her neck to look out of the window, where Anna, who was sitting by the door, was staring in dismay. 'What's up?'

'They've found out,' Anna said, turning to face them, her face etched in shock. 'There's a huge crowd outside, and there's a local news van.'

They all stared at each other in dismay. 'You're kidding?'

Holly wound down the window and stuck her head out to get a better look. 'Oh, no! You're right, Anna. But how?' She sank back into her seat and Anna hastily shut the window.

'Rachel's going to be devastated,' Nell murmured. 'How the heck has this happened?'

'I suppose it was always going to be tricky, keeping it a secret,' Izzy mused. 'Someone as famous as Xander—and then having Joe Hollingsworth and Charlie Hope as guests was always a risk too.'

Joe Hollingsworth was a former chat show host and

television personality, who lived with his partner, top comedian Charlie Hope, in nearby Kearton Bay. They were good friends of Xander's, so it wasn't surprising that he'd invited them to his wedding, although it did mean that it would cause further excitement among the celebrity-hunters and press, should they discover it. The wedding arrangements had been shrouded in secrecy, so it was frustrating that details had somehow been leaked. Holly hoped that Rachel and Xander wouldn't let it spoil their wedding day.

The car drew to a halt outside Kearton Hall, a beautiful Elizabethan country house. As they nervously climbed out of the car they were temporarily dazzled by camera flashes and overwhelmed by calls from waiting fans and reporters. Holly thought they must be absolutely devoted to Xander. Why else would they stand outside in the snow? She couldn't help but feel sorry for them.

'This way please.'

A young woman with dark hair and a pretty face hurried towards them. She was looking rather flustered at the unexpected turn of events, and ushered them inside into a grand room, which featured a massive fireplace, where Holly was relieved to see a roaring fire burning. All around, portraits of aristocratic looking men and women from centuries past gazed down at them, but there was a warmth to the room too, particularly as it was beautifully decorated for the season, with a large Christmas tree and festive decorations. Holly fleetingly wondered if Lewis had any hand in the floral displays dotted around but had no time to dwell on the question.

'If you could just wait here in the Great Hall I'll be with you in a moment. I must greet the bride,' the woman said, before hurrying back out, no doubt to try to offer some protection to Rachel when she arrived with Abbie.

Riley and Connor, looking extremely handsome in their tuxedos, hurried in, looking a bit annoyed, followed by a distraught-looking Janie.

'You've seen it all then?' Riley asked, as he embraced Nell. 'You all look fantastic, by the way. Really stunning.'

Connor nodded his agreement, and they all murmured their thanks.

'This is a catastrophe isn't it?' Anna said, as Connor pulled her into a hug.

'How's Xander taking it?' Izzy asked.

Riley rolled his eyes. 'He's not a happy bunny, but he went into full professional mode. Honestly, you'd never have known how gutted he was. Polite and charming to a fault. His agent was furious though. She's demanding answers and, to be honest, I wouldn't want to be the one who let the cat out of the bag. I get the feeling she takes no prisoners.'

'Where *is* Xander?'

'He's taken his place in the wedding room.' Connor grinned. 'Charlie Hope's keeping everyone entertained. He's clearly decided that Xander's going to enjoy today whether he likes it or not.'

'Good for him.' Anna peered nervously toward the door. 'I hope Rachel's not too floored by all this. It was absolutely the last thing she wanted, poor thing.'

At that very moment, the huge, oak door opened, and Abbie, Rachel and Sam stepped inside, brushing off the snow, followed by the wedding planner, who slammed the door shut firmly behind them.

Janie hurried to Rachel's side. 'Oh, Rachel, what an awful thing to happen!'

'It's okay, Mum. Just one of those things,' Rachel said. 'We always knew there was a good chance news would get out. We'll just have to get on with it.'

'Can I, on behalf of everyone here at Kearton Hall, apologise for what's happened here today,' the young woman said, her face showing her distress. 'I promise you that we've done our utmost to keep this wedding under wraps, and I honestly can't imagine how news has leaked out.'

'Well, clearly someone opened their mouth,' Riley said with a shrug. He and Connor exchanged looks. 'I guess there was always the chance it would happen.'

'We have a very loyal and professional team here,' the wedding planner said. 'I have every faith in their discretion.'

'I wouldn't worry,' Connor said. 'I'm sure your staff can be trusted.'

'Let's not get into this now,' Rachel said firmly. 'I feel a bit sorry for them all to be honest. They must be freezing cold out there.'

'Lady Boden-Kean has requested they be given hot chocolate and mince pies. I hope you don't mind.'

'Not at all. I think that's a good idea. Don't want anyone getting hypothermia.' Rachel smiled, ever the nurse. 'Today isn't the day for an inquest. What's done is done, and I just want to get married, thanks very much. Don't look so worried, Tally. I'm sure there's a good explanation for all this. At least they can't get into the house, so they won't have access to the wedding or reception, and that's the main thing.'

'They won't. We have our regular security team on hand, and they're very good. We use them for all our events,' Tally assured her.

'I believe you. To be honest, I can't worry too much about all this right now. I just want us to exchange our vows and have a great day with all our friends and family.'

'Absolutely,' Tally agreed. 'And with that in mind, can I ask anyone not in the wedding party to take their seats so we can begin?'

Janie hugged Sam and told him how smart he looked, then kissed Rachel and murmured that she'd never looked more beautiful. Then she, Connor and Riley hurried out of the Great Hall.

Rachel took a deep breath.

'Right then,' she said, sounding astonishingly calm. 'Let's do this.'

***

Lewis thought that, whether she realised it or not, Holly completely outshone everyone else in the room. Although she was dressed identically to the other three bridesmaids and the matron of honour, she looked far more beautiful, in his opinion, than any of them.

Even the bride, who was wearing the most stunning gown, with a white faux fur stole that made even him gasp—and God knows, he was no expert on wedding dresses—struggled to compete with Holly.

Of course, he realised, he could be well be biased. The fact was, as he watched her walk down the aisle, nervously clutching her small bouquet of white roses, his heart had swelled so much with pride that it felt as if it were blocking his throat, and for a moment he'd struggled to breathe. That, he supposed, was the moment he'd accepted that he'd fallen in love with Holly. He didn't know whether to laugh or cry.

He'd wondered, for a long time, if he'd ever be able to put his trust in another human being, and not only in them but in himself. Loving someone, he'd fathomed, meant letting them in, and he'd never been sure he'd be able to do that, having learned from a very young age to put a guard up, protect his feelings, keep a safe emotional distance.

He'd often thought that it would prove impossible for him to trust someone enough to give them his heart, but what he'd realised these last few weeks was that it wasn't just about trusting the other person. It was more about trusting himself to be good enough for them. It started and ended with that. Did he feel that he was enough for another human being to accept him just as he was, and let them see the real person inside?

It had taken many years of learning about and understanding how people like his father operated. He'd had to keep a safe distance from him, for his own sake. He'd learned to deal with the criticism from aunts, uncles, cousins, who thought he treated his father with an appalling lack of consideration.

'But he's getting old,' they insisted, 'and you're all he's got left really, since your mum died. Why don't you make more of an effort to see him?'

He'd tried, once or twice, to explain how his father's very presence wore him down, exhausted him, put him on guard and tore at the fragile self-esteem it had taken him years to repair.

'But that's just the way he is,' they insisted. 'He doesn't mean anything by it. You're too sensitive, that's your trouble.'

He'd been told that all his life, and so had his mother. But they didn't know, didn't understand, what it had been like living with this narcissist who controlled every aspect of their existence, dominated every action, and shaped the way they'd come to view themselves.

He knew his father was getting older now, and he knew that it was expected that he should put their "difficulties" aside and accept the man for what he was, but Lewis had no intention of doing so. He couldn't. He'd spent too long repairing the damage, and he was no longer prepared to put his own mental health at risk to please someone who had done his very best to make life as miserable and soul-destroying as possible.

Having reached this point in his life, Lewis realised that, at last, he felt able to let someone else in. He trusted *himself* finally. He was good enough. And it seemed that he'd found himself, just as he'd found Holly. It was a comfort and a joy to him to realise that he'd come so far, and that he was capable of loving and accepting love after all, but it was a bittersweet discovery; Holly had her own battles to fight, and he wasn't even sure if she'd realised yet that she was at war.

He craned his neck, looking for Jonathan, while wishing at the same time that he could just forget about him, at least for the duration of the wedding ceremony.

There he was, not playing by the rules but wearing his usual suit. At least, Lewis thought, glancing down at the tuxedo he was wearing, his fingers automatically stroking his bow tie, he'd managed to do better there. He tutted to himself as Jonathan totally ignored Holly, not even glancing in her direction. His attention was all focused on the bride and groom, and Lewis thought he was behaving like a total prat as he pointed his phone at them, evidently taking photographs.

He could barely wipe the smile off his face when a man appeared from nowhere and leaned towards Jonathan, muttering something in his ear. Jonathan looked pretty fed up, and Lewis felt a pang of satisfaction as he put his phone in his jacket pocket with obvious reluctance. There was a strict policy of no photographs or filming at the event, other than by the official photographer. Trust Jonathan to flout the rules.

As the wedding ceremony began, the bridesmaids took their seats beside their respective partners, and Lewis felt a flash of sympathy for Holly who got barely a nod from her so-called boyfriend. The prat didn't deserve her. He wished, with all his heart, that she could see it.

The wedding went smoothly, despite its shaky start.

Xander and Rachel both seemed incredibly calm, and neither of them stumbled over their vows. Sam played his part brilliantly and looked extremely proud of himself.

Lewis noticed, with some amusement, that several of the guests spent more time gawping at Charlie and Joe than at the happy couple. The power of celebrity.

He deliberately didn't look in Jonathan's and Holly's direction again. It wouldn't do him any good, after all. He was determined to enjoy the day and keep out of their way, for Holly's sake, and for his own. Seeing her with that Neanderthal wasn't doing his blood pressure any good. His craving for a cigarette was particularly strong today, which came as no surprise. With a resigned sigh, he reached into his pocket and pulled out a pear drop. He would deal with his increasing dependence on sugar at a later date.

Chapter 15

Holly's nerves were jangling, and she had no idea why.

The wedding had gone smoothly, despite the initial shock of finding fans and reporters on the doorstep of Kearton Hall. Two security men, Gav and Dave, had apparently done a sterling job of keeping them away from both Xander and Rachel—and Joe and Charlie—and had made certain that no one gained entrance to the Hall itself. The windows in the room that was used for the ceremony were screened by blinds so no sneaky pictures could be taken. Luckily, it appeared that only the local news had got wind of the wedding, and Penny had, with Xander's and Rachel's blessing, gone outside to inform the reporters from the regional news programme and a couple of local newspapers that, if they behaved themselves and caused no trouble, the happy couple would pose for pictures and say a few words after the wedding.

A message had been sent to the wedding party from Lady Boden-Kean informing them that, as the weather was worsening, she had taken the precaution of opening the tea room in the grounds and allowing the fans and reporters to camp out in there until the interview had been given, which both Xander and Rachel had been most relieved about.

Tally had led everyone back to the Great Hall, where the photographer took all the official shots. It was a magnificent backdrop for the photographs and Holly thought Xander and Rachel looked every inch the perfect couple. Xander with his movie star good looks, and Rachel, looking so ravishingly beautiful in her white silk gown with its long sleeves and tiny pearl buttons at the cuffs, long, full skirt and high neck, that she could have been a Hollywood actress herself.

After that, the guests had returned to the banquet room, and drinks were served while Xander and Rachel kept their promise and headed out to the tea room to greet the crowds. A brief interview had been given, hands shaken, photos posed for, and most of the fans and the television crew had, after congratulating the bride and groom and wishing them a merry Christmas, drifted away home, no doubt persuaded in part by the increasingly heavy snowfall which would, in due course, make getting home extremely difficult, if not impossible.

No one had made any disparaging remarks about Holly being too fat for her dress, and she had to admit that, as the afternoon wore on, she'd stopped thinking about her appearance, becoming more interested in having conversations with her friends and sneaking rather awestruck glances at Charlie and Joe.

She and Nell had both remarked how strange it was that, despite being huge fans of Xander's and feeing rather star-struck when he'd first arrived in

Bramblewick, they rarely thought about his acting career these days, seeing him simply as Rachel's partner and one of the gang. She supposed Charlie and Joe were only normal human beings too, but it was hard to see them that way and, to be fair, Charlie was the life and soul of the party, a born performer who was in his element chatting to guests and cracking jokes, while Joe rolled his eyes good-naturedly and took more of a back seat in the proceedings.

Yet, despite all that, she had a growing feeling of unease that she couldn't quite shake off. She'd tried to analyse it but found no solutions. Something was nagging away at her, preventing her from fully enjoying the day. She wished she could figure out what it was.

Perhaps, though, it was simply that Lewis was in the room. She sneaked a glance at him, and butterflies danced in her stomach. He looked amazing in his tuxedo and bow tie, and she would have happily stared at him even longer than she'd stared at Joe and Charlie. But at the back of her mind was the troubling question. How had Lewis afforded a tuxedo?

Yes, she knew they could be rented, but even so... He hadn't even had the money to buy himself a hot chocolate at The Castle Keep Café in Helmston that day. He'd made lots of excuses, but she'd seen the expression on his face when she'd caught him counting out the change in his hand under the table. He'd not had enough money, and she didn't believe a word he said about it simply being cash that he was short of, and that he could use his debit card if necessary. He'd admitted to having only twenty pence and a button in his wallet and, though she knew he was joking, she wasn't convinced it was far from the truth. She knew the tyres had been an expense he could have done without, and she also realised that he wouldn't get paid again until the end of the month, which meant he'd be pretty much broke all through December.

So how had he spared the money to rent a tux, even if he hadn't bought one?

She felt a prickling of unease, as Jonathan's warning about his strange behaviour with Lulu came back to her. Had she paid for the suit? It didn't really matter if she had—not in itself. But was it a symptom of a much bigger problem? What else was Lulu paying for? How had he persuaded her to part with so much money when she'd not spent a penny on luxuries in all the years Holly had known her? And why had he taken her to see a solicitor?

She bit her lip, feeling troubled. Lewis leaned against a wall, chatting easily to Nell and Riley. She smiled, despite her worries, as she noticed the slight bulge in his cheek and realised he was sucking a pear drop yet again.

He really was lovely, she thought. So kind and gentle. Being around him was a relaxing experience. She never felt pressured or confused when she was with Lewis, and he always made her feel like he was really interested in her and cared about her. But that, she thought, was part of the problem. *Why* was he so nice to her? Why did he want to spend time with someone like her anyway? What was in it for him? She'd often wondered that, and after Jonathan's revelations she was very much afraid that the answer was Lulu. It wasn't her he was interested in at all, but her friend.

She hugged herself, confused and uncertain. Did that even make sense? And was Lewis really that man? Because no matter how much she tried to warn herself to be careful, she couldn't reconcile such devious behaviour with the man who was standing across the room, smiling warmly at her friends and looking so at home and at ease with them that he couldn't possibly be up to no good. How could she even think it?

Out of the corner of her eye she saw Jonathan approaching and switched on a smile, her heart sinking as she noticed the scowl on his face.

'Are you okay?' she asked brightly, even though she knew it was a silly question. His expression told her that he was far from okay.

'Just bin told off by Laurel and Hardy over there,' he muttered, nodding to the doors where the two security men were standing, arms folded, their faces like stone as they watched him. 'All I was doing was trying to talk to a mate on the phone. Talk about paranoid. Like I haven't got better things to do than take photos of this lot.'

'I suppose they just have to be ultra-careful. We did all agree not to take pictures after all.'

'I know that! I'm not stupid. I told you; I was trying to talk to Josh, that's all.'

Josh again! She was beginning to wonder if his relationship with Josh had more depth and commitment than the one he had with her.

She panicked as he lifted his phone.

'Stop it! You can't get that out here,' she snapped. 'Can't you just do as you're told for once?'

He glared at her. 'Are you serious? I want to talk to a mate, and there's no law in the land can stop me.'

'But you know what we agreed!'

'What *you* agreed! I didn't even get asked, and since when do you speak for me?'

'Jonathan, please.'

'Right, mate, that's it. You've had your last warning.'

Jonathan's face was a picture as the mobile phone was snatched from his grasp and shoved in the security man's pocket. 'What the hell do you think you're doing?'

'I told you, not five minutes ago, that you couldn't use your mobile phone in here. What are you, chuffing stupid? You know the situation. Everyone else here is sticking to the rules, so what makes you so special, eh?'

'Who do you think you're talking to? You can't take my phone! I was making a call, that's all.'

'Yeah, and who were you making a call to, eh? *The Whitby Gazette*? *The Sun*? *The Daily* chuffing *Mail*?'

'Don't be so stupid.'

'Stupid, am I? And I suppose Dave over there was stupid, too,' the guard said, jerking his thumb in the direction of his colleague, 'when he spotted you taking photographs of the wedding ceremony earlier?'

Holly paled. 'Oh, Jonathan, please tell me you didn't.'

'Of course I didn't! Why would I take photos of them? I barely know them.'

'There's a whole bunch of people outside this place

who barely know 'em, mate,' the guard said. 'Doesn't stop them standing outside in the snow like loonies for hours, just hoping for a glimpse of them does it? And let's face it, those photos would fetch a few bob wouldn't they?'

'For the last time,' Jonathan snapped, 'I wasn't trying to take photos of them. I was expecting a phone call from my workmate about a job we've got coming in, and I had more important things on my mind than Xander sodding North and his nuptials.'

Holly gave the guard an appeasing smile. 'I'm ever so sorry about this, but I really don't think Jonathan has any interest in taking photographs. By all means keep the phone until the end of the wedding if it will put your mind at rest.'

Jonathan gasped. 'Says who? It's my phone, not yours! I say who keeps it.'

'Actually,' said the guard, 'I say. And thank you, love,' he added, nodding at Holly, 'I'll do that. Enjoy the rest of your evening.'

He smirked at Jonathan and strolled back to join his friend, who was grinning widely as if he was all too aware of what had just taken place.

'I don't believe you did that,' Jonathan snapped. 'How dare you?'

'It's just for a couple of hours,' Holly pleaded. 'What does it matter if it puts everyone's mind at rest?'

'Josh is expecting my call,' he said, sounding petulant. 'No one has the right to take my phone from me. I might sue them.'

It was on the tip of her tongue to tell him to grow

up, but she said nothing, not wanting a scene in the middle of the wedding reception.

'I may as well go and get a drink then,' Jonathan grumbled. 'I'm not standing here on my own like a lemon all night.'

'You're not on your own, you're with me,' she pointed out. 'Or don't I count?'

'I'm always with you,' he snapped. 'But don't you ever think how fed up I get with this?'

'With what?'

He ran a hand through his hair, looking exasperated. 'For God's sake, Holly, you just don't get it do you?'

As his voice increased in volume, Holly glanced around nervously, dreading people's disapproval. 'Shh. Keep it down, for goodness' sake.'

'Oh, that's right. Mustn't upset your precious friends must we? Except they're not your friends are they? And you just don't see it.'

'Please, Jonathan, not here, not now,' she pleaded, as several people turned their heads in his direction.

'Why not here? Why not now? Why do you care so much what they think? They don't give a monkey's about you or your feelings. You know what happens when I go out with my mates? I'll tell you. We all stand together, and we have a laugh. A real laugh. I'm never on my own, never. But what happens when we go out with your so-called friends? We end up stuck by ourselves, just me and you. They drift off and stand apart from us, no doubt gossiping and whispering about you.'

'Please, please be quiet,' she begged him, seeing the

very people he was discussing exchanging worried glances. She had no doubt they'd heard every word. The hum of conversation in the room had disappeared, and she was all too aware that most of the guests—if not all—were now listening to Jonathan's tirade. Even the two security guards were eyeing them with interest.

'Why? In case your friends hear me? You call those friends? Open your eyes, Holly. They don't care about you. They don't even like you. They just use you. You're their entertainment, the butt of their jokes. You're the one in the group who's only there to make the rest of them feel better. Look around you. Can't you see that while they're all together, you're the one on the outside? I told you, no one likes you. All you've got is me, and yet I'm the one you treat like dirt. You run around after them, trying to make them like you, trying to please them, but when it comes to me, forget it. You let me down, you mess me about, you neglect me, yet you can't do enough for your so-called pals who are nothing. *Nothing*.'

Holly tried very hard, but the sob escaped anyway. She was mortified. This was Rachel's and Xander's wedding day and he was doing the very thing she'd most feared. How could he cause a scene on their special day? And how could he say such cruel things to her, in front of everyone? She'd never be able to face them again. She closed her eyes, partly to stop the tears escaping, and partly to shut out the image of so many shocked faces staring at her.

'Holly, it's okay.'

An arm went around her, and she smelt Jo Malone's

Pomegranate Noir, which she knew Riley had bought Nell for her birthday.

She knew because Nell was so thrilled she kept banging on about it and making all her friends sniff her wrist.

Like she knew Anna had a secret crush on David Tennant and had confided in her that one of the things that first drew her to Connor was that he reminded her of him.

She knew Rachel was wearing a locket with her father's picture inside, and that she'd chosen this date for her wedding because it would have been his birthday and she'd wanted him to feel part of it.

She knew Izzy was beside herself with excitement because she'd bought Ash tickets for a West End show he'd wanted to see for ages and couldn't wait to give them to him on Christmas morning.

And she knew that Abbie was secretly having piano lessons as a surprise for music-loving Jackson.

She knew other things too. She knew Anna worried secretly that Gracie would never love Eloise; Nell fretted sometimes that Riley would one day want to return to his family in the Highlands, even though he'd assured her he was completely settled in Bramblewick; that Rachel still had nightmares about her previous marriage to Sam's violent and manipulative father; that Izzy still felt guilty because she knew her parents would love her to have a child, even though neither she nor Ash wanted children; and that Abbie lived with the fear of her breast cancer returning, despite her specialist's optimism and her own medical knowledge.

She knew all these things about her friends because they'd told her. Because, whatever Jonathan said about them, they did make her a part of their lives. They trusted her, included her, confided in her.

If anything, she realised with a sudden shock, it was she who had pushed them away lately. She was the one who didn't tell them what was going in her life, who never revealed her innermost fears. She was the one who had isolated herself, and it was because she was ashamed. She didn't like what she'd become, and she hadn't wanted them to realise how bad things had got. How low she'd sunk.

Jonathan was wrong. Her friends had *always* been there for her. It was she who'd not been there for them. And yet they were still here for her. She opened her eyes and saw them gathered around her, their faces full of concern. Anna held her hand. Rachel's arm was round her waist. Nell's hand was on her back. Izzy's and Abbie's eyes were filled with tears.

And there was Lewis.

'It's all right, Holly. Please don't cry.'

'Oh, and here he is. Prince Blondie strikes again.'

Jonathan's sneering tones snapped Holly back into the present. 'Jonathan, you've said enough. Stop it.'

'Said enough? Said enough? I've barely started. Look at them all, suddenly bothered about you. Amazing. You know, you've never once stuck up for me when they've ignored me, pushed me out. They've always acted like I'm not good enough for them, but then, how can I compete, eh? I'm just a mechanic. I'm not a doctor, or a teacher, or a world-famous actor. Of course they're not going to speak to me. I'm a minion, a peasant. Not good enough for your stuck-up so-called pals.'

'Ooh,' Charlie Hope said loudly, 'someone's got issues.'

'That's not true, Jonathan,' Anna said calmly.

'I think you've got a bit of a chip on your shoulder there, pal,' Riley said coolly.

'I'm just a gardener,' Lewis said. 'They've always been perfectly pleasant to me.'

Jonathan rounded on him furiously. 'But you're not just a gardener, are you? What *is* your story anyway? You, poncing around with your secateurs and your gardening gloves. Who do you think you're kidding? You don't fool me with that posh accent. There's something dodgy about you and I'd like to know what you're up to.'

Lewis raised an eyebrow. 'Up to? I'm not up to anything.'

'No? Really? So, you're not ripping off the old woman and conning her into giving you all her savings then?'

There was a shocked silence, and Holly's heart thudded in terror.

'What are you talking about?' Jackson said at last. 'I don't know where you get these crazy ideas, but Lewis is as honest as the day's long.'

'Absolutely,' Abbie snapped, glaring at Jonathan. 'Keep your vile accusations to yourself.'

'Vile, am I?' Jonathan said, his face purple with rage. 'Crazy ideas are they? Well, ask Holly then. She'll tell you. Took the old bat to York, didn't he? Got her to spend a load of money and then took her to see a solicitor.'

'What if I did?' Lewis said calmly. 'I've done nothing wrong.' He looked steadily at Holly. 'You know that don't you?'

'Why would she know it?' Jonathan demanded furiously. 'What is it with you and her anyway? Always hanging around her, pestering her. Go and get your own girlfriend, pal. She's taken.'

'She's not a possession,' Lewis replied and Holly detected, for the first time, a slight tremor in his voice. 'She's a woman with her own mind, her own thoughts and feelings, and she can make her own decisions, even though you do your level best to make sure she can't.'

'I'm warning you,' Jonathan snapped, 'keep away from her. If I find out you two—'

'Don't you dare!' Now Lewis had raised his voice. It was the first time Holly had ever heard him sound anything other than totally calm and in control. She stared at him in surprise.

'Dare what? Dare accuse you and her of going behind my back? I've seen the way you look at each other, don't think I haven't. Don't treat me like I'm stupid. No one fools me. I see it all. And I've been watching you two. I reckon you've been cheating on me for weeks.'

'Jonathan!' Holly cast pleading glances at her friends. 'I haven't, I really haven't.' She reached for Jonathan's hand. 'How can you say things like that to me? When have I ever—?'

'He's judging you by his standards,' Lewis said coldly.

'What's that supposed to mean?' Jonathan shook Holly's hand away and squared up to his rival. 'You're asking for a punch in the mouth, mate.'

'I'm not your mate,' Lewis said. 'And I mean, just because you're up to goodness knows what behind Holly's back, it doesn't mean she's doing the same to you.'

Holly's mouth fell open. 'What do you mean? What's he been doing?'

'Nothing,' Jonathan snarled. 'It's him, causing trouble, telling lies like he always does.'

'So you deny there's anything between you and that girl from the party?'

Jonathan's eyes widened. 'You—you what? I don't have a clue what you're talking about.'

'Then, after trying to sneak her outside at Abbie's house, it's just a coincidence that I saw her standing outside the café in Helmston that day, glaring at Holly as if she hated her?'

Holly turned to Jonathan. 'Is this true?'

'What girl?' Nell demanded. 'What are you talking about?'

'There was a girl at the party,' Lewis said patiently. 'Gina, I think her name was, and he was talking to her for ages when Holly disappeared.'

'Aye,' Riley murmured. 'I remember that all right.'

'I went outside, and I found Holly there. We were talking and then the door opened, and Jonathan and Gina practically fell outside together. When he saw us, he babbled some excuse about them looking for Holly, and when Holly didn't seem to believe him, he turned the tables on us and accused us of being up to no good. Just like he's doing now.'

'Unbelievable!' Jonathan threw up his hands and looked around at them all. 'Utter rubbish. Are you really listening to this?'

'Holly and I bumped into each other in Helmston and called at The Castle Keep Café for a hot drink. She told me Jonathan was working all day, which was why she'd ended up on her own. Then he barged into the café, having seen us together, and demanded to know what we were doing together. He insisted Holly had got it wrong, and he'd only been working in the morning. While they were arguing, I looked outside and saw Gina standing on the pavement opposite, glaring in at us. When she realised I'd seen her, she couldn't get away fast enough. I'm pretty sure they'd been together, until he saw Holly in the café with me.'

'Blimey,' Charlie gasped, 'this is better than Hollyoaks.'

Joe dug him in the ribs as he, along with everyone else in the room, waited to see what happened next.

'Jonathan?' Holly's voice was faint, and she felt dazed. All her doubts about the phone calls and the supposed overtime came flooding back. Who had he really been trying to ring that day? Was Josh just a code word for Gina?

'It's all rubbish,' Jonathan yelled. 'You're a liar!'

'Right, mate, I think it's time you were leaving.'

The two security guards clasped Jonathan's arms

tightly.

'I'm not a liar,' Lewis said.

'You *are* a liar, and a conman,' Jonathan blurted. 'You've just put this on me, cos you're trying to make them all forget about the money and the solicitor. You're stealing off Lulu. Go on, admit it.'

'I'll do no such thing,' Lewis said. 'It's not true, and you know it.'

'Right, that's enough,' said Dave. 'Time to go.'

'Ask Holly!' Jonathan refused to budge, his eyes fixed on Holly as she stared back at him, horrified. 'Go on, Holls, tell them. You know what he's up to don't you?'

They all turned to look at her and she felt a wave of nausea as Lewis's eyes met hers.

'You know it's not true, don't you?' he said quietly.

She could feel Jonathan's anger and desperation as the security guards tightened their grip on his arms. Everyone was staring at her, waiting for her answer. She couldn't let Jonathan down could she? But she didn't believe Lewis was a thief either.

And yet...

'Holly?' Lewis's voice sounded croaky. There was a puzzled look in his eyes, as if he didn't understand what was taking her so long.

'I—I—' Her legs shook, and her stomach churned. 'I don't know, but... Lewis, how did you afford that tuxedo?'

There was a stunned silence. Lewis stared at her as if he couldn't believe what he'd just heard, and Holly almost crumpled with shame. The minute the words left her mouth she regretted them. She would do anything to take them back, but how could she now? Instead, she gazed at him pleadingly, her eyes begging him to forgive her.

'Exactly!' Jonathan said triumphantly. 'Answer me that one, eh.'

Lewis fastened his jacket, adjusted his bow tie, and turned to Jonathan. 'It belongs if you must know, to my boss, Sir William. He lent it to me. And now that I've answered that question, I think it's time for me to go home.'

He turned to a stunned looking Rachel and Xander and shook their hands. 'Thank you so much for inviting me. Congratulations to you both.'

'Thank you,' they murmured in unison. 'And you're very welcome.'

Holly watched in dumb misery as Lewis nodded farewells at all their friends, then left the room without so much as a glance in her direction.

'Thank God for that,' Jonathan said. 'Good riddance to bad rubbish. Now, can you let go of me?' He shook his arms, but the security guards held on tight.

'Personally,' said Dave, 'I think you've outstayed your welcome. What do you think, Gav?'

'Too chuffing right,' Gav agreed. 'You've been a pain in the proverbial since you got here, and I'm sick of dealing with you, quite frankly. Mind,' he added, nodding at Xander and Rachel, 'it's your day, your call.'

Holly's friends turned to her, their expressions sympathetic but resolved.

'I think,' Xander said firmly, 'that you're both

absolutely right. Time to go, Jonathan. You've done your best to ruin our day, but you're not going to spoil another moment.'

'And we don't believe a word you said about Lewis,' Abbie added.

'The only one who can't be trusted here is you,' Jackson told him.

'His eyes are too close together if you ask me,' Charlie called. He folded his arms knowingly. 'Always a bad sign that. My mother warned me about it.'

'Right, mate, you heard them,' Dave said. 'Let's be having you.'

They marched him towards the door and Nell put her arm around Holly. 'I'm sorry, Holls, but enough is enough.'

'You must see the truth now?' Anna said gently. 'I'm ever so sorry, sweetie.'

Holly didn't know how to respond to any of it. She couldn't think straight. All she knew was, she needed answers. Before they could stop her, she broke away from her friends and ran after Jonathan.

The security guards had led him through a side door to avoid the few straggling fans and solitary reporter that still waited outside the main entrance in the hope of seeing Xander, Joe or Charlie.

'Out you go, chum,' Gav said cheerily. 'Here's your phone back. Don't say we never give you anything.'

'And a very merry Christmas to you,' Dave added.

They began to shut the door after him, halting as Holly hurried up to them.

'Going after him, are you?' Gav said sympathetically.

'Best of luck with that.'

'I'd have let him stew,' Dave admitted. 'Still, it's your call. Hope it all works out for you, love.'

'Thank you,' Holly murmured.

'Merry Christmas,' they chorused, and the door clanged shut behind her.

Holly crunched her way through the snow, shivering with cold, despite the fur stole. She saw the shape of Jonathan ahead of her. He was hunched against the cold, and she could hear him uttering curses as he walked.

She was about to call out to him when her heart almost stopped. Lewis was up ahead. He was quite plain to see, as the light from an upstairs window shone on him, illuminating him against the darkness. He was leaning against a brick wall, and she was shocked to see the puff of smoke that revealed he had a cigarette in his hand. After all this time!

Jonathan had clearly seen him too, as he straightened, and his steps slowed a little. Fearing carnage, Holly tried to walk faster, not easy in the snow with court shoes.

In the still, cold air, the voices carried easily, and she winced as she heard Jonathan say, 'Waiting for my girlfriend, are you? I wouldn't bother. She's seen you for what you are, mate.'

Lewis took a long drag on his cigarette, and it seemed ages before he dignified the remark with a reply. 'Oh? And what's that exactly?'

Jonathan hesitated. He glanced around as if assessing his chances of escape, and his gaze fell on

Holly. Seeing her there seemed to give him courage—or make him more foolish. He folded his arms and stood in front of Lewis, his whole demeanour challenging.

'A dirty, lying thief,' he sneered. 'A conman, a crook, a pathetic loser who can't get his own girlfriend so hangs around mine, like a puppy begging for crumbs from the table. You're a joke, mate. A pitiful joke. And you know what else? You're—'

Holly wasn't sure if she actually heard the thud of Lewis's fist meeting Jonathan's jaw, or if she imagined it. What she knew, for certain, was that Jonathan landed on his back in the snow and lay there, stunned for a few moments, while Lewis stood over him.

'I've been wanting to do that since the day I met you,' he told Jonathan, without a trace of regret in his voice. He glanced up as Holly reached them but said nothing to her.

She fell on her knees in the snow and checked Jonathan's face for injuries. 'Are you okay? Can you talk?'

'He hit me. Did you see? I'll sue him. I'll have him locked up.'

'You're fine,' she told him, relieved.

'Same old Jonathan,' Lewis said, taking another drag of his cigarette.

Holly shook her head, hardly able to believe that he'd held onto it while punching Jonathan. 'What are you doing, smoking?'

'I always carry this,' he told her. 'It's like a challenge to myself. I call it my Trophy Cigarette.'

'And now you've smoked it,' she said mournfully. 'Why?'

'Sometimes,' he said, 'even a pear drop won't cut it.'

'I'm sorry,' she murmured. 'I really am.'

'Forget it.' He turned away. 'I'm going home. Work in the morning. Merry Christmas to you both.'

'Lewis!'

He didn't answer but trudged away into the darkness.

Jonathan struggled to sit up. 'Merry Christmas? I'll give him merry Christmas!'

'Oh, shut up, Jonathan,' Holly said wearily. 'Give me your arm and I'll help you up.'

Though she'd quite like to have left him lying in the snow. He'd got everything he deserved. But really, she thought bleakly, she deserved just as much. How could she have questioned Lewis's integrity like that?

She should have known he was no thief, and the stupid thing was she did know, deep down. Her answer had been born more from not wanting to throw Jonathan to the wolves than from any genuine mistrust in Lewis. Now he would never forgive her, and she'd lost his friendship forever—a friendship, she realised, that meant everything to her.

It may have been Jonathan that Lewis punched but she sensed it was she who had really stirred his anger. He must hate her. She couldn't think of a single way to show him how sorry she was. Oh, Lulu was going to be furious with her!

Chapter 16

'Well, that was an event, wasn't it?'

Holly gritted her teeth as Jonathan flicked the kitchen light on and threw his keys casually on the worktop. 'Fancy a brew?'

How, she wondered, could he be so casual about everything? He'd ruined her friends' wedding day, jeopardized Lewis's reputation, and made a total fool of her in public, yet there he was, talking cheerfully about it all as if it had been some sort of jolly jape and suggesting a cup of tea. Like that would solve anything!

As he sauntered over to the cupboard, she had to use every ounce of self-control not to scream at him. Instead she said coolly, 'How's the jaw?'

He turned around, rubbing his face as if he'd suddenly remembered it hurt. 'Not too bad. Got a punch like a girl, that bloke.'

Not from where she'd been standing, she thought grimly, and if she knew Lewis, she was pretty sure he could have done a heck of a lot worse if he'd chosen to. She wondered what he was doing now. She really hoped he hadn't given in to temptation and bought a packet of cigarettes on his way home. Bad enough that he'd used his Trophy Cigarette. She could only cross her fingers that he was well-stocked with pear drops. She felt guilty enough for practically accusing him of theft in front of everyone; she certainly didn't want to be responsible for him getting some awful lung disease.

'Is it bruised?' Jonathan queried. 'I could go to the police you know. He could spend Christmas behind bars and serve him right.'

'It's not bruised,' she assured him, even though she could see that his jaw was purpling. 'And what good would that do? Don't you think you've done enough?'

'Meaning what?'

She shook her head. 'I'm not here to talk about Lewis,' she said.

His eyes narrowed. 'Oh, so what are you here for? I thought you'd come back 'cos you're my girlfriend. Didn't realise you had an ulterior motive.'

She took a steadying breath. 'I'm amazed you invited me back,' she said bravely.

'What do you mean by that?'

'Well, your flat seems to have been out of bounds to me for ages. Always an excuse, some reason why I can't visit. Feels strange to be here after all these weeks.'

He tutted. 'Don't be soft.'

'So,' she said, mustering all her courage, 'what's really going on with you and this Gina?'

Jonathan groaned. 'For crying out loud, are you joking? You're seriously going to believe Blondie over me?'

'I'm simply asking the question,' she said. 'I want the truth. Is there something between the two of you?'

'What do you think?'

'What I think,' she said slowly, 'is that it's a bit of a coincidence that she was standing outside The Castle Keep Café staring at us on the very day you were supposed to be working all day but then showed up in Helmston.'

Jonathan turned his back to her, opening the cupboard door and taking out a couple of mugs. 'Tea or coffee?'

'I don't want a drink,' she said. 'I just want some answers.'

'Fine, suit yourself.' He shrugged, taking a spoon from the drawer. 'You know, you've only got his word that she was even in Helmston that day. Did you see her? Because I certainly didn't.'

'No,' she admitted. 'I didn't see her.'

'There you go then. He's made it up to cause trouble, that's all, and you fell for it. Told you he was a liar.'

Holly chewed her lip thoughtfully.

Jonathan's face softened. 'Aw, love, don't look so miserable. You know I love you. This is all about your insecurities, that's all. Not surprising, the way people treat you. But you need to understand that I'm not the enemy here. I'm the only one you can really trust, the one who's got your back when other people let you down.' He smiled at her. 'Come here, you.'

Holly went towards him and took the hand he held out to her.

Jonathan pulled her close and kissed her gently. 'Hey, wait 'til you see what I've got you for Christmas,' he said. 'You'll love it.' He glanced at the clock. 'Nearly Christmas Eve already.'

'My favourite day,' she murmured into his shoulder.

He drew back. 'Christmas Eve is your favourite day? Why not Christmas Day? That's the day you get your presents, remember.'

'Christmas Day is inevitably a disappointment. It's all arguments and presents you didn't really want and too much food and bickering over the television and a ridiculous amount of alcohol.'

At least, it was in our house. She couldn't remember a single Christmas Day that had passed peacefully and happily.

'Christmas Eve is much better. There's all that optimism. You can still believe that something wonderful is about to happen, that Christmas Day will be magical and special. It's all in the anticipation. The reality always disappoints.'

'Bloody hell.' Jonathan pulled a face. 'You suck the joy out of everything, you know that?' He shrugged. 'Still, that's you, and I love you anyway.' He gave her a suggestive wink. 'Forget the tea. How about we go into the bedroom and bring Christmas Eve in together?'

She smiled. 'Sounds like a great idea,' she told him. 'After you.'

He leered at her as he grabbed her hand and led her across the hall. Holly took her time, slowly and carefully removing her shoes and unclipping the stole.

'Blimey, don't rush will you?' He was already in bed, his clothes dropped carelessly on the floor.

'This is my bridesmaid's outfit,' she reminded him. 'I have to be careful with it.'

'It's just a dress, Holls,' he pointed out. 'Not like

you're going to be wearing it again, is it?'

'Guess not.' She wrinkled her nose suddenly. 'Not being funny, Jonathan, but aren't you going to have a shower first?'

'I had a shower this morning,' he protested. 'What are you saying?'

'Just that it's been a long and eventful day,' she said. 'Plus, you've been fighting. I shouldn't think you're as fragrant as you could be. It will only take five minutes.'

He scowled at her, clearly not convinced, and she added coyly, 'Who knows? I may even join you in there.'

His face brightened and he leapt out of bed. 'Fair enough. Early Christmas present, eh? Give me two minutes.'

She waited, her heart thumping. She heard the bathroom door open and then the sound of running water. Hardly daring to breathe she hesitated, waiting for the shower door to click shut. As soon as she heard it, she rushed round the bed to where his discarded clothes lay on the floor. Frantically, she rummaged through his trouser pockets and pulled out his mobile phone.

There was no password or pin on it, and she almost gasped out loud in surprise. She'd fully expected it to be harder to get into than a Gringott's vault. She supposed he was so confident she'd never question him that he'd seen no need to protect his privacy. And he'd been right. Until now.

She scrolled frantically through his contacts but there was no Gina listed. There was, however, both a home number and a mobile number listed for Josh, yet when she checked, they were both actually mobile numbers. She strongly suspected that the "home number" for Josh was really Gina's number, and there were certainly plenty of logged calls from it. Strangely enough, however, there wasn't a single text from it, which either meant she was being paranoid, and the number really was a home number which, for some reason, had a remarkable similarity to a mobile number, or, more likely, Jonathan had deleted every single message in that thread.

She pulled a face, wondering what to do. Should she risk calling the number? But if Josh answered she'd feel an idiot, and not only that, but he'd probably tell Jonathan what she'd done and that would cause a real ruction.

As she considered what to do, her gaze fell on the gallery icon and, half dreading what she might discover on there, she tapped it. Her mouth dropped open and she fought down a wave of nausea.

'Oh my god!'

'Are you ready, babe?'

His voice, calling out to her in obvious expectation, made her sick to her stomach.

'You utter creep!'

Jonathan, his hands slippery with shower gel, frantically turned off the shower. 'Eh? What's up with you?'

'This!' She waved the mobile phone in the air, almost breathless with rage.

'What?' He frowned and she saw him desperately

trying to think what incriminating evidence he'd left on there. 'Has she just rung? Look, Holls, it's nothing to do with me. She's obsessed. I keep telling her to get lost but she's not listening. There's nothing between me and her, I swear it.'

Holly stared at him as he stood there, covered in gel, hair dripping wet. She curled her lip in disgust. 'So, you *are* seeing this Gina then.'

'What?' he blinked, bewildered. 'I've just told you—'

'I know what you told me,' she snapped. 'I also know what you're really saying. I'm not as stupid as you think I am.'

'Look, Holls—'

'Forget it,' she said, holding up her hand. 'I honestly don't care anymore, and that's not what I was talking about anyway.'

'Huh? Then what are you banging on about?'

'These.' Her hands were shaking as she scrolled through the photographs. 'The security guards were right all along. You were taking loads of photos of the ceremony. There's even a video of Xander and Rachel cutting the cake! How much were you planning to sell these for, eh?'

He didn't reply. He turned the shower back on and calmly rinsed off the shower gel as if she wasn't even there.

Holly was trembling with rage as she continued to work through all the pictures. How could he be so deceitful? A thought struck her, and she tapped the text icon again. She'd been so busy looking for Gina's messages that it hadn't occurred to her to check anything else, but she soon found the evidence she'd been seeking.

'You told all these people about the wedding! You've texted just about everyone in your contacts list. I'll bet it was you who rang the papers too, wasn't it? Wasn't it?'

He turned off the water and reached for a towel. Wrapping it around his waist, he stepped out of the cubicle and took the phone from her hand. 'Finished?'

'How much?' she whispered. 'How much did they pay you?'

He grinned. 'Not a single penny.'

'I don't believe you!'

'I don't care whether you do or you don't.' He shrugged. 'It's a fact. I didn't ask for any money, and they didn't offer any.'

'Then why? What's in it for you?'

'What do you think?' He gave a shout of laughter. 'It was a pleasure. All I wanted was to wipe the smug smiles from those two self-satisfied gits. Mr and Mrs Perfect with their perfect wedding. Just like the rest of your so-called friends. Looking down their noses at me and thinking they're so much better. You all telling me that I couldn't do this, couldn't do that. Wear a tuxedo, for crying out loud! How pretentious is that? Don't get your phone out. No phone calls. No pictures. Don't tell any of your family or friends about the wedding, or else. Or else what? Who do they think they are, eh? Well, I taught them a lesson, didn't I? Spoilt the day and I'm glad. Whenever they remember this, they'll remember me. Serves them right.'

'Oh, my god.' Her voice cracked as she tried to speak. 'You're horrible. Loathsome. What did I ever see in you? Why didn't I realise what you were really like before this?'

He barged past her into the bedroom, and as she stood there, too shocked to even move, he returned, thrusting her stole and her shoes into her arms. 'There you go. You can clear off now.'

'Wh—what?'

'Get out, go on. Girls like you are ten a penny, love, and to be honest, I've lost interest. I've had my fun but you're just boring me now. Besides, Gina's only ten minutes away and she'll be over the moon when I tell her I've finally dumped you. So go on, get out of my face.'

The hatred in his eyes took her breath away. Feeling like she was in some sort of nightmare, she stumbled out of the flat, flinching as the door slammed behind her.

It was only when she was standing outside in the snow, shivering with cold, that she remembered she had no money on her, and no way of getting home.

Chapter 17

Holly couldn't think what was happening for a moment. Someone stroked her hair and she inwardly cringed, convinced in that split second that she was with Jonathan. Then realisation dawned and her eyes snapped open. She almost cried with relief as Lulu's face came into focus, her wrinkled face smiling gently at her, her eyes warm with sympathy.

'Morning, love. I was going to let you sleep a bit longer, but then I thought maybe you'd get dehydrated, so I've brought you up a cuppa.'

Holly struggled to sit up. 'What time is it?'

'Just gone eleven,' Lulu told her. 'How are you feeling?'

'Like an idiot,' she admitted. 'I'm ever so sorry I woke you up last night. Can't believe I left my bag at the wedding reception.'

'It doesn't matter,' Lulu assured her. 'It's safe, by the way. Abbie rang me this morning to tell me she'd picked it up for you. It's at The Gables and she'll drop it round for you after work.'

'Work!' Holly gasped in horror. 'I'm supposed to be at work today.'

'Not a problem. Connor told me last night that I was

to tell you not to worry, that they'd manage without you for one day, and that you were to rest up today. Mind you,' she added, nudging her gently, 'he said you were to be back sharpish the day after Boxing Day.'

'Poor Connor,' Holly murmured. 'What must he think of me, dragging him away from the wedding to come all the way to Whitby to pick me up?'

'What he thought,' Lulu said firmly, 'was that he'd like to do what Lewis did and give that ex of yours a good thump.' She frowned, suddenly looking anxious. 'I take it he *is* your ex?'

'Oh, he most definitely is,' Holly said with a shudder. 'It's over, Lulu, and there's no going back.'

There really wasn't either. As if being abandoned with no money and not even a coat, miles from home wasn't bad enough, the shame of having to ring Anna for help would stay with her forever. She'd left her mobile in her bag, and Anna's was the only number she could remember. She'd had to find a phone box, reverse charges... she must remember to ask Anna what the call had cost her and thank her for accepting it. She didn't know what she'd have done if her friend had refused.

Connor had been brilliant, arriving in an incredibly short time, given the weather, which proved he'd left the wedding immediately to collect her. He even had a blanket in the boot of his car, which he wrapped around her as he settled her in the back seat.

'I always carry an emergency winter survival kit,' he explained. 'You never know round here, especially with this sort of weather. This is the first time I've had to use it though. Now, you try to get some sleep while I drive us home.'

He was so kind, and Holly couldn't thank him enough, nor could she apologise any more than she did.

'Honestly, don't worry. We were about ready to leave anyway. Xander and Rachel left just after you to go to their hotel, and we're all pretty exhausted. Even Charlie Hope has stopped making jokes. He was falling asleep at the table and nearly ended up with his head in a tiramisu.'

Holly appreciated his attempts to lift her spirits, but she couldn't smile. She had to tell him the truth about Jonathan and the photographs, and why Xander's and Rachel's secret wedding had been ruined.

'They're going to hate me,' she said miserably. 'And I can't blame them.'

'Honestly, Holly, they don't hate you. They're not fond of Jonathan, I'll tell you that much, but if you want the truth none of us are. We've been praying you'd see the light for months. We've been so worried about you. He's just not a good person, simple as that.'

'I know that now,' she replied quietly. 'But I'm going to have to confess to them aren't I? They need to know how their secret was blown.'

Connor tapped his fingers on the steering wheel, seeming to consider. Eventually, he sighed. 'No need to tell them, Holls. They already know. We all do.'

She gripped the blanket, confused. 'What? But how?'

'It wasn't difficult to work it out. When we arrived at the Hall Jonathan turned up around the same time, and a couple of the people waiting outside called to him by name. He obviously knew them, but he tried very hard to pretend he didn't. Couldn't get inside fast enough. And then there was all that business with the phone. The security guards tipped Xander off that he'd been filming and taking pics. They wanted to smash his phone, but Xander told them to leave it. He said it wasn't worth it. So you see, none of this will be news to them and you really shouldn't worry. They're far more concerned about you.'

She'd swallowed hard, unable to find the words to reply, and had spent the rest of the journey staring out of the window at the swirling snowflakes, wondering what she'd done to deserve such amazing friends.

Connor had parked outside Cuckoo Nest Cottage and led her carefully to the front door, which was when she'd remembered that she didn't have her bag, which meant she didn't have her key either. Reluctantly she'd had to ring the bell until Lulu slowly made her way to the door to let her in. Poor Lulu's face had been a picture when she saw Holly standing there, wrapped in a blanket, while Connor ushered her inside, murmuring to Lulu that he'd explain in a minute.

Lulu had insisted that Holly go straight to bed, and Holly had been too exhausted to argue. Yet lying in bed, she found herself unable to sleep. Everything that had happened that day replayed itself in her brain, and she cringed at the memory of how badly she'd treated Lewis, and how gullible she'd been over Jonathan.

She could hardly believe that, after the disgusting way he'd behaved at her friends' wedding, he'd honestly thought that she would forgive him so easily and would be willing to spend the night with him. How little he thought of her. How little respect he had for her. She remembered him leading her to his bedroom, a smirk on his lips. He'd had no doubt that she was his for the taking she realised.

And then it had hit her.

The bedroom!

It was exactly as it was the last time she'd been in there, and yet hadn't he insisted that he'd redecorated it especially for her when she'd agreed to move in with him? She was certain he'd said that, because she'd felt so guilty that he'd spent all that time and money doing something he hated for her benefit. He'd lied! And if he'd lied about that, what else had he lied about?

It was at that moment that Holly had opened the door of her bedside cabinet and reached for the diary. While downstairs Connor was no doubt filling Lulu in on the events of the day, Holly carefully read the words she'd written, day after day, but had never dared look back on. Her eyes filled with tears, and she blinked them away, desperate to read to the end, determined to absorb every painful sentence, even though it meant reliving the arguments, the sarcasm, the cruel put-downs and the endless confusion. And as she read, the fog began to lift, the confusion evaporated, and Holly at last began to understand just what had been happening to her for the last eighteen months or so.

He wasn't her boyfriend. He was her abuser.

And Lewis had known, had understood, had tried to get her to see the truth. Why else would he tell her to keep a diary? Except, he hadn't told her. He'd asked her. He had far too much respect for her to ever demand anything from her, she knew that for sure.

Holly put the diary back in the bedside cabinet, turned out the light, and pulled the duvet up to her chin. As she stared up at the darkness, she heard the front door open and close, then the sound of a car driving away. Slow footsteps on the stairs, then the creaking of her bedroom door. She lay quite still, hoping Lulu wouldn't switch on the light. The door closed again, and Lulu shuffled off to her own room. As the door closed, Holly finally allowed the tears to fall, and they kept on falling until she fell asleep, utterly exhausted.

'You'll be all right, you know,' Lulu told her now, handing her the mug of tea. 'You're better off without him, trust me. Aw, love, don't cry. It will be all right. He was no good, no good at all. I'd wring his bloody neck if I could get me hands on him. He's not worth the tears.'

'I'm not crying for him,' Holly sniffed. 'How am I ever going to face people, Lulu?'

'There's no need to worry about that,' Lulu promised her. 'They're your friends. They're just going to be as delighted as I am that you've finally seen the light and that lowlife is out of your life at last.'

'But Lewis,' Holly whispered. 'What about Lewis? How will he ever forgive me?'

'Aye, well.' Lulu adjusted the duvet and sighed. 'That's a bit trickier, I'll grant you. What possessed you, love? How could you think that lovely lad would take my money?'

'I didn't,' Holly admitted. 'Not really. I just—Jonathan said—'

'I don't care what Jonathan said,' Lulu said. 'That lad's shown me nothing but kindness. And how the heck do you think he's pinched me money, when I never had any money to pinch? I'm sorry to disillusion you, love, but a state pension's hardly worth trying to fleece me for, and I've no other income, that's the truth.'

'But all the things you bought in York?' Holly rubbed her forehead, confused. 'Surely they can't all be from a grant? And besides, it takes ages to apply for things like that, and for the money to come through. It doesn't make sense.'

'It wasn't from a grant,' Lulu said flatly.

'What? But you said—'

Lulu shook her head. 'No, I didn't. What I said was, there are grants for them sort of things, and that's true. I never said that's how I'd got them. You joined the dots there. Mind you, I didn't correct you, I'll admit that much.'

'Lulu! How sneaky.' Holly sipped her tea thoughtfully. 'But the solicitor? What was that about? Did it have anything to do with Lewis at all?'

Lulu eyed her for a moment, then blinked away tears.

Holly put the cup down and reached for her in alarm. 'Lulu, what is it? I'm sorry. I didn't mean to upset you, really I didn't.'

'Oh, I know that, love. Like a granddaughter to me,

as I've always said. You'd never do owt to upset me on purpose, like I'd never do owt to upset you. You're all I've got, Holly. All I've ever had since my John died, and you know how much I love you, don't you?'

'Of course I do. I love you, too.' Holly was almost too afraid to ask. 'Is something wrong? Something you're not telling me? You're not—'

Lulu smiled through her tears. 'I'm not ill, if that's what you're worried about. Just me arthritis and me fat legs as usual. Nothing new. But one day, love, well... the fact is, I'm not getting any younger, and that's why I asked Lewis to take me to see the solicitor. You see, I had to make sure. I had to know that, when I'm gone, you're going to be all right, and that Cuckoo Nest Cottage will be looked after. So what could make more sense than leaving you the old place in me will?'

Holly couldn't speak for a moment. She simply stared at Lulu, stunned.

'Don't swallow too much air,' Lulu advised her. 'You'll get hiccups.'

'I can't accept that!' Holly gasped. 'Lulu, it's too much.'

'Don't be so daft,' Lulu said, waving a hand dismissively. 'It makes sense. What would happen to this place if you didn't take care of it, eh? And who else am I going to leave it to? I'll tell you what, Holly, I've slept a lot sounder in me bed at night, knowing that you're both going to have each other when I'm gone. And the fact is, you belong here. You're another little cuckoo, just like John's granny. This cottage is your home. Maybe it's more yours than it ever was mine.

Any road, I'll hear no more about it. The will's done and signed and witnessed, and that's final.'

Holly put her arms around Lulu and hugged her. 'I just don't know what to say. Thank you so much. I don't know what I'd have done without you all these years.'

'The feeling's mutual,' Lulu assured her. 'Now then,' she added, as she pulled away and wiped her eyes with the sleeve of her cardigan, 'I know what you're dying to ask me next.'

Holly blew out her cheeks. 'I kind of do, but it seems really cheeky, especially now.'

'Go for it,' Lulu dared her.

Holly couldn't help but laugh. 'All right if you insist. Where *did* you get the money from, if you have no money and you didn't get a grant?'

Lulu nibbled her thumb nail. 'Well the thing is, I did promise I wouldn't say owt.' She tutted suddenly. 'Ah, well, what does it matter now? And I reckon you need to know, seeing as you're flinging accusations all over the place. It was Lewis. He gave me the money. Every penny.'

Holly was thoroughly confused. 'What? But how? He's broke.'

'He transferred it all from his bank account to mine, love. Thousands of pounds. I argued, believe me, but he wouldn't take no for an answer. And when he explained it all, I understood, I really did. You know me. I'm not one for accepting charity, but the way he told it, it was like I was doing him a favour.'

'I don't understand.'

'No, well.' Lulu looked uncomfortable. 'Fact is, I don't think it's my place to tell you. I think that's his right, don't you? And I think he's earned it.'

'I suppose you're right,' Holly acknowledged. 'The problem is, I doubt very much that he's even talking to me, and how can I blame him?'

'I reckon,' said Lulu, 'there's only one way to find out. Why don't you finish that tea, then get yourself showered and changed? Lewis is at work today, but he's finishing at one, with it being Christmas Eve. You should go and see him. Talk things over.'

'Tell him I'm sorry.'

'Aye, that an' all. He's never struck me as a spiteful lad, nor a stubborn one. If you're genuinely sorry, I reckon he'll forgive you. What do you think?'

Holly paused, but she couldn't deny what her heart was telling her. Lulu was right. Lewis would listen to her, and he would accept her apology, she was sure of it.

'I think you're right,' she said, reaching for the tea as her stomach fluttered with a mixture of nerves and excitement. 'I'll go and find him this afternoon. It's the very least I can do.'

Lulu put her hand on Holly's arm, stopping her from drinking. 'Lewis is a good man,' she told her. 'I know it's early days but, well, maybe one day there'll be two of you in the nest, eh?'

Holly's face heated up and she hardly knew what to say to that. 'Who knows?' was the best she could manage in the end.

It was a crazy dream on Lulu's part, and Holly

understood why her friend would want to see things tied up neatly with a shiny bow. But real life wasn't like that, and she'd hardly endeared herself to Lewis with her recent behaviour. Even if he forgave her, there was certainly no guarantee that he'd even see her as a friend again, never mind anything else.

She couldn't deny that the thought of living here in Cuckoo Nest Cottage, as part of a couple with Lewis was enough to make her heart leap in joy, even if reality did push it firmly back in place within seconds. But she had to be realistic. There was no place for fantasy and wishful thinking in her life. Not anymore.

***

Freshly showered, hair dried and makeup carefully applied, Holly spent a great deal longer than was strictly necessary choosing what to wear.

'Oh, for goodness' sake,' she said in the end, exasperated. 'What does it matter? You're going to be wearing a coat anyway.'

She peered out of the bedroom window and shivered at the thought of stepping outside. The snow was falling fast again and showed no signs of stopping. 'And a hat, and a scarf, and gloves,' she added. Not exactly sexy, but then, she wasn't trying to attract him was she? She was simply going to ask him to forgive her, so what difference did it make whatever she chose to wear?

She smiled as two young children raced over the bridge, heading towards the village. They hurled snowballs at each other as their mother followed on behind, pushing a buggy. No doubt she was heading to the shops to make some last-minute purchases. Maybe she'd ordered one of Nell's pork pies, or a Christmas cake. She and Lulu had collected theirs a couple of days ago and they were all ready for the big day, Lulu's online shop having been delivered a few days before.

'Christmas Eve,' she murmured, shaking her head slightly. 'My favourite day of the year.'

Would it still be her favourite day by the time night fell, she wondered. It all depended on Lewis really. She sighed and pulled a camel-coloured sweater and a pair of brown leggings from the wardrobe. She had a pair of brown knee-length boots that would go well with them, and would keep out the snow, too. 'That'll do,' she said firmly. 'It's not a fashion show.'

It was funny, really, how much depended on this meeting. She'd texted all her friends as soon as she got out of the shower to apologise to them all for everything that had happened, and especially to Xander and Rachel. Without exception they'd all replied, assuring her that she had nothing to be sorry for, that they loved her, and that they wished her a very merry Christmas.

Each couple had promised her that, if she felt like dropping in any time over Christmas, she would be very welcome. Well, not Izzy and Ash nor Xander and Rachel, but only because they'd all flown off on honeymoon: the first couple to Spain, and the second to a secret destination that even Rachel knew nothing about. Holly was quite relieved about that. At least there was no way that Jonathan could spoil that for them. She was so lucky to have such understanding and loyal friends.

But Lewis—well, she wasn't so certain of the outcome. Oh, she knew he would forgive her, at least on the surface, and she was positive that he'd be very kind and understanding and say all the right things. But that meant nothing if he didn't really believe her, if he didn't really forgive her, deep down in his soul. He'd told her before that he didn't lie and he didn't play games, yet she'd thrown that promise back at him as if his words meant nothing. She cursed herself for her own stupidity. All because, for that moment, she'd actually taken pity on Jonathan. Of all people!

No use worrying about that now. She pulled on her clothes, pulled a comb through her hair, and double-checked that her mascara wasn't smudged and that she didn't have lipstick on her teeth, then she ran downstairs, sniffing the air with appreciation as she did so.

'Oh my goodness, that smells absolutely gorgeous!'

Lulu was standing by the cooker, and she beamed in delight. 'I know. Thought I'd cook the turkey today to save us all the palaver tomorrow.'

'I told you I'd cook the turkey,' Holly said.

'Oh, I know you did, but you're doing everything else,' Lulu said. 'I just wanted to be able to say I've done something, at least. I've just basted it but it's not due out for another hour and a half. Do you think you'll be back by then? Only it's a bit heavy you see.'

'I'll be back,' she promised. 'Don't even try to lift it

out of the oven.'

'I'll hold you to that,' Lulu said. As Holly fastened her coat, she looked at her hopefully. 'Are you going to ask him for Christmas dinner?'

'Heck, Lulu, I don't even know if he'll be speaking to me yet,' Holly said.

'Oh, there's no worries about that,' Lulu assured her. 'I've got a feeling in me water. He's another cuckoo, you see. You two belong in this nest together.'

Holly shook her head, baffled. Sometimes Lulu had the strangest ideas. As if Lewis was a cuckoo!

'Right, wish me luck,' she called, heading towards the door.

'Luck,' Lulu called. 'But I'm telling you now, you won't need it.'

Holly rolled her eyes, but her fingers were tightly crossed as she left Cuckoo Nest Cottage and headed towards the village. There was a For Sale sign outside her old home, and she wondered fleetingly who would buy it. A new neighbour. Would it feel strange, having someone live in the house she'd grown up in? She realised that it made no difference to her. That house meant nothing. Cuckoo Nest Cottage was home.

She crunched through the snow, which was ankle deep in parts, glad that she was wearing knee-high boots. She dug her hands in her coat pockets, surprised and delighted to discover her gloves. She'd been looking for those for ten minutes. She pulled them on and plodded onwards, hoping that Lewis had gone straight home and hadn't decided to go into town. The snow made everything seem eerily silent, and the only sound that she could hear was her own breathing.

As she neared the main street though, voices reached her, floating on the cold air. Children squealing with delight as they jumped up and down in the snow; a dog barking as he tried to fathom what this strange white substance was that kept landing on his nose; frazzled parents lugging bags of shopping, calling greetings to one another as they passed, collars turned up, faces pink with cold.

Spill the Beans was heaving, which didn't surprise her. It was always busy at this time of year, and Christmas Eve was probably Nell's busiest day of all. So many people out shopping, popping in for a hot drink and a toasted teacake to warm them up. Many people had placed orders for Christmas fare and would be collecting them that day. Others would simply have succumbed to the lure of the delicious displays in the window, unable to resist the pull of a chocolate yule log or a tray full of mince pies.

The café door opened, and Holly glanced in as a middle-aged couple stepped out, heavy bags of shopping clearly weighing them down. She smiled at them, then stopped dead as, behind them, she caught a glimpse of Lewis. He was sitting at one of the tables and he wasn't alone. Opposite him, a young attractive woman was smiling warmly at him. Her hand reached out and squeezed his arm and then... the door swung shut and Holly could have yelped in frustration. What now?

She crept over to the window and pressed her nose against the glass, hoping it didn't get stuck with the bitter cold. She squinted into the café, trying to make out just what Lewis and the mystery woman were up to. They'd looked very close.

'Holls?' The door, she realised with a start, had swung open again, and she groaned inwardly as Nell called to her. 'Thought it was you. What are you doing staring in like The Little Match Girl? Come in, have a drink.'

'I, er, no thanks.' Holly began to back away.

Nell let the door swing shut and hurried over to her. 'It's okay, Holls. Yesterday's forgotten. None of us blame you, you do know that?'

'I know,' Holly said, casting nervous glances through the window.

'We love you,' Nell said, hugging her. 'We couldn't believe that pig left you stranded in Whitby like that, although why we were surprised I don't know. Anyway, enough about him. He's in the past, thank heavens. Come in and have a coffee, eh? Gingerbread latte? You love those.'

'Honestly, I can't.' Holly shook her head desperately and tried to see if she could catch a glimpse of Lewis again, but he remained frustratingly out of sight.

Nell looked bewildered and peered through the window over Holly's shoulder. 'What are you—oh!' She gave her an understanding smile. 'Yeah, he's in there. I get it.'

'I was on my way to his flat. I owe him a huge apology,' Holly told her. 'But he seems to be with someone. Some woman.'

'Yes, they've been there about half an hour,' Nell

told her. 'Although I think they'll be leaving soon. They've finished their drinks and they're just hogging the table now.' She tutted. 'I should tell them to shift really, we're so busy. Too soft, that's me.' She winked and Holly couldn't help but ask.

'Do you know who she is? Have you seen her before?'

Nell's lips twitched with amusement. 'Should I have seen her before? And no, I don't know who she is. Although,' she added thoughtfully, 'I'm pretty sure I heard him call her Tanya.'

'Tanya!'

'Yes, should I know her?'

'No, no.' Tanya! Lewis's florist friend. The one who'd made her bouquet for her, the day she moved in.

'Are you sure you don't want to come in?' Nell urged her, shivering. 'It's flipping freezing out here.'

'No, honestly. I'm going to head back home.'

'But don't you want to see Lewis? I thought you came here to apologise to him.'

'I will. Another time.'

Nell sighed. 'Okay, Holls, whatever you say.' She leaned forward and kissed her on the cheek. 'Merry Christmas. Love you lots.'

'Love you, too, Nell. Give my love to Riley and give Baby Aidan a big kiss from me. Merry Christmas.'

As Nell pushed open the café door, Holly turned and began to trudge, as fast as she could manage, back towards Cuckoo Nest Cottage. Her thoughts wouldn't be stilled, as much as she tried to suppress them. A gnawing fear that Tanya was important to Lewis made her impatient with herself.

So what if she was? What difference would it make in the long run? It wasn't as if she herself had any sort of future with him, was it? Especially not after yesterday and her monumental blunder. And she couldn't even blame him if he was engaged or something. He'd never said he wasn't. He'd never commented on his private life at all. And she'd been so obsessed with Jonathan and her own stupid, pathetic life, that she hadn't even bothered to ask. Said it all really.

Her breath came out in clouds, and she felt like a dragon, snorting smoke into the atmosphere. But that image just made her remember Lewis's attempts to control his nicotine craving with pear drops, and how her cruelty had made him turn to cigarettes after all that time being strong. Just another thing he could blame her for, she supposed.

She wondered if he was ranting about her to Tanya. Tanya! That name conjured up someone very glamorous and confident. All false nails and lip gloss. Though she was a florist, wasn't she? And that didn't really fit with that image. *Oh, for goodness sake, Holly, just give it a rest. None of it matters!*

She saw Cuckoo Nest Cottage ahead and wasn't sure whether to feel relieved or depressed. She'd be glad to get into the warmth, but how was she going to tell Lulu that she'd bottled it? And what if Lulu insisted she go back and speak to him, even in front of this Tanya woman? Lulu wasn't cruel, but she could be very stubborn, and if she thought she knew what was best for Holly...

'My God, you can shift when you want to.'

Holly spun round, her legs weakening with shock as she saw Lewis, struggling through the snow behind her. His ears were pink with the cold and the tip of his nose was practically glowing like Rudolph's. She almost pointed that out to him but decided against it on balance. She'd done enough damage.

'What are you doing here?' she asked breathlessly.

'Chasing you. I thought I'd catch you up ages ago, but you really know how to cut through snow don't you? Are you in training?'

'How did you know?'

'Nell told me. She said you were looking for me to apologise but then you saw Tanya and chickened out.'

'She didn't!' Holly's face grew so hot that she was surprised the snow around her didn't melt. 'Well, this is embarrassing.'

He finally reached her and stopped, taking a few deep breaths then coughing.

'That's because of the smoking,' she reproached him.

'I had one cigarette,' he protested. 'Not even that, really. More like half. It's the cold air, that's all. It's nearly killed me getting here so fast.'

A tiny hope flickered, like a candle flame spluttering in a draught. 'What's your hurry?' she asked, trying to sound nonchalant. If he needed to ask her about Lulu or something like that it would crush her.

'Well,' he said, cupping his hands and blowing on them to warm them, 'what do you think?'

She kicked at the snow, not sure what to think or say.

He waited a moment then sighed. 'Come on,' he said, and linked his arm through hers.

They walked in silence, and he led her onto the bridge just past the cottage. Lewis let go of her arm and leaned on the railings, seeming not to notice or care that his arms were now deep in snow.

'I still haven't heard your apology,' he pointed out eventually, just as the silence grew deafening.

Holly supposed she deserved that. 'I'm sorry,' she said, her voice low with regret. 'Really I am. I should never have doubted you or asked you that stupid question in front of everybody. I don't know why I did. I'm an idiot.'

'You're not an idiot,' he said. He straightened and turned to her, brushing the snow from his sleeves. 'It's really important to me that you understand though, Holly. I'm not a liar. I told you that. And I don't play games. I can't abide them. I've had a lifetime of it, and I can't take any more. I live my life now in the most straightforward and honest way possible. It's the only way to be happy, trust me.'

'I know that,' she said. 'I've always known that. I even knew it yesterday when I said what I said. It was just a stupid, misguided sense of loyalty to a man who didn't deserve it.'

Lewis blew out his cheeks and gazed over her head into the distance.

'Is it over?' he asked at last.

'It's soooo over,' she assured him. 'I read the diary

last night. We went back to his flat, you see, and I managed to get hold of his phone. It was him who tipped off the press and a load of his mates about the wedding, but I believe you all knew that anyway.'

He nodded. 'Now that you mention it.'

'So I confronted him and, well, basically he told me how little I meant to him, then chucked me out on the street. Connor had to collect me. Embarrassing.'

'He left you all alone in the dark, in Whitby?' Lewis's voice was harsh with an emotion she wasn't certain of. Was it anger, or was he really that upset for her?

'Yeah he did. I didn't even have a coat or my purse. What a gentleman, eh? Oh, and you were right about Gina too. He confessed, or as good as.'

'I'm sorry. I really am.'

'I'm not. I needed to hear it. Anyway, when Connor dropped me home, it suddenly occurred to me that he hadn't decorated the bedroom after all. He'd made such a big deal about doing it as a favour to me because I'd promised to move in with him, and it was all a lie. I knew then that I hadn't promised any such thing and that I had to be sure what else he'd been lying about. That's when I read the diary.'

'And knew for sure?'

Holly nodded, appalled to find hot tears suddenly spilling down her cheeks. 'I don't know why I'm crying,' she said as Lewis gently wiped them away. 'I know what he is now, and I know it was all a lie. I understand. I get it. He doesn't deserve any tears.'

'You've had a huge shock,' Lewis told her. 'It's going to take you some time to come to terms with it all.' He hesitated, as if unsure whether to voice his thoughts.

'What is it?'

'I don't want to alarm you, but you have to know that Jonathan won't just let you go as easily as this.'

'What do you mean? He's the one who threw me out, remember? And he's got Gina now.'

Lewis shook his head slightly, a rueful smile on his lips. 'It doesn't work like that. He'll expect you to beg him for another chance. When that doesn't happen, his ego won't allow it. He'll do everything he can to get you back under his control. He'll be charming, contrite. He'll make you a thousand promises with no real intention of keeping them. He'll tell you everything you've longed to hear for so long. You need to be prepared for that.'

'But it's too late. I don't want him back, and I won't fall for that again. I can see it now—the games he played, the way he manipulated and lied to me. I don't want to go back to that, ever. Why would I?'

'I just thought you should be aware of what's coming our way,' Lewis told her gently.

'*Our* way?'

'I've got your back,' he told her, squeezing her hand.

Holly sniffed and peered up at him. 'I know it,' she murmured. 'But, Lewis, how do you know so much about all this? You seem to get it so easily, and you knew about keeping the diary, which was so useful in the end. I just wish I'd read it earlier,' she admitted.

'You read it when you were ready for it,' he said, digging his hands in his pockets. 'At least you wrote everything down. I wish my mother had done.'

'Your mother?' Holly shivered. 'You mean—your father...'

'Was just like Jonathan,' he finished for her. 'Oh, he was a more subtle, sophisticated version, but in essence they were the same. That's why I couldn't stand it, seeing him do to you what my father did to my mum. He broke her, you see. Destroyed her. She was still completely in his power when she died.'

'Oh, Lewis, I'm so sorry.'

'He did it to me too,' he continued, not looking at her. 'All through my childhood he spun his web, trapping me there like a helpless fly. It took me years to figure out what was happening, and I might never have done it if it hadn't been for Tanya.'

'Tanya?' Holly ignored the twinge of jealousy. There were bigger things at stake here.

'We were at college together,' he explained. 'You see, I always loved gardening. I think it was because Mum loved it too, and I only ever really saw her happy when she was out there in our garden, planting and digging. I associated it with joy and freedom. Dad had no interest in it and never bothered us. We could be alone out there, pretend everything was normal and okay. Even have a laugh sometimes. Long before I left school, I'd made up my mind that gardening was my future.'

'I see,' Holly said. 'So you enrolled at horticultural college.'

'Eventually. I had quite a difficult time persuading my father of course. He wanted me to be like him, go into finance. Live his sort of life: a flat in London, a house in Surrey, the little wife waiting patiently at home to be patted on the head at weekends, obeying every command. I told him I'd rather die, and I meant it. It was the first time I'd really stood up to him and I think we were both a bit shocked. Neither of us knew what to do with that turn of events.' He managed a brief smile.

'Anyway, Dad finally realised I wasn't going to budge, and I enrolled at the college. That's when I met Tanya, and we became great friends. College could have been a fun time, but...' He broke off and shook his head.

'But what?' Holly asked gently.

'Mum got ill. Seriously ill. Dad used her illness to apply pressure on me to quit. Told me I was making her worse with all the stress. I didn't know what to do. Tanya listened. She heard it all—everything I'd been through as a kid, the way he spoke to me, the way he twisted everything I said, made me feel bad, inadequate. She got it. She understood the way he'd made me feel, and she even knew the name for it. Gaslighting. She brought me books that detailed what happened in such cases. It was like reading about my life—about my mum's life. Suddenly everything began to make sense. I can't even begin to tell you how it felt.'

Holly trembled. 'I don't think you have to,' she said.

Lewis reached out a hand and touched the side of her face for a moment. 'Sorry,' he said. 'Of course you'd understand.'

'So, did you confront him?' Holly asked anxiously.

He hesitated then shook his head.

'Why not?'

'Are you going to confront Jonathan?'

Holly shook her head. 'No way.'

'Why not?' He threw her question back at her, but he did it gently.

Holly considered. 'I suppose because I think it's pointless. He'd just dismiss everything I said, twist it around to make me sound mad, and I'd end up confused and unsure again. I suppose I'm scared of him. Of his power. And there's a part of me that doesn't want him to have the satisfaction of knowing how he's made me feel.'

'Same,' Lewis said briefly. 'And yes, it does make me feel ashamed sometimes, because I think I should be stronger, but then I know, deep down, that my own sanity and mental health is more important than my pride. I won't put myself in harm's way any longer. It's about staying safe at the end of the day.'

'And your mum?'

'I tried to tell her, but she was too upset. She wouldn't have it, and she wasn't well enough to pursue the matter. The one thing she did insist on, though, was that I didn't quit my course. Whatever he said, however he tried to make me feel like I was letting her down, I knew he was lying. Mum really wanted me to be a gardener. She knew I'd find peace through it, and she was right. I think she'd be pleased and proud of me now, and that keeps me going.'

'I'm sure you're right,' Holly said. 'So, do you have anything to do with your dad?'

'Not really. Not since Mum's funeral, which doesn't make me popular with the more distant relatives, but tough luck. Of course, Dad wasn't prepared to let go that easily. He was convinced I'd fail at gardening and would come begging for a leg up the corporate ladder. He didn't attend graduation, but he did visit me at the flat in Staithes once. Poured scorn on it, of course. Called it a hovel. Needless to say, he'd completely missed the point that I'd moved as far away from him as I could manage. He was too busy telling me how I'd failed, and Mum would be ashamed. He insisted I couldn't manage on my pathetic earnings, but I told him I didn't need his help.'

'I'm sorry. It must have been awful.'

'It was almost funny. By then, I was much more clued up on the way he operated. He started sending me money. Three thousand pounds every month, like clockwork, straight into my bank account.'

Holly gasped. 'You're kidding!'

'Nope. I sent it back to him. He returned it. I sent it back again. This happened four times. Then I thought, okay, you want me to accept this money, I'll accept it, and I'll make damn good use of it.'

Holly frowned. 'How do you mean?'

'Every quarter, I donate the whole lot to a different charity. Dad's hard-earned cash has supported women's refuges, abused children, animal shelters, a local hospice... you name it. He'd be furious if he knew.'

'You mean, you've never kept a penny for yourself?'

'Not a penny. I'd honestly rather starve. Luckily, it's never got that bad.' He grinned at her. 'I set up another bank account for my own earnings and outgoings. The old one is purely for Dad's money, and I never dip into it. I'm sure you can guess now where Lulu's stair lift and all the other stuff came from.'

'Oh gosh!' Holly clapped her hand over her mouth, then began to laugh. 'I get it.'

'Yeah, Dad paid for everything. He'd be delighted. Not.' He shrugged. 'He gets to feel good, thinking he's still got power over me, and I get a whole wad of bank statements that I can hurl back at him if he ever starts trying to threaten or manipulate me because of his so-called generosity.'

'You think he will?'

'One day, probably. *Do this or you won't get another penny*, that sort of thing. He'll be feeling quite secure in the knowledge that he's making me increasingly dependent on him, you see. He's going to get quite a shock if he ever plays that card.'

'So, it's sort of an insurance policy? Not spending the money I mean.'

'I suppose so partly. But it's a great feeling, too, knowing that money's doing so much good. And I love it if I hear about someone who really needs a helping hand, and I think to myself, *okay, I know where that money's going next quarter*.' He smiled softly. 'You should have seen Lulu's face. She argued for ages at first, until I explained everything. Once she understood why I wouldn't keep the money anyway, she softened. Especially when I pointed out that, by letting me pay for it all, she was freeing up much-needed funds that would have been used in a grant for her, that could go to someone else, someone who had no other means of getting the help they needed. After that she saw it as her duty to agree. Plus, of course, I did happen to mention that it would make life a whole lot easier for you too.'

'I wondered how you'd talked her into it,' Holly said admiringly.

'I had to do something,' he explained. 'It would break her if she had to go into a nursing home. Cuckoo Nest Cottage is where her heart is. I had to make sure she could stay there in comfort for the rest of her days.'

'Lulu was right about you,' Holly said. 'You really are a good man. I have an invitation for you, by the way. She asked me to invite you for Christmas dinner tomorrow. What do you say?'

He leaned against the railings of the bridge, his back to the water. 'I don't know,' he admitted. 'What do you think?'

'Me?' Holly kicked at the snow, feeling awkward. 'I'd quite like you to come, obviously, but if you have other plans... I mean, Tanya or someone.'

Her eyes met his and she saw the twinkle and relaxed.

'Tanya and I are just friends,' he said. 'We met up today because her husband's here for a job interview. He's a vet, and the local surgery is looking for someone to join the practice. Tanya drove here with him, and we arranged to meet for a coffee while she waited for him.'

'I'm sorry,' Holly said. 'I didn't mean to imply—'

He suddenly took hold of her hand and held it tightly. 'Like I said, I don't lie, and I don't play games. I'm young, free, and single. Well, free and single anyway.'

'Me, too,' she said softly.

He stroked her fingers, then with a muffled exclamation that she didn't quite catch, he pulled her to him and kissed her.

'You know I said I'd wanted to punch Jonathan since the moment I first saw him?'

She nodded, her heart pounding as he twisted a strand of her hair between his fingers and gazed at her with such passion that she felt quite faint.

'Well, I've wanted to kiss you from the moment I met you,' he confessed. 'It feels like forever, and I thought the day would never come.'

'And was it worth the wait?' she asked, knowing his answer already.

'Totally,' he confirmed. 'Although, I should really try it again, just to make sure.'

Holly stood on her tiptoes and wrapped her arms around his neck as his lips found hers again.

'So,' she breathed at last, 'will you come to Christmas dinner tomorrow?'

'Love to,' he said, smiling.

'Lulu's going to be so happy,' she told him, imagining her friend's delight at this unexpected turn of events.

Lewis nodded, and she saw the serious look enter his eyes again.

'What is it?' she asked, afraid. 'Have you changed your mind?'

'About you? About us?' He shook his head. 'Never. But, Holly, you've been through a lot. We both have. You're the first girl I've ever let through the armour, and I've had years to adjust. What Jonathan did—it's changed you. A lot. Everyone says so. It's going to take some time for you to trust again. Not just me, but yourself. I don't want you to cling to me because you think you must be with someone to validate your existence. You're a bright, kind, warm, witty, and utterly beautiful human being, and you need to know that before we make any promises. You must be sure that it's me you want, and not just someone—anyone—who's kind to you and makes you feel good about yourself. Do you understand that?'

Holly blinked back tears. 'I think so,' she said slowly. 'You mean, I need to work on myself and my own self esteem first. Does that mean we can't see each other for now?'

'No! God, no.' He pulled her close again. 'Look, we'll take this as slowly as you need. We'll go at your pace, and I'll wait for as long as it takes. You've neglected your friendships, and you've lost all confidence in yourself and your abilities. I don't want this—us—to be everything to you, the way your relationship with Jonathan became everything. You have friends who love you and want you back in their lives. You need to have fun, with and without me.'

Holly tilted her head to one side, thinking. If Jonathan had said that, about having fun without her, she'd have been terrified. It was different with Lewis. She could trust him, and she understood what he was saying. He wanted her to find herself again and that was all right, because she wanted to find herself too. She'd missed the old Holly more than she'd realised.

'What?' she asked, feeling a surge of joy as she noticed him smiling fondly at her.

'You look so adorable when you tilt your head like that,' he told her.

'Do I?' Holly shook her head, dazed. 'I don't think Jonathan ever told me I looked adorable.'

'I'm not Jonathan.'

'No,' she said. 'You couldn't be more different if you tried. And that's why I—' She broke off, afraid of scaring him away.

'You can say it,' he said softly. 'If you mean it. I feel the same, you know.'

'You do?'

'Of course I do. I love you, Holly. I think I've loved you almost from the beginning. I'm not afraid of that. It makes me very happy.'

She smiled shyly at him. 'I love you, too.' She leaned on the fence again and watched the water flowing in fascination. It had travelled a long way through the moors, at times barely a trickle, and had become a beck that would find its way to the river and, eventually into the sea. This tiny, insignificant stream would be part of something huge and quite magnificent. Everything mattered, she thought suddenly. Everything and everyone. All had their part to play to create the bigger picture. Nothing was unimportant. Not a single blade of grass. Not a single person.

I matter.

'I've always wanted to learn to drive,' she said at last. 'He used to tell me I'd be useless at it, but I think I'd be good.' She turned to face Lewis, and saw him standing, hands in pockets, watching her with a love that he was no longer bothering to disguise. She felt a sudden lightness, and a reckless courage that reminded her, without warning, of the woman she'd once been.

The one who'd stood up on a stage in a room full of strangers and belted out karaoke songs, not caring that she had a terrible singing voice and that some people were laughing. Because they'd been laughing *with* her, not *at* her, and back then she'd understood that, and it had all been part of the fun. Somehow, she'd lost that ability to be happy and to make others happy. She'd withdrawn, closed off.

She'd forgotten how to be brave.

'I'm going to train as a phlebotomist,' she told him. 'Did I mention that?'

Lewis's eyes sparkled brighter than the lights on the Christmas tree as he smiled.

'I think we're going to be all right, Holly,' he said.

Holly's hand reached for his, and their fingers entwined. 'I think so, too.' She moved closer to him, and he held her as she rested her head on his shoulder. They stood quietly, at peace, watching the snowflakes drifting down over Cuckoo Nest Cottage.

One day, the place would be hers she realised. It was hard to believe, really, although there was a part of her that had always known it was where she belonged. It was home, and Lulu was her family. And now she had Lewis too. She knew, beyond doubt, that they would all live together in this little nest one day. A family. Always.

She felt a tingle of pleasure as Lewis kissed the top of her head. 'I'm so glad I moved to this village,' he murmured. 'Bramblewick is the best place on earth.'

'You're right, it is. And we have the best friends, too,' Holly agreed, thinking not only of Lulu, but of Anna and Connor, Nell and Riley, Rachel and Xander, Izzy and Ash, and Abbie and Jackson, the people who loved her, and had stayed loyal to her, no matter how many times she'd pushed them away. 'We're so lucky. Life is perfect.'

She simply couldn't imagine a single thing that would make her world more pleasurable. Then she heard a rustling sound, and her face broke into a grin.

She knew what was coming next.

'Have a pear drop,' said Lewis.

To find out more about Sharon Booth and her books visit her website

www.sharonbooth.com

where you can also sign up for her monthly newsletter to get her latest news, cover reveals, release dates, giveaways and more.

Also by Sharon Booth

There Must Be an Angel

When Eliza Jarvis discovers her TV presenter husband, Harry, has been playing away with tabloid darling Melody Bird, her perfect life crumbles around her ears.
Desperate to get away, she heads to the North Yorkshire coastal village of Kearton Bay in search of the father she never knew, with only her three-year-old daughter and a family-sized bag of Maltesers for company.
Eliza is determined to find the man who abandoned her mother and discover the reason he left them to their fate. All she has to go on is his name–Raphael–but in such a small place there can't be more than one angel, can there?
Gabriel Bailey may have the name of an angel but he's not feeling very blessed. In fact, the way his life's been going he doesn't see how things can get much worse.
Then Eliza arrives with her flash car and designer clothes, reminding him of things he'd rather forget, and he realises that if he's to have any kind of peace she's one person he must avoid at all costs.
With the help of a Wiccan landlady, and a quirky, pink-haired café owner, Eliza's soon on the trail of her missing angel, but her investigations lead her straight into Gabriel's path.
As her search takes her deeper into the heart of his family, Eliza begins to realise that she's in danger of hurting those she cares about deeply.
Is her quest worth it?
And is the angel she's seeking really the one she's meant to find?

If you love Bramblewick, you'll love Kearton Bay!

Printed in Great Britain
by Amazon